ACHERON RIDE

Acheron Ride

book one
Millie Leigh

MayhemNovels LLC

one

Graves Valley was a prison, but Elliot couldn't kill a fellow inmate to leave. She couldn't hop on a ChaosMotors bike and decapitate another rider and win first place. On the track where anything could happen, getting murdered was high on that list.

Drowning would be worse, though.

She had stayed away from the Covington ChaosMotors Championship as long as possible. Unfortunately, her boss chose her to do the article. At least she could pick her own team. She researched the Covingtons and some riders and compiled a list of the less violent teams. Three teams told her to fuck off so far. Elle's future as a photographer was looking grim.

Her boss, Randy, at ChaosMotors Magazine was a real piece of work. As much of a hard ass as he was, Randy was the person she needed to impress if she wanted that promotion from Journalist to Front Page Photographer. That's all she'd dreamt of since she snapped her first blurry photo. Her mother had planted her passion for photography. Always with a camera in hand. So Elle bit her tongue and kept her head down. One day she would make enough with her front-page photos to pay her dues and leave Graves Valley. One day.

Humphrey Graves created the Valley. Made to reduce the crowds in the prisons, his idea sparked something in the president. The prisoners in Graves Valley farmed and harvested crops to send to Sunset Cove, the neighboring town free of walls. Then the Valley began to send them the medicines they invented. Their purpose was to make non-criminals' lives better while they rotted away inside the walls.

Elle swayed in the grass of Covington manor to try and calm herself. Gasoline and dirt danced on the tip of her tongue. Roughly two hundred Chaos bikes parked in the mud. She took her camera from her side and began to shoot the pristine property before the sun went down.

She waved at her friend and coworker, Nate, from across the lawn. He was slender, with poofy light brown hair and soft eyes that hid behind tortoiseshell glasses. He wore khakis and a crisp button-down shirt. Nate had been her friend for a couple of years, and if it wasn't for his calm demeanor, she wouldn't be where she was now.

He approached her and made sure she knew to stay in the middle of the crowd when Cyra began her speech. When it came to Cyra it was better to stay hidden and blend in. Don't attract attention to yourself.

"Cyra Covington, our Superior," he rolled his eyes and lifted his camera to get a shot of the entrance to her manor. Riders waited for her arrival on the steps. "You know, she wouldn't have won the election if she wasn't related to Humphrey Graves himself?"

"Blood related?" Elle was surprised she'd never heard of this. But Cyra had been Superior before she arrived.

The Valley went by blood. If you died inside, your blood got everything, including what was due. Which made sense to Elle on the rumors of Cyra slaughtering her children when she won the election. It meant she could choose who the position passed to when she died.

"Yeah, wild isn't it?" Nate turned to take a couple more shots. "See you inside. You got this." He left her with a shoulder grab of reassurance. His main focus was Cyra tonight. Randy made sure of that with the prospects of front-page potential.

Elle slung the camera strap over her shoulder and stuffed her hands in her pockets. The smooth silk fabric of the inside brushed her fingers. The exterior maple color reminded her of the trees in her backyard growing up. When she touched the silk, she could imagine the wind in her hair as her sister pushed her on the tire swing. The jacket had calming powers, and she used its familiarity often.

Elle kept her eyes on the floor and entered the home. The manor could house hundreds, but the riders crowded in the main entry. White marble covered the walls and floor. Hefty diamonds hung from the chandeliers above them. Elle tried to capture a decent photo of them swinging. Couldn't get a good angle. The walls were smooth and clean. A platform was set up between the two wide curved staircases that led to the loft. Twelve gigantic marble columns went from the ground up to the ceiling above the second story.

The contestants looked out of place in a room like this. Most of them were in layers of black and brown. Dirt covered their rough hands and scruffy jaws.

When The Championship first began, the only riders were the farmers. The ones who worked the hardest. It evolved to be a race for the lowest of the lows. The ones who knew they'd never see outside the walls again.

It was difficult to leave the Valley. Even if you committed a lighter crime. Only way out was to pay your debt or race. The Championship guaranteed your freedom. The riders varied from murderers to sex traffickers and some even rapists. The people who should've gotten hanged instead of joining the other mates in the Valley. She pitied the ones to go against them.

A three-member team waited by the entrance. They were each in black leather, which was normal for riders, but they all had neon blue hair. She nodded toward the one staring at her. He didn't look away. Her fingers tightened on her camera. The two ignoring her, disappeared into the crowd while the other stopped in front of her. His three-inch mohawk caught her eye first, although his smile was more out of place in the room packed with riders. Weary, she held her hand out to greet him.

Eyes on her camera, he gripped her with a sweaty palm. "Hey, I'm Gage. You look a little lost. Are you a reporter or something?" he asked. She shook once and let go. He didn't seem like he wanted to hurt her. Riders were often in the news for fighting with an unlikely victim.

"Journalist," she corrected. "I work for ChaosMotors Mag. Elle."

His teeth jutted out of his mouth when he smiled, and his lips curled up to show his gums. He was thin and lanky, and his ears stuck out.

He searched the room to find his team in front of the stage, and Elle got a good look at his jacket. A large logo covered the back in bold teal font, Blue Falcon, it read. Right above it was, in fact, a blue Falcon. The wings reached from one shoulder to the other in a magnificent sweep. He turned back to face her and looked her up and down.

"Is this your first year?" she asked to fill the silence.

"Third. But it feels like the first every year. My boyfriend, Josh, got me to join." Gage motioned to a man on his team. A full belly and a round chin, he grinned at him. Half of his head had thick long sapphire hair, and the other half was shaved down to his scalp. "I'll never be able to repay him. For most of us, it's the reason we breathe."

The Championship for these riders was life or death. It wasn't a sport or game. For them, it was worth risking their lives. She couldn't imagine having that outlook herself, however she understood it. Cyra Covington gave the winners a ton of money and some fame but also a free ride past the checkpoint. There were only two ways to enter Graves Valley; be born in the walls or brought in handcuffs through the checkpoint. Fingerprints and scans that Cyra required made you never forget you were a prisoner. Her prisoner.

Covington's men guarded and monitored the walls in full-body black armor and helmets. A gun on their hip or in their hands at all times. Everyone called them the Guard. They walked the perimeter of the Valley and followed every order given by Cyra. Inside the manor tonight, Elle could spot twenty in the front room alone.

People who were born inside the Valley were still considered criminals. Your parents were criminals, so you must be one too. Everything went by blood. So, once your parents died, all their dues were added to yours. You might not have committed a crime, but you owed Cyra what was hers. If you were lucky, you owed less because you were born inside and not brought in. That wasn't the case for Elle. Her dues were hefty.

Elle explained her situation of trying to get a team for an article. Gage pointed out a few other teams and warned her of their worst qualities.

"Team Trick is filled with alcoholics, but Team Freak." He whistled through his teeth. "They love to dose riders with psychedelics at the race parties. And once a team makes a fool of themselves, it usually ends up in a magazine."

Gage lifted his pointer finger to the left side of the room where a large team gathered in black hoodies. One waved at Gage and he scoffed as he looked away. Elle locked eyes with the man and he smiled at her. His canine teeth were sharpened to a point. She shivered as she turned away.

The room became louder and commotion broke out behind them. Gage tugged Elle closer to the stage. Her instincts were right about him, after all. He put himself between her and the tussling young men.

Guard broke it up in seconds, and Elle kept her eyes away. Even after all these years, she still wasn't used to the Guard beating the others.

"Well, I wish I could help you out, but Josh would kill me if we were in a magazine. His family doesn't approve of the races, so he's trying to keep it secret for as long as possible. You might want to try Team Halo or Halfpipe. They're assholes, but they like the spotlight." He shrugged and crossed his arms over his chest.

Elle thanked him as she grabbed her phone to take note of the names. Gage pointed out the captain of the first team he mentioned. She squinted to see the man with long brown curls to the left of the stage. He was easy to place in his all-white attire. She thanked Gage again before his team called him over. He waved as he crossed the room to his blue-haired posse.

Gage kissed his boyfriend on the cheek, and his face lit up. Elle smiled as she watched them share a private moment in a room full of hundreds. These two men were riders in a deadly race, surrounded by their opponents, and still willing to show affection towards each other. No care about who saw them.

She brought her camera up again, and the room grew silent. Cyra must be in view. People called her the warden. Really she was the executioner. Everyone in the Valley despised her. She was malicious, ruthless, barbaric. They died and suffered for her to have a good show. Each year brought more disassembled bodies and homes. And gifted her more wealth and fame. The people feared her. That depiction seemed to be vital to her.

Long white hair came down to her hips, and her blue eyes were large and contrasted with her pasty skin. A cream gown draped across her, and a string of diamonds strewn around her neck. According to Graves Valley News, she was seventy-three years old but didn't look a day over fifty. Once in an interview, she told them it was due to her low stress. Elle believed that. Everything that caused her stress, she disposed of.

Cyra climbed the three steps onto the stage, and the room went silent. She could hear Cyra taking each step even though she was in the back of the crowd. A man stood beside Cyra in a white suit and tie. Thick eyebrows and thin lips. Elle guessed he was in his late forties and wondered what his relation to Cyra was. If Elle believed the rumors, which she did, he couldn't be her son. He could be the one she hand-picked to take over the throne, though.

Cyra cleared her throat and began her yearly speech, "This marks the one-hundred-seventy-fourth Covington ChaosMotors Championship. I challenge you all to be sharper. Faster. More resilient." Everyone cheered. She held her hand up, and the noise ceased. "The reward has increased. ChaosMotors is giving fifty million and a brand new residence in Sunset Cove. GVN has scheduled five interviews the week after the last race. Grave Wheels will be gifting handmade leather jackets with your team logo. The first rider to cross the finish line on the fourth race wins for their team. Are you ready?"

The crowd became deafening. A loud bang came from the ceiling as a thousand clear balloons fell. Some burst midair with white confetti. Everyone cheered and started bouncing them around. Hope filled their eyes as the possibility of leaving the Valley in a couple of weeks dawned on them.

The pieces fell like snow. Elle thought back to those winters with her father. Catching flakes on her tongue in Sunset Cove. Her mother captured the photos that would live forever in her mind.

Elle turned her sight back to Cyra and yelped when someone rammed into her. She had to readjust, but as she lifted her lens to the loft, she froze. A woman about her age with long black hair and dark skin cracked her knuckles in front of her chest. The blonde with her attempted to hit a balloon off the rail, delighted as she tried.

However it was the man between them that held Elle's attention. Smooth tan skin and short black hair with strands hanging in his dark eyes. His teeth gripped his bottom lip as he looked below. He was stat- ue-still with his arms resting on the railing, tilting to look down at the stage. Like most of the riders, he was in all black, but she couldn't see the team logo. A gasp slipped from her when he made eye contact, and she squeezed the capture button. Cursing herself, she glued her eyes back to Cyra.

"Each team must be between three and six riders. You must arrive on your own bike. If you enter with four and two perish, you may find a willing soul to replace your fallen. First race will have thirty teams competing, the second will have fifteen, and so on. Few rules exist on the track, but there are lots of fine print for weapons." She paused and continued with an unamused sigh. Exhausted from repeating her own regulations. "Remember, if your team wins and one member succumbs to the track, their share will go to the names on their beneficiary form. And that is why we continue the race each year, is it not?" She shouted the last sentence, and the crowd went wild again. This time she didn't wait for them to quiet. "In five days, the first race will take place."

Members of the Guard marched from the back hallway. Each with an automatic weapon in their grip. Then a group of them came from the front door, and the crowd made a path. A Guard bumped Elle's elbow, and she collided with someone. The rider dropped a glass, and the liquid splashed her arm. She jerked her camera away to save it from ruin. Her arm already smelled like the sweet watermelon drink. Gross. She tried to wipe it off but it was sticky.

A Guard rammed their baton into the rider's leg, and he dropped to his knees. Then the barrel of a gun was on the rider's forehead. Elle wanted to look away but couldn't. It was her fault.

"They just dropped their drink!" a rider across the hall yelled over everyone.

The Guard didn't care. No tolerance for stupidity. He knocked the rider over the head with the butt of the gun. Blood splattered the wall beside Elle. The rider slumped to the tile floor in front of her. She hoped he wasn't dead. His teammates pulled him out of there.

Swimming with images of her past, Elle stumbled through the bodies. Sweat dripped in her eyes and coated her palms. Her parents' faces flashed before her. The ghost of a gunshot rang in her ears. Being dragged kicking and screaming in cuffs to Graves Valley.

two

Elle attempted to stay behind and take photos of the empty manor, but the crowd pushed her outside. The camera was back to her eye as the riders exited. A couple of teams even posed. Most flipped her off. She expected it.

She wandered back to the field of bikes to convince a team to do the article. No success. A team Gage had spoken of, Halfpipe, walked down the steps. Elle went to approach them when the small blonde from the loft caught her eye. Elle adjusted her camera at her side so she could put her hands back in her pockets. The girl headed straight for her.

"Hey, are you taking pictures for a newspaper?" she asked in such a soft voice that Elle almost didn't hear her.

The girl wore mud-covered boots, and her dark pants had rips in the knees from years of wear and tear. Her pin-straight hair hung just above her shoulders. Jealousy washed through Elle as she had to sweep her waves into a ponytail every morning.

"I'm writing a four-page article for ChaosMotors mag. A few teams backed out. Are you interested?" Elle smiled as innocently as she could. This might be her big break. She'd worked for years under Randy to get to where she was. This one article could change her life.

The girl grinned. "Absolutely. I'm Alexandra, everyone calls me Lex though. I'll ask my team. That would give us great press whether we win or not. Right?"

"Yes." Elle nodded. She seemed excited, but Elle wasn't sure about her teammates. At least she could still get information from her.

"Sorry, you didn't mention your name."

"Elle," she said. Lex was about to respond but got interrupted when her teammate with long hair came up to them. Elle took a step back when she realized the girl had her hands in fists and her eyes trained on her.

"Vero, this is Elle. She needs a team to write an article about the race. Wouldn't that be great for us?" Lex smiled. Elle didn't think the other girl would smile back anytime soon.

"Drake won't like it," she spat. Her hair swayed behind her as her steps halted.

"I'll talk him into it. What do you say?" Lex asked. Vero glanced from Lex to Elle before she nodded once and backed up. Vero's eyes stayed on Elle like she was preparing for an attack. She was protective of her friend. And herself. Elle couldn't blame her. She didn't know her.

Lex turned around to wave her other team member over. Elle could feel her heartbeat in her stomach. The shakes came back in her hands. The silk wasn't working. At least Vero seemed to have calmed down. She looked relaxed with her back against the small tree nearby. The dark-haired man got a few feet away before he inspected Elle and paused on her camera. She should learn to hide this damn thing when meeting new people.

"Drake, listen," Lex started.

"No," he grumbled. Elle felt the first pang in her chest. She was inches away from her dream.

"She's from ChaosMotors Magazine. She needs a team to write an article about. This could be great for us!"

"No," he repeated.

He walked toward a slim black Chaos bike with a clear seat and large handlebars. Buttons lined the middle, and there were bars on either side. Elle tried not to stare at it. She had never seen one this close before.

"Nobody knows who we are. What could it hurt?" Lex whined and wiped her hand over her forehead. Frustration clear on her face.

"Don't play dumb, Lex." He spoke through his teeth, but Elle could hear him despite their distance. Vero pulled Elle's arm, and the air left her lungs in a huff.

"What's your angle?" Vero asked.

"Excuse me?" Elle yanked her arm free.

"What's in it for you?" Drake stepped to her.

They were trying to force her into a corner. It wasn't going to work. She had come this far. "Progress in my career. A chance to be a full-time photographer. Not a writer. If your team does well, this will get me there." She tried to smile, but it vanished when Drake laughed condescendingly. "What's so funny?"

This captain was about to bury all her hard work in a ditch without a second thought. He didn't know her. Didn't understand. Years and years of writing and research and late nights. She glowered at him. He was patronizing her.

"You're like a damn puppy. Nipping at the riders as they go by. And you want us to trust you with our personal business?"

Trust issues. Great. Still, she could work with that. "You don't have to tell me your personal business. You can review my article before I send it in."

"That's fantastic!" Lex said as she looked at her teammate.

"I am not here to ruin anyone's life. Have you ever been to a race where the crowd shouts your name?" Elle asked. He stiffened and rolled his eyes. She assumed that would excite the male ego in him. She was wrong. Seemed he didn't want the attention like the other riders she knew of.

"Come on, Drake, let Lex have her puppy," Vero said. Elle glared, which made Vero chuckle. "Might even be fun. She seems feisty."

"Cut it out, V. Don't be mean," Lex said and patted her friend's arm.

Vero sighed. "Whatever. I'm on board with an article. Could help get us some fans. But you're the captain." She pointed at Drake and waved as she left the group and walked to a small black pickup truck across the field.

"You'd let us review what you write?" Drake asked. Elle sensed a glimmer of hope. Couldn't let him see that.

"Yes," she managed not to squeak out.

"And if I ask not to be in any photos?"

She'd have to work on that. "It might help your team if you're in the photos."

He hadn't listened to her. His leg swung over the bike, and he braced himself.

"To be clear, I'm doing this for Lex. I could give two shits about you. If you do anything to hurt either of these girls, I will cut your head off with my pocket knife. Got it?" His eyes were slits as he peered over at her.

"Yes, but."

"See you tomorrow," he interrupted.

"Hey!" she yelled, and he stopped to look back at her as if she was insane. "I figured you'd want to know, considering your main concern is to help them." She motioned to Lex and the direction Vero walked off to. "If you're in the photos, it would do just that. You're the alpha of the group. Girls will come running. You could turn them into real fans." She crossed her arms over her chest. Finally, he listened.

He tilted his head toward her. "You think I'm hot?"

Elle laughed at the sky. Turns out this guy was worse than the riders she knew of. "I'm saying the teens will think you are. Don't you re-member Ryan West? Team Grip? I was never interested in The Championship, and I remember his name. That's what I'm talking about. Press only gets you so much. The fans are what make you immortal."

"I don't remember him," Drake said.

"I do. He was smoking hot." Lex sighed longingly.

"Exactly. Hot guys on bikes make the ladies' panties drop. Hot guys in The Championship? Even better. Just sleep on it. Like I said, you can review everything before I send it in."

"I'll think about it," Drake grumbled. He didn't wait for a response as he sped off down the driveway. A mix of dirt and grease wafted around in his absence. The silence that came ended with a frustrated groan from Lex.

"Real friendly guy," Elle said.

Lex roared with laughter. "He's not so bad once he opens up. But it took years for him to crack his shell with me."

"Why did you stay?"

She smiled. "I met Drake in school. By then, he'd already been in three or four races. I asked him to teach me how to ride."

Elle didn't understand. She'd read up on The Championship. Especially the rules and regulations. "I thought the starting age was eighteen?"

Lex lifted one side of her mouth. "Most people don't know the basic rules." She was impressed Elle had done her research. "He snuck in. It was before teams were mandatory. He says it was easy." Lex shrugged. "But he took me to a track and let me ride his bike. He didn't have many friends, so I assumed he wanted some company."

"Or he had a crush on you." Elle brushed their shoulders together, and Lex giggled.

"Just the opposite. I thought he was dreamy. Until I realized he was more brother material than boyfriend." She scrunched her nose at the thought.

"I have one of those too. Completely understand." Elle smiled, thinking of Nate. When they first met, he'd shown her around the office and protected her from Randy as much as he could. Now they spent most of their time photographing empty fields and each other for practice.

They stopped in front of the truck Vero sat in. She had her phone to her ear and waved her hands around as she spoke.

"Yeah, my friend even forced us to go to the lookout once." She gagged, and Elle laughed.

"The one where you can see over the Guard wall?"

Elle had heard of that place. You could see city lights if you went at night. If you went during the day in autumn, you could see the colorful trees in the distance. She should plan a trip there soon to see the red leaves.

"Yeah, and it was beautiful. We stayed for hours. We also had an awkward conversation about how we would never be an item, and we have never brought it up again." She laughed as she thought back. "We found Vero four years ago, and it has been the three of us ever since."

A group of riders zoomed past on their bikes, and Elle jumped at the sound. One went by balancing on his back wheel. Show off. To their credit, they kept it up way longer than she had expected. Impressive. Still a showoff.

Lex smacked her hand on the truck window. Vero leaped out of her skin and flipped her off. Lex laughed before she turned her attention back to Elle.

"How did you meet Vero?" Elle asked softly. She didn't want her to hear from inside the truck. She stayed cautious of the crabby girl.

She dropped her voice even lower. "Drake met her first. I should let her tell you about that though. It's more personal."

"They were together?" Elle went wide-eyed. She did not see that coming.

"Oh, nonono." Lex shook her head. "Sometimes I wonder if they should be together with their dang mood swings. But they're close now. I don't think he could cross that line with her. He'd have to risk their friendship, and he's done that before."

"What happened?" Elle asked.

"Why? Thinking of asking him on a date?" Lex winked.

"Never." Elle scoffed. "He seems like an ass. I'm curious because he didn't want his picture taken."

"Drake is..." She paused, and Elle could see the gears turning. She rolled her eyes before she sighed, "a mystery. He was in a relationship with another rider once. It didn't last long. Team Beehive."

Beehive? She recalled that name. They were in the race last year.

"Isn't that the team..." she started, and Lex nodded.

"Yeah, they all died last year in The Championship. Drake didn't even seem sad. He just processes things differently, I guess."

"Keep telling yourself that," Elle mumbled. They laughed together again. Lex reached into the truck and grabbed a pen. She scribbled on a small white napkin and handed it to Elle. It was a phone number and an address.

"Meet me tomorrow morning. We're usually there by nine but come by whenever. You can see how we work and what we do to prepare for race day. The garage is on private property. Drake doesn't like anyone knowing where it is, so keep it to yourself," Lex said.

"Not a problem." Elle slid the napkin into her jacket pocket.

"I think we're going to be great friends." Lex gave Elle a hug and jumped into the driver's seat. Elle turned and started to head back to her car in a slight panic. She was not prepared to make friends. She didn't need friends right now. She needed this article to do well. Eyes on the prize.

Don't lose focus.

three

E lle got to Bernie's Coffee Shop, and three baristas greeted her with big smiles. Cinnamon rolls must be the pastry of the day, she could smell them the moment she walked in. They made her latte, and she took her usual seat by the trash can. Before reaching into her pocket, she surveyed the room. She slipped the small round silver tin under the can. Bernie would find it later.

Elastaderm was a healing ointment in the Valley. Only obtainable at the hospital. And only used on injured Guard. If caught with a tin of it, instant execution. They called it Blue Sludge on the street due to its shade of sapphire. For a healing cream, it could do a whole lot more. It couldn't grow a whole limb back but, on a small cut, it would stitch the skin together in an instant.

Once, her neighbor was bitten by a venomous snake, and it took a while longer, but he didn't die. She always wondered what would happen if you ate a spoonful of it. A shudder ripped through her at the thought of the taste.

It was almost impossible to get your hands on it with the Guard keeping watch. So, of course, she found a way to make her own. Elle followed some lab techs into a known warehouse that made the cream. She learned that day how small she was. Fitting inside an air vent was something she never thought would be useful. It took her a year of trial and error before she made a usable batch. Finding suitable substitute products was the challenging part. Now, she could buy three of them at the corner store, and the rest she could pluck from a garden nearby.

Elle would have to take a trip to pick up a bundle of calendula flowers soon. It wasn't an easy trek there, and not because of the hills.

She closed her eyes as the images flashed before her. Evelyn pushed her on a tire swing and hauled her through a field of blooms. Grassy knolls and playgrounds were a distant memory. She opened her eyes to allow reality to sink back in. Her sister would never see those flowers again. Elle would never hear her voice again.

She straightened her back and jammed her hand in her pocket. Another gulp of coffee helped soothe her mind. Count to ten. She had work to do.

It took over an hour to transfer the photos from her camera to her laptop. The one she'd taken of Drake by accident appeared on the screen, and she groaned. He looked striking as he leaned on the railing with his teeth gnawing on his lip. Too bad his personality was appalling.

Bernie stepped through the door and waved to her in the corner. She gave him the knowing salute. He nodded back. It was their code, so he knew there was a tin of Elastaderm waiting for him.

Bernie had been a friend since she was a kid. He was a large graying man, so pale she wasn't sure he ever saw the sun. His polo shirt was always tucked into his pants. Elle found out he was born in Graves Valley, and it made her appreciate him even more. He never took his position or situation for granted. Always telling her she should feel blessed to be alive. Even if it was inside these walls. He always tried to make everyone else's day better. Guard be damned.

Elle edited four photos before she checked the clock. She waved at the three behind the counter as she headed to her car. It was a tiny silver four-door that she never kept clean, and she loved it. Rust and all. Her phone dinged as she put the address Lex had given her into the map. She'd never heard of that street, but her gut told her to trust the blonde.

Once she pulled onto the dirt and gravel road, doubt started to creep in. They were going to murder her in these woods. A garage emerged in the clearing. A plain large white rectangle with one door on the left side. A gravel driveway stopped a few feet from the door. The black truck parked to the side. Trees surrounded the building with red leaves. Huh. Maybe she wouldn't need to make a visit to the lookout after all. Elle couldn't pass up the opportunity to snag a couple of shots with her phone. The clouds in the background partly hid the rising sun.

Lex waited at the door for her. "Cmon! I want to show you my bike!"

Elle surveyed the area once more before she followed her inside. Lex grinned wide as she closed the metal door with a grunt.

The garage was one big rectangle with high ceilings. Dark walls met the beige cement of the floor. Tools hung on peg boards by each station. Two large workbenches scattered with parts of handlebars by the back door. Paint cans covered a square table next to her and even though they all had lids she could taste them on her tongue. Metal scraps lined the wall and filthy rags spread throughout. As cluttered as it was, she had seen worse at home. Some of the boys' rooms, anyway. Yet it still smelled better here.

Vero and Drake were in the far right corner working on a red bike as Lex gave her a short tour. Lex pointed at her teammates. "That is Drake's workstation. This is mine." She motioned to their left. "Over there is Vero's. Back that way is the bathroom and the office we never use." Lex continued around the room. "Then we have the track out there." She turned toward the back door. They walked to the table of paint, and Elle stopped short.

Boxes of coal were underneath. Fireballs were common in the races, and this was the cheapest option to do it. A stack of torches leaned against the wall next to an assortment of spears. Elle knew The Championship was violent but couldn't picture Lex shooting a spear at someone. However, she could imagine Drake shoving one through her chest. The sound of her ripping flesh as he pulled it out of her lifeless body made her shiver.

Lex got her attention when she picked up a stack of sketches from the floor. She placed them on the table under a can, and Elle got a quick look at them. The real talent on the pages left her surprised.

"These are amazing," Elle said. "Did you draw them?"

"No, Vero's the artist. She paints our bikes every year." Lex cocked her head across the room. Vero had half her body under a motor. Drake stood next to her and handed her a screwdriver.

His shirt and dark jeans were coated in dirt and grease but he looked calm today. More relaxed. The photo of him surfaced in Elle's mind, and she bit her lip thinking of his. She shook her head and tried not to pinch herself. Remember how awful he is. He could still rip the article away from her.

Lex caught her staring and dragged her out the back door. Elle stopped to take Lex's photo as she smiled at the sun. Her bright pink dress clashed with the field in the center of the track. It was all dirt. It was undeniable they made the track themselves. The jumps and ditches were in rough condition. Puddles coated it with mud. Elle walked around to take photos while Lex asked about the article.

"Will it come out after The Championship is over?"

"No, no. The public will see it before the second race."

"That's great news! I hope you can get enough info before then," she said. Her hand covered her forehead in worry.

"I'm sure it'll be fine. Like I said, it's mostly about The Championship in general. I have basic questions, but the fans care more about what you look like and how The Championship will affect you. Cyra's only concern is getting more people interested in racing."

"Right. Yeah. Of course." Lex nodded and fixed her eyes on her frayed shoes.

"What?" Elle asked, her apprehension evident.

Lex looked over her shoulder at the door. "We don't say her name here."

"And by 'we' you mean... Drake?" Elle followed her gaze.

"Yeah, that's what I mean," Lex whispered.

Elle wasn't sure what that meant. Nobody liked Cyra. At the same time, to not say her name was ridiculous. Had Drake done something to Cyra? If he had, how did he live to tell the tale? She could be in more danger here than she realized.

She cleared her throat. "Understood. So, did you make the track?" she asked, and Lex seemed to appreciate the subject change.

"No. Well, I kinda helped. Vero and Drake will say otherwise. It's rough," she said. She grabbed the end of her dress and started to fidget.

"I noticed you could use a different wood on the ramps, and maybe." She stopped when she heard herself start to babble.

"What? Go on."

"Nothing. Not my place to say." Elle held her hands up in front of her.

"You can say it, Elle." Lex grinned at her. "It's just me."

Despite being tied back, Elle's auburn hair blew in her face, and she tucked some of her bangs behind her ear. Lex stayed quiet. Encouraging her to speak her mind. Elle didn't feel like she had to hide behind her camera around Lex. Her words were soft as she eased into her suggestion.

"Well, if you used spruce wood, it would be more efficient and stronger than the pine you are using here." She pointed to the ramp closest to them.

"And how do you know this?" Lex asked.

"I have a brother who builds things. He used to construct half pipes for skateboarders and BMX bikes, but now he designs ramps for riders," she explained.

"Interesting. I'll pass along the info," Lex said.

Later, Lex brought Elle inside and took a photo of her bike. It was obvious which one was hers. The sunshine yellow gave it away. First thought Elle had was how thin it was. Couldn't be more than five inches. She could easily weave around riders on the track on this.

It had a smaller handlebar across the front with yellow buttons on the sides near the engine. The seat matched in color and had a headrest on the back which was unusual. Seeing as Lex was so tiny, she figured it might help protect her from riders and debris during the race.

On either side of the front wheel was a sheet of metal surrounding it. Needle-sharp thick spikes came out of it like a porcupine. Elle stepped closer with her hand outstretched.

"Don't touch that!" Lex shrieked.

Elle jumped back and dropped her hand. Her breath wavered from the scare. "What's it for?"

"These pop the tires of the riders who try to side-swipe you. Don't touch anything. You might kill yourself in here," Lex warned with a delicate tone.

"Let her touch whatever she wants," Drake muttered from across the room.

"Shut up," Elle snapped at him. The girls laughed.

"You know, at first, I thought she'd be boring, but she certainly has a mouth on her," Vero said to Drake. He chuckled and the sound echoed off the walls.

"We can hear you," Lex said.

"I don't care!" Vero shouted back. She grabbed another tool from Drake's hand and he sat down beside her to assist.

Lex nudged Elle's arm. "Go on, sit on it."

"Are you insane? You just said not to touch anything," Elle said. She imagined pressing a button on accident and the entire garage exploding.

"Sitting on it won't kill you. I want to see how it will look with you on it. You're taller than me."

"I already know the answer, Lex. Like a damn giant."

"She can stay!" Vero yelled. Elle knew they were joking with each other but a wave of relief washed over her at the words. Maybe Vero would come around sooner than she thought.

Lex rolled her eyes and pleaded with Elle. "C'mon, it'll be a second."

Elle gave in and placed her camera down on the closest table, minding the tools. She didn't trust it on the floor of this place. Lex motioned for her to sit, and Elle swung her leg over the middle. She sat, and her head was above the seat, and her feet were inches past the pedals. A familiar shutter came from beside her. Elle turned to see Lex with her camera. Her mouth went dry.

"Oh, that will be deleted immediately." She tried not to yell at her for touching her camera, but Lex placed it down on the table. Her baby was safe.

"No! You look great."

It was hard to be upset at someone who smiled as much as she did. Elle bit her tongue.

Lex and Elle joined the others across the room. She stayed quiet as the three worked on the blood-red bike. This had to be Vero's. It was sleek and sexy. Thin wheels lined with silver and black handlebars with a simple black seat in the middle.

Newer ChaosMotors models were slim and didn't have any wheels. They hovered over the ground when riding and had legs extend from the base when it wasn't in use. Elle couldn't wait to see some of the other more interesting bikes at the first race. Hopefully, she would be able to take photos of them before The Championship began. She didn't have much luck outside Cyra's manor.

"Screwdriver," Drake said. Lex searched the long wooden table for a minute before she handed it over.

"How do you prepare for a race exactly? You never know what kind of weapons they're going to use against you or how the track is going to be," Elle said. She took out her phone to take some notes.

"Prepare for the worst," Vero said.

"Work out, mediate, and try to picture yourself dodging bullets," Lex added.

"Show up. Cross the finish line first," Drake said. Vero laughed.

"What about the track out back? How often do you use that?" Elle asked.

"Every day, as the race gets nearer. Last year, we had a bad storm right before the first one," Lex recalled. "So we couldn't use it. Other teams have a practice track inside their garage, but we make do with what we got. We still kicked ass." Lex nudged Vero's boot. "I'm sure we'll win this year."

"Are you always this positive?" Elle snarked, and Drake let out a dry chuckle.

"Yes!" Lex sang out with a grin.

Vero wiped her hands on a rag and coughed into her fist. Bruises covered Drake's forearms, and sweat decorated the back of his neck.

"Socket wrench," Drake said and focused on Vero with his hand out to Lex. She inspected the tools on the table and did a third once over before Elle reached over and handed it to Drake. He did a double-take, and Elle noticed Lex was staring at her now too.

"Sorry," she said and looked at Lex. "I'm not supposed to touch the tools, right?"

"No, no, I'm shocked you knew what that was," Lex said.

"Oh," she said, feeling that tightness in her stomach again. Should've kept her hands at her sides. Focus on your job. The magazine.

"You need a socket wrench often?" Drake asked, raising an eyebrow.

"My brother does," Elle said.

"The brother that builds the ramps?" Lex pointed over her shoulder at the back door.

"Different ones." She thought of Skylar and Pedro, the two that were constantly making things out of nothing. They were thirteen and obsessed with blowing things up. Including her old radio. Twirps.

"You have a lot of siblings?" Vero asked.

"Too many," she said.

It was amazing the way the team worked together, even though they were so different from each other. Almost like a machine themselves. Gears turning at different speeds to cross the finish line at the same moment. It reminded her of the time Nate photographed a group of Guard for Cyra to promote the position. Elle held lights as he walked behind them, and they moved together to get the job done.

Guard weren't just chosen by Cyra all the time. Some mates applied for the position. They figured it was a better chance at survival if they were on the team doing the most killing. Elle could never do that.

Drake handed Vero the wrench. Then he looked up at the clock on the wall. He mumbled a curse to himself as he threw a rag at the table and ran toward the door. He shoved a shirt into a backpack and bolted outside.

"Bye!" Lex yelled after him.

"So, you mind if I ask you some questions while you work, Vero?" Elle stole Drake's spot on the floor and Lex plopped down to join.

"I guess." Her tone seemed lighter now. Maybe she had warmed up to her enough. Elle held her phone in her hands to continue her notes.

"Why do you want to win?"

"Money, obviously." She scoffed. "Get out of this hell hole. Hardly any of us at this age get sent here. We're all born here. How unfair is that?"

"Do you believe everyone sent here deserves to be here?" Elle asked. Would she think Elle deserved to be here? Not that she would blame her for thinking that. She would understand.

"I guess? I don't know," Vero said, sitting up. She turned her dark eyes on Elle.

"Elle, were you not born here?" Lex whispered with wide eyes. Elle didn't have to answer. They knew.

"Shit," Vero murmured. Wiped her face with a rag before she threw it across the room toward a bag of dirty ones.

Elle shrugged. "It's alright. How could you know?" She tried to brush it off.

If you were born in the Valley, you couldn't escape until you were eighteen. And with no family to live with on the other side, how were you supposed to find a home? Nobody could afford their dues to begin with. Unless you crossed the finish line first, of course.

"Shit, dude, I'm sorry. I gotta learn to keep my mouth shut. I shouldn't have assumed." Vero started to bite her thumbnail.

"You didn't say anything I haven't heard before," Elle said. "You made a broad assumption. Not an aimed one."

Vero went back to tinkering with the bike. Her hair was on top of her head in a big knot. She wore a dark tank top that showed how muscular she was. Elle couldn't be more impressed. Her dark skin shined with sweat, and she wiped her arm with another rag before she broke the silence. "You just seem so vanilla."

Lex laughed. "Yeah, Elle. How'd you end up in the Valley?"

Elle never told anyone this much about herself. Let alone her past or her journey across the checkpoint. These girls were looking for an explanation, and they answered her questions. It was only fair.

"It's a long story. I grew up here for the most part."

"They brought you as a child?" Lex covered her mouth.

That was the worst thing for someone who was born in the Valley. Watching children enter the checkpoint. Elle remembered the groups of people crying as the minors crossed in front of her. The boy who went through first screamed for his mom on the other side, but there was nothing they could do. They were guilty of their crimes, and they would live in the Valley for it. There were rumors of family members committing crimes to enter the Valley on purpose. Now that was risky. Elle knew this wasn't the only Valley around. They could send them to Frost or Ashbury Valley. There were a dozen others.

"Yes," Elle said, and the memories of her family started to trickle in. She shook her head. "Do you mind if we—"

"Yeah. Go on, what were you asking me?" Vero moved her hand dismissively.

"What will you do if you win?"

"Move to Sunset Cove, into that big house they have waiting for us. Then marry someone rich who knows how to cook." Elle noted she said someone and not a man. She smiled at that. However, it was a typical answer. Probably not a real one. She was okay with that.

Lex jumped to add her answer. "I would build my own house right next to Vero. Pay a whole crew to make us our own track in our back-yards."

"And what about Drake? Where will he live?"

"He might stay in the Valley," Vero said.

"What? No. No way. He'd live with one of us for sure," Lex stammered. "He would live with us. How could he not?"

"His family is here, dude," Vero replied and gave Lex a look. Elle didn't miss it. The girls were having a silent conversation. Elle took a mental note. She might be in over her head after all.

"They could come with us. There is nothing in the rules that says family members have to stay. If we can afford it, we can all leave. Pay their dues too."

"So what would you do if Drake decided to stay?" Elle asked.

"He wouldn't do that," Lex repeated.

"Send him money to get a better garage," Vero said.

"How about a therapist?" Elle mumbled, and they all laughed.

It was strange to talk with the two girls. Lots of smooth conversations as they worked and took breaks to eat snacks. Eventually, they moved outside to watch the moon rise above them. Lex wanted Elle to see the white flowers at night. She wasn't disappointed.

Elle took photos with her night vision lens before they decided to lock up. She strolled over to her car as the girls slipped into the black truck. They beat her to the end of the driveway and she let them. She didn't want to go home yet. A small part warned her to be wary of them. Not only were they riders, they were also not well known. There was no information on them. That was dangerous in the Valley. They could kill her or bury her alive, and nobody would even know. But the other part of her wanted to see what being their friend would be like. Could they even picture her as their friend?

Vanilla. She didn't fit in.

The windows down made her thoughts trail off to her siblings. Not the ones she spoke of today. Her brothers and sister she'd never see again. The ones she lost. The ones who would never see her grow up. They would love it if she somehow made friends with this unlikely group. She might not fit in, but Elle felt like they were starting to accept her. Well, two out of three ain't bad.

four

Even though there was a lot of work to do, she was desperate to see Sarah. Elle wanted to see the kids, of course. However, what she needed was a hot cocoa and a hug. Her car squeaked when she put it in park in the driveway. Yes, she had moved out at eighteen and got her own apartment, but Sarah's Little Hearts was home. It started as a group home but now was more of an orphanage. It was rare these kids had parents that were still alive. It was even rarer that someone in the Valley wanted to adopt them.

Little footsteps came running as she opened the car door. Elle bent down for the young boy to wrap his small arms around her neck. She scooped him up and walked him inside. His dark chocolate eyes stared with amazement as she told him about meeting riders in The Championship. A group of older kids greeted her, and one of them took the boy off her hands.

"Ma is in the kitchen," one of the teen girls yelled as she ran out the front door with a net and a silver bucket. One thing you learn growing up in a place like this—you're better off not asking.

The house was beaten up. Just like all of them. Only two ways to end up at Little Hearts; your parents died in the prison, or you were arrested and sent here as a child. The building had character. Some of the stairs had lumps, while the boards on the floor had grooves. Holes in the wall were normal, with all the kids throwing things or running into them. It echoed with voices, and Elle swore ghosts roamed the halls at night. She imagined them as her friends when she was a child. Always spoke to them in the middle of the night. Hoping one day they'd answer her.

They never did.

Elle steered toward the back of the house and ran into Samuel in the hall. The newest member of the clan. Six years old and a head full of thick light curls. He had his red baseball cap on like usual. He screamed bloody murder anytime someone tried to take it off him. She patted his head and got down to his level to ask how he was doing. He rambled for a few minutes about the Valley and his parents in Sunset Cove, but she knew how that felt. She tried to be helpful. Wasn't sure what to say. Living here, things didn't get better. Elle knew you had to deal with it and try to make it easier as time went on.

The walls beside them were caked with dirt, and the floors had muddy footprints. Elle would have to clean a bit before she left today. Sarah let out a frustrated grunt, and Elle rushed into the kitchen, towing Samuel along with her. Sarah had her head in the fridge and was moving things around like a mad woman.

"If you're looking for the milk, it's on the counter next to you, Ma." Elle smirked as Sarah turned around, and her eyes locked on the gallon. She huffed and shut the door.

"How you do that, I will never know." She paused and wiped her hands on her apron. Sarah's copper hair was in a messy bun, and perfect ringlets fell around her face. Freckles covered her nose and cheeks. Her slender frame towered over Elle. More wrinkles crowded her forehead than the first time they met. It made her even more beautiful.

"Now come and give me a hug, dammit." Sarah crushed Elle into her chest.

Elle finished her mug of cocoa and showed Sarah the photos she had taken at the manor. She forgot about the one of Drake and groaned as she shut her laptop. Sarah's eyes doubled in size.

"Don't even think about it. He is a complete—jerk." She corrected her language when she remembered Samuel was still in the room. Sarah shooed him outside to be with the other boys.

The kitchen was where Elle spent the most time. Between cooking meals and cleaning or doing homework and chatting with Sarah. The large oak table had mismatched chairs around it. The dark one that wobbled on three good legs had been Elle's favorite since one of the older girls climbed on top and announced her sexual orientation to the entire home. A week later, she ran away. Elle never saw her again but thought of her often.

"He looked handsome." Sarah nudged Elle's arm as she sat down beside her.

"Sure, until he opens his mouth," Elle said, and Sarah laughed.

"Honey, sometimes people give a bad first impression."

"Not this time, Ma. Trust me." Elle's laptop hummed on the table. Stain circles of past mugs covered the top. Nicks were sanded down on the sides of the table so the kids didn't get splinters. Elle ran her fingers over the mark where she'd been to blame.

"Alright, I'm just saying. I want grandkids before I die." Sarah rubbed her shoulder.

Elle gagged and shook her head with her tongue out.

There was a bouquet on the counter, and Elle gave Sarah a raised brow. Since she was a kid, Christopher had been coming by the house. And Elle was the only one who seemed to know it wasn't to see them. He'd do any odd job they needed for a home-cooked meal, which included many PB&Js.

"I know." Sarah hummed as she looked at the vase.

"I told you he was in love with you," Elle said.

"Oh, stop it. He is not in love with me." She gave a dramatic pause. "Well, alright, he might be." Sarah smiled into her hands, pink covering her cheeks. The sink beside the flowers overflowed with dirty dishes. Elle stood and started to scrub them.

"I'm happy for you," Elle said.

Sarah walked over to help. "Have you been eating, honey? You're looking thin."

Elle didn't miss the conversation jump. She rolled her eyes at her subtlety.

"Yes." She gave an exasperated sigh. "I'm just stressed. It's this article. Randy is putting so much pressure on us all. Plus, putting these people under a microscope is not fun. Then there's the jerk. At least, the girls have been alright. Well, one has been great, the other just okay. Nate got some amazing photos of Cyra, though," Elle rambled, and Sarah smiled when she finally stopped to take a breath. Sarah took the clean plate and dried it with a towel.

"Honey, you're talking fast. I can tell it's stressful. Just make sure you're doing your breathing exercises and taking time for yourself. Remember what Dr. Gordon said."

Elle took an intentional deep breath to show Sarah her calming ways. Sarah nodded.

"I've been thinking of that day more," Elle admitted. The bowl in her hand felt heavier as she placed it in Sarah's.

"Of the accident?"

"Yes and I know I need to concentrate on my future, not my past. I need to let my family rest. I know. I know," Elle recited.

"You deserve a life. Remember that too." Sarah gave a slight smile.

"And they didn't?" Elle refused to believe that.

"That's not what I'm saying. You don't deserve to be here, but I'm glad you are. You make my life better. Sweeter for sure." She pinched her cheek, and Elle recoiled. "Don't live in the past, honey. Today is a gift. That is why it's called the present."

Elle grabbed her camera as she locked her jacket in the car. She went around the back of the garage toward the sound of wheels in mud. Lex waved like crazy as she sped past. Drake went around the track and picked up speed with each lap. Vero was off to the right under a tree with a wrench in one hand and a can of beer in the other. She gave Elle a lazy salute.

Drake maneuvered off to the side, and Elle held her breath as she approached him. Maybe today would be different.

"Hey," she said.

He nodded toward her but didn't speak. He didn't shout, so she assumed they were on okay terms. For now.

Drake let out a long exhale and turned toward her. "You have questions for me? Interview nonsense?"

Hm. She wasn't expecting this. Elle kept her eyes on Lex going over another jump. She landed it without flaw and hit the accelerator harder.

"What made you start racing? Lex said you were young," Elle asked and half-expected him to ignore her anyway.

"I started riding when I was twelve. By fifteen, I was racing in The Championship. This year will be my tenth race. Every year it gets more challenging because of the other riders. Not the track. People don't understand that their first time."

She couldn't imagine being in The Championship that little. She could barely lift the laundry basket back then, and this guy was riding around dodging ax blows and spears to the head. The red leaves swayed in the trees beyond the track, and Elle reached for her phone to snap a photo. Figured it might be rude. She kept her hands at her sides and tried to stay focused.

"How did you survive when you were so young? I imagine you were pretty small."

"Being small has its advantages. You can go faster. Easier to weave around riders or obstacles on the track. I didn't ride to win that year. I rode for the experience."

"You wanted a near-death experience?" Elle snorted.

"Yeah, I guess one wasn't enough for me." He chuckled to himself.

"I understand that." Her words came out soft. Thinking of her family. The reason she was sent to Graves Valley.

"What's that supposed to mean?" he snapped at her, and she winced. His fists clenched at his sides. She was over his mood swings already. He was worse than the kids at home.

She rolled her eyes. "Your whiplash is exhausting."

"You think you know what it was like to be out there?" Was this his attempt at trying to get her to leave?

"I never said that." Elle crossed her arms in front of her. Get it all out. She leaned in even closer to him and refused to lose eye contact. "You're so overprotective of your friends. But at fifteen, you were in this deadly race for adults... to do what? Die?" she asked and saw the light turn on behind his eyes. She guessed it. And regret it. His eyes were daggers on her as he took a step forward. This was it. He was going to murder her here. He would filet her flesh from her bones like a fish.

"Try and let the past go," she murmured. He took a step away from her. His eyes began to clear. He rubbed his palms on his dark jeans.

She was still so close. Before he stepped back again, she studied his face. Until now, she thought his eyes were brown. Really they were a dark blue. She had only seen the ocean once but remembered its clean salty scent. Its color. She was looking at that hue right now. His breath became normal. "And the beast rests once again," she said.

They were silent for a few minutes. He swayed on his feet. Elle waited for him to speak first this time.

"Do you do that a lot?" he asked. "Say whatever is on your mind."

"No." Elle's cheeks began to flush. "I try to bottle that stuff up," she joked.

He smirked. His words were softer now. "You are not what I expected, Elle."

She struggled not to hear him say her name over and over in her head. Watching his tongue hit his top teeth to form that word. Elle.

Elle focused on Lex completing two more laps before she checked on Vero. She polished off her beer and crushed it against the tree. Elle never imagined her life taking this turn. She hadn't even been in the same room as a rider, let alone watch them practice or work on their bikes. Now she was in their space and getting to know them, just to watch them kill each other later. Never in a million years would she have predicted this as her future.

"What else do you need from me?" Drake asked.

"I need to tell people why they should care about your team more than another." She said. Her phone stayed in her pocket. She didn't want to spook him by writing anything down.

"No team is better than another. We are all on the same playing field. Most can't afford to buy a new bike, so we make our own. Our team should win because of Lex's ability to put a smile on someone's face in the middle of this shit hole. And Vero, she's a badass. She will do anything to be first place."

"And you?"

"I'm the asshole who will kill someone for them to get ahead." His eyes on hers again told her exactly who he meant.

"So you're the hitman?"

"Exactly."

"Even though you're the one who keeps these two going? I can see it in the way they talk about you and the team," she said. He went rigid beside her. "Don't worry, I still think you're an asshole." He chuckled, and his stance eased. He marched back to his bike and saddled up. Guess the chat was over.

Vero dropped a tool in the grass, and Elle hesitated a moment before joining her in the shade. Two crushed beer cans and a half-full water bottle mixed in with the pile of tools.

"You take photos for a living?" Vero asked as soon as her ass hit the dirt. "How does that work exactly?"

"Well, I write for a living. I want to be a photographer. Not a journalist. This is my stepping stone," Elle answered. Vero tweaked her engine before revving it again. She didn't like the sound, Elle assumed, because she went back underneath. "Can I ask you a more personal question?" Vero nodded before she continued. "What do your parents say about you being in The Championship?"

"Nothing. They're dead." Elle was about to apologize when Vero raised her hand. "It's fine, Elle. Happened a while ago. What do your parents say? They want you to follow your dreams and all that?" she groaned as she tightened another bolt.

"Nothing. They're dead," Elle repeated.

Vero chuckled. The sound reverberated off the metal above her. "At least you have a lot of siblings."

"Right," Elle said. A hush fell between them. Their eyes locked, and Elle knew she understood.

"You think I could see some of your work?"

Elle nodded and brought up her photography website on her phone. "I prefer photographing people. I like moving them around and making changes to shift the view and mood. Usually, I make my friend Nate model for me. He's a photographer too. So he stands well. My mom was way better. Amazing actually. So I think I latched on to that when I was little. You know what I mean?"

"My dad was a mechanic." Vero laughed, and Elle nodded.

"Exactly." She smiled and took a moment to scroll through her photos. Vero sat up and scrubbed her hands on her pants before she scooted closer to Elle.

"Damn," Vero exhaled. Her eyes scanned the screen. Elle looked off at the track as Drake and Lex hopped off and started heading in their direction.

"Hey, we're going to the store. You wanna come?" Lex shouted at Vero.

She shook her head but waved them over. "Yo, come look at this!"

Lex ran, but Drake took his time. Lex sat down between them and swiped Elle's phone out of Vero's hand. She gaped at the photos.

Drake stood behind Elle and raised a brow at the girls. Vero snatched the phone back and threw it up to Drake. He stayed silent as he viewed them. Elle started to sweat.

"She's fantastic, right?" Lex said.

Vero nodded at Elle. "Not bad, Vanilla," she whispered.

Elle smiled at the girls. She turned back to Drake and cursed herself for leaving her jacket behind. She needed to take her private life back. She stood and looked over his shoulder to see which ones he was looking at so intently.

"Alright, you can be honest. It's not for everybody," Elle said and tried to take her phone out of his hand, but he stepped away from her.

"I'm not done," he mumbled, and Lex cheered as she stood.

"Yes! He likes them! We should do a photoshoot tomorrow! Where should we go?" Lex's excitement exploded. Her arms flailed as she hopped on her toes.

Elle wasn't sure how to take Drake studying her work. All her accomplishments were in his hands. Did he think they were too artsy or too dark? Too light? The landscapes were her favorites. He didn't seem like the kind of guy to appreciate the way a shadow appeared on the left side of a tree trunk. Like the willow tree. Wait.

"I know a place. I'll show you," Elle said, and Drake handed the phone back to her. She pulled up a photo that was in her locked album. It was of the willow tree near the lake with a dock. It was black and white, and the fog was coming off the water. There were benches on the other side of the water that you couldn't see in the distance.

"What! This is perfect," Lex exclaimed. Drake winced. Lex took the phone back to show Vero.

"Calm down, Blondie," Vero said, pulling her finger out of her ear.

"Can you do some in color and a few in black and white?" Lex asked with a wide smile.

"Of course," Elle said, and Lex handed her phone back.

"Tomorrow?" Lex asked Drake, and he didn't answer. He gave a slight shrug and according to Lex, that meant yes. She jumped and threw her fist in the air. Vero laughed and put her head back under the bike.

Elle loved her enthusiasm inside this terrible place they called home. Might rub off on her. She didn't hate the Valley as much as some, but she definitely didn't jump around like Lex did.

Drake waved his hand toward Lex. "Let's head out."

Lex followed him and waved goodbye to Vero and Elle.

The two of them stayed by the tree so she could continue working. Elle didn't mind the wind blowing her hair around or the tree line whistling back at them. The sun came down over their heads as they chatted back and forth. Vero filled the silence with random facts about her bike. Elle assumed nobody ever cared to listen. She would never squander her passion. She wanted to learn more anyway and stayed longer than she anticipated.

Elle helped Vero lock up the garage before she drove home. To keep her mind off the photo shoot, she forced her thoughts to Bernie's flavor of the day. Secretly she wished tomorrow would be her favorite; lavender honey.

five

E lle stopped at Bernie's on her way to the office. She needed fuel if she was going to see Randy today. He'd ask for an update, and she wasn't ready for his reaction.

Taking her last sip of coffee, she dropped it in the trash before getting into the elevator at the office. She hated this building. Everything was brown. The walls were dark wood. The floor was a light beige tile, and the ceiling used to be white but was now tan from age.

She pressed eight, and it flashed at her like the decrepit light bulb it was. No rhythm to its madness. She clutched her laptop to her chest, and the doors opened on three. Four people got on before Nate and he squeezed past them to stand with Elle.

"Hey, kid." He smiled at her.

She detested the nickname and he knew it. "Ready for Randy?" she asked him.

He ran his palm down the front of his fleece sweater and fixed his glasses on his nose. Nate gave her a finger gun. "You're gonna kill it in there."

"Yeah, my career, probably." She shrugged at his questioning eye. "The article is what I'm worried about."

"What team did you land on?" he asked, and the elevator stopped on six to pick up three more people dressed in jeans and T-shirts.

"Evolution."

The elevator filled fast and Elle protected her camera with her palms. The group in front of her whispered back and forth about the upcoming Championship and the news channels' constant flow of facts on different teams and ChaosMotors.

"Never heard of them," Nate said.

"Exactly. They need the press. I could use that to my advantage."

"Unless they suck and get killed at the beginning of the first race." He snickered, and she gave a half smile.

"I hope not. I'm quite fond of them."

"Oh?" he questioned her. "She has interest?"

"Shut up," she said, and he laughed. "I'm making friends. Kinda."

"Friends? You?"

The doors opened at eight, and everyone filed out. They stepped out last and Elle led Nate down the main hall to their office. The room was wide and filled with cubicles and old white laptops in rough shape. Elle's small chestnut desk sat next to Nate's. She placed her computer down as he rifled through some paperwork. His head popped up at the sound of a door slam.

"Time's up," he said, and she nodded.

"Elliot!" Randy called from the front of the office, and everyone froze. He refused to call her anything other than her full name. She looked up at him, and he signaled her to his office. She gathered her things. Nate slapped her on the back, giving her encouragement.

Elle hoofed it to his office. He didn't like to wait. He was already sitting behind his desk with his clear reading glasses on. He peered up at her, and she closed the door behind her.

"Update?" he asked.

She sat down across from him, and as she opened her mouth to respond, he interrupted.

"Team?"

"Evolution," she said.

"Who?" he barked. "Elliot, I specifically remember telling you to pick a good team."

"You told me to choose a team that was willing. I asked seven before this one approached me. They've been racing for years. I figure I can use the article to get them known. A new team, but a team with experience, might bring more readers to the magazine."

"Take any photos yet?" he asked, holding out his hand for her computer chip.

She handed it over. Only some of the photos were on the chip. None of the team. She promised Drake they could see them first.

"I've only edited a few. We're doing a photoshoot today. I'll get more shots of the entire team," she started to ramble then bit her tongue. Randy hated when she rambled. He sighed and plugged the chip into his computer. He'd keep it until she saw him again.

"Photoshoot better be good. Now get out of my office."

"Yes, sir." She left in a hurry and sat down next to Nate. He was about to speak when Randy called his name. He gave her a small smile.

"See you later. I'll be gone before you get back," she told him, and he waved as she packed up her things. She needed to get out of this shit room. Even her chair was brown. She shook her head as she left.

Elle caught Drake's eye in the rearview mirror from the back seat of the truck. She rubbed her brow slowly with her middle finger, and he smirked. Crops and fields replaced the buildings out the window. The far side of the Valley was full of farmland. Everything went to Sunset Cove. Not the mates.

When the Valley was first created, and everyone inside was a criminal, they referred to them as 'mates.' Inmates. In the prison. Now people use it as derogatory. Especially the Guard.

Elle thought things had gotten better inside the Valley in the last hundred years. Looking out at those fields, she wasn't so sure. Too many of them broke their backs to fill others' tables.

The truck stopped, and Elle caught Drake staring at her again. This time she glared until he looked away first. He jumped out and went to the back to help Vero grab the bikes from the trailer. Elle strolled over to the willow tree and placed her hand on its trunk. It took a minute for the memories to stop. She steadied herself and smiled up at it.

"Hello, old friend," she said.

"Talking to trees now?" Drake said, and she jerked.

"Don't scare me like that," she said, hitting his shoulder. Great, now he knew she was attached to a damn tree. "Yes, I was talking to the tree. It's because we go way back. I know your little pea brain couldn't possibly understand."

Elle didn't give him a chance to respond. Didn't want to hear his opinion on the one thing she had that was solely hers. When she'd come here it was to talk to her parents. Her brothers. Her sister.

She left him by the trunk and walked over to the best spot for great lighting. Vero and Lex came up behind her, and she directed the three of them to put the bikes on a diagonal and then told them where to stand.

"So, I will take photos for the magazine and some for Lex's fridge. Drake said he didn't want to be in them, so we will take some where you can't tell what he looks like."

"You're not going to edit a woman's face on my body or anything, right?" Drake asked.

"Stop talking. You're giving me good ideas," Elle said.

Vero lost herself in a fit of laughter. She was in full leather gear with no sleeves and sleek knee-high black boots. Lex had a dark dress that kept folding up at the hem. A small yellow flower tattoo revealed itself above her ankle that Elle hadn't noticed before. She unfolded the bottom of Lex's dress and peered at Drake.

"What do you need to fix on me?" he asked.

"You're a lost cause," Elle said, and the girls laughed. She made him drop to his knees, and the girls wouldn't stop giggling.

He started his retort but she interrupted him.

"Shush. Trust me," she said, and he looked up at her. He nodded once. It surprised her. She told him to crouch and lift one knee and rest his wrist on top. She tilted his arm a fraction of an inch.

"Relax. Think of something else," Elle told him. "You look tense."

"I am fucking tense," he said through his teeth.

"Think of that girl who tried to dance with you!" Lex laughed into her hands.

"That's not calming. That pisses me off." Drake sneered.

"A girl tried to dance with you? Poor girl." Elle chuckled and got down to his level. "I don't know. Think of your first kiss." He looked right at her.

"Not *our* first kiss, babe. Look over there," she said, and he snickered.

She grazed his jaw with her fingers and pointed toward the dock. Elle stood back up and fixed Lex for the last time. She stepped back and adjusted them from her camera lens.

The grass swayed in the breeze with the long strands from the willow tree. The fish in the lake would splash every once in a while but for the most part, the water was still. Elle could smell the groups of honeysuckle behind her.

Lex seemed more than willing to do whatever Elle asked. Vero started to whine after about an hour. Drake moaned and groaned after every photo, so it was hard to tell what he was thinking.

"Just a little longer, I promise," Elle said.

"Can you be in one?" Lex asked.

"Absolutely not." Elle took another photo.

"That's bullshit," Drake said. "I didn't want to do this. And I'm in every one. Your turn."

"Yeah, Drake can take a girls' pic!" Lex said.

Elle didn't trust him to hold her prized possession. She was looking down at the camera in her hands. It would only be a second. But still.

"I won't hurt your child," Drake said. Somehow he guessed what she had thought. She lifted the strap over her head and handed it to him.

"Okay, but be gentle," she said, and he pretended to drop it. She choked on her exhale and reached for it. He smirked at her.

Elle glared, fuming. "Don't ever do that again, you fu—"

"Calm down. Now, go stand next to Crazy and Blondie," he interrupted, and Vero flipped him off. Elle tried to level herself as she went to stand by the girls. Drake lifted the camera to his face.

"Okay, and then Elle, get down on your knees—no, I'm just kidding," he said, and the three of them burst out laughing. He snapped a photo, and Lex yelled at him.

"Hey! No. I look dumb!"

"I can't fix that," he said, and Vero laughed. He made them all smile for a serious one before he gave Elle her camera back. She sat down in the grass to review them. Drake tried to peek. sSe brought it to her chest.

"I can't see?" he asked.

"You can review all the photos after the edits," she promised. She looked at the small screen, and it was the photo he had taken of the three of them laughing. Her breath caught in her throat. It had been years since she'd seen a picture of herself where she looked happy. A genuine smile on her face.

The family photo in front of the fountain. Sunset Cove. Her mom held Elle in her hands, and Ezra had a red balloon tied to his wrist. Everest stuffed his face with ice cream. The six of them laughed when they saw Evelyn sticking her tongue out.

This photo of the three girls had that same energy.

She closed her eyes and turned the camera off. The point of this article was not to make friends. Her career was on the line. Her future.

The sun had begun to descend. Lex had her feet in the water at the end of the dock. Drake sat beside her with his knees up to his chest and his hands laced in front of them. Vero was laying down on the dock behind them, covering her eyes with her arm. Elle snapped a photo and knew Lex would like that one. She smiled and settled down next to Vero. Drake dipped his fingers into the water and flicked them at Lex. She squealed and tried to get him to stop. They sat in silence for a while, and the crickets became louder as it got darker.

"Dinner at ours?" Lex asked. "That goes for you too, Elle."

"Oh. Uh." Elle thought fast. Either accept and realize that Lex was becoming a friend, or reject and look like an ass. It's just dinner. "Sure, alright."

Vero sat up and started to mess with her hair and let out a heavy sigh. Her strands were going everywhere in the wind.

"Do you ever put your hair in a braid?" Elle asked.

"No, I don't know how," Vero snapped at her. I guess hair was a touchy subject. She tried not to take Vero's aggression personally.

"I can do it for you. If you like it, I'll teach you how to do it yourself," she offered. Vero thought about it for a minute before allowing Elle to work her fingers into her scalp. By the time she finished the simple braid, Vero was smiling.

"It looks so cute!" Lex said, and Vero nodded once at Elle. She realized that was the closest thing to a 'thank you' she was going to get. She was fine with that.

Cattails lined the lake beside the dock and a couple of ducks floated past them in the water. Elle remembered feeding the birds here with Sarah last summer. A few of the kids came with them and Christopher brought the rest with him later that night. The kids were fascinated by the fireflies Elle caught for them.

"Did you look at the photos Drake took? Did they come out okay?" Lex asked.

"They look good. He's a natural. If he weren't such an ass, I'd say he could be my assistant on future shoots," Elle joked.

Drake turned toward her. "Don't want to associate yourself with a criminal, I get it." Lex went pale. "What?"

"Drake," Lex sighed.

"It's alright." Elle got up from the dock and started heading to the truck. "Shoot's done anyway. Everyone ready to go?"

"Elle," Vero said, but Elle stopped her.

"Seriously, it's fine." She looked over at him. "What's insane to me is you're the one who said we're all on the same playing field, must only be on the track. What about the other dozen Valleys?" Elle said. Vero stopped in her tracks. They were all quiet for a minute.

"How do you know there's so many other Valleys?" Lex whispered.

"My grandfather was sent to help build a few of them when I was still in the Cove," Elle said, and Drake stiffened.

"You were in Sunset Cove?" Drake went wide-eyed. Vero smacked the back of his head before the two of them began to pack the bikes on the trailer. Lex held the door open for Elle before jumping in the passenger seat. She was grateful that Lex knew she needed to get away from him, even if it was only for a minute.

Drake was silent on the way back to the garage. He didn't look in the rearview mirror. He didn't add to the conversation. Vero helped him bring the bikes inside, and then Drake headed out to the track. Vero joined Elle and Lex but fixed her eyes on the door.

"I think we broke him," Vero said. "He hasn't said a word, dude."

"I'll go get him," Lex said, taking a step until Elle caught her arm.

"No, I'll go," Elle offered. "Clearly, it's about what I said." The door slammed behind her as she walked out. In the dark, she found Drake hunched over the first ramp. He always looked so miserable.

"Lex, seriously," Drake mumbled.

"I told her I'd come talk to you," Elle said, and he whipped around. His eyes were daggers again, but she stood her ground. She needed to clear the air to work with him. Listen and bite your tongue.

He stood straight and narrowed his eyes on her. "I've never met anyone who wasn't scared to challenge me."

"Scared? Of you?" She cackled. "Should I be?"

"Yes, but you're not. And you don't know me. I know. But I also don't know you. And I haven't decided if I want to."

"Because you don't like me hanging around your friends? Or because you believe I'm going to leave after my article is out?" she asked.

"I have my reasons," he answered. She expected that.

"Because you're a criminal? And nobody else in here is?" She narrowed her eyes at him.

"Okay," he said and gave a half smile. "Okay, I'll try my best not to assume anything about you and try not to be such a dick." He paused. "Only if you admit something to me."

Admit something? What kind of game was he playing? "What?"

He gave a sinister smile. "You have to admit that I looked pretty damn sexy in those photos you took today," he whispered, and she went beet red. "I noticed you blushing."

What an ass. "Actually, I was blushing because of the very first thing I noticed at the manor."

"Oh?" he said, intrigued.

"I saw the three of you on the second level. Know what I saw first?" she said. She brushed her hand on his bicep. He tensed but kept still. She locked eyes with him and leaned closer. "Vero."

She was halfway to the garage when he started to laugh.

six

Drake did not join them for dinner at Lex and Vero's. Elle was not surprised, though she found herself feeling disappointed. She wasn't sure what to make of that.

They sat down with Vero at the table and passed the bowls around. Pasta, mashed potatoes, and peas. Elle hated peas but didn't want to be rude, so she put one scoop on her plate.

"Well, you handled today very maturely. I thought for sure you would fly off the handle." Lex smiled before she put a glob of potatoes on her plate.

"Everyone was born here if you ask Drake. Being sent as a child messed with his brain. I'm sure you can relate." Vero chewed on her pasta and took a sip from her can of beer.

"Everyone has their own shit," Elle started. "Most of us have a sob story to tell, and if you ask me, not one is worse than the other. We shouldn't be working against each other or separating ourselves into groups."

"So, what happened to your parents?" Lex asked.

Sarah popped into her mind. Dr. Gordon and all his wisdom. She needed to let go. On shaky ground, she pushed through. "They died. That's how I got here." Elle paused. "It was a car accident." Bile rose in her throat. Her vision started to blur.

The horn blared in her ears, and the van went over the railing on the bridge into the water below. The windshield smashed into a million pieces. A big slice cut straight into her mother's neck, and blood spilled down the front of her. Elle could see it in the rearview mirror. The water poured in, and soon, her father and brothers were under too. Her sister screamed, but no sound came out, just a mess of bubbles. Her older brother, Everest, took his last breath. His body shook in a way that jerked him entirely. Pounding on the window beside her made the vehicle shake. A young boy tried to break the glass. He was holding something in his hand. Elle couldn't make out what it was. Once it shattered, he yanked her to the surface as Elle watched her family drift to the bottom of the lake in their coffin.

"Elle?" Vero said, probably for the fifth time. "Yo, you good?"

"I don't talk about it often." She crossed her arms in front of her. Took a deep breath. "I have breathing exercises that help."

"You don't have to tell us," Lex reassured her.

"We ended up in a lake. A boy pulled me out. But everyone else..."

They stared. It was part of the reason she never told anyone. Dr. Gordon tried to convince her it wouldn't be like this every time. She didn't believe him.

"Someone saved you?" Vero asked.

"The Guard murdered him before taking me here. They charged me with my family's death." Elle brought her fork up to her lips and forced another bite into her mouth. "Someone had to pay what was due. Someone had to pay for their deaths."

Then Lex started to shout. "You didn't do anything! That's bull!"

"Try telling the Guard that. Or Cyra." Elle scoffed. "I wouldn't have had anyone to stay with in the Cove anyway."

"When's the last time you told someone about your family?" Lex asked.

"When I first arrived. I saw a therapist for years. Video calling. Then Cyra stopped allowing calls to the Cove," Elle said. Her chest began to tighten. She needed to stop the conversation, and luckily, they let her. Lex droned on about the photoshoot to Vero and how she couldn't wait to see the edits.

Elle helped clear the table when they finished. Her peas rolled around the edges of the plate. She started to say her goodbyes when Vero convinced her to stay. She hadn't taught her how to braid yet. Elle couldn't help her smile. Vero led her into the bedroom at the end of the hallway.

It was a typical room: bed, dresser, two nightstands, a closet filled with leather, and a full hamper. Gloves and helmets lined her closet shelf. But her nightstands were both covered with sketchbooks and charcoal.

Elle silently asked permission by holding it up to Vero. She shrugged. The drawings were dark. Demons with guts and blood pouring out of them in thick red paint. They were all sharp teeth and hollow eyes. Intestines ripped apart. Necks snapped in two. She couldn't believe the imagery. The talent was unbelievable.

"These are amazing, Vero."

She scrunched her nose and shrugged. "It's only a hobby." Vero sat on the edge of the bed, and Elle put the book back on the table.

"Some people would pay a pretty penny for those. No doubt," Elle said.

"Thanks," Vero mumbled.

Elle joined her to start on her braid. Her hair was thick and dark. Elle had worked with worse at Little Hearts. She was glad Vero liked it.

Lex dove on the pillows to join in on 'girl time' or whatever it is she called it. They were quiet as Elle taught Vero what to do. When she finished, Vero stood to look in the mirror. She undid and then redid it herself twice before smiling at herself. She sat back down next to Elle and seemed lost in thought.

"I had a boyfriend once," Vero said barely above a whisper.

"What happened?" Elle asked, and Lex looked away.

Vero rolled her eyes and chuckled. "Drake. My knight in shining armor."

"Oh," Elle said. The shock sinking in.

"I'm surprised he stepped in, considering he was even more of a handful back then. But when I was in the hospital, Drake was the one who came to see me. Every single day. Then, he brought Lex. That's how we met." Vero smiled at her friend. Lex brimmed with tears near the headboard. "I owe Drake my life. I race for him. For Lex. There is nothing I love more than these two idiots." She paused, and they laughed.

"But now there's purple hair." Lex winked at Vero, and she blushed.

"Purple hair?" Elle asked.

"Vero has a crush." Lex giggled.

"Dude, that topic is off limits," Vero snapped. Lex threw a pillow at her, and she caught it before whipping it back at Lex's head. Soon they were stifling laughs into their palms to not disturb the neighbors.

Elle got home late and pulled her hair over her shoulder to brush it. Thinking of Vero's smile when she tied off the braid. She threw her own in a bun and climbed into bed.

Randy was displeased with her lack of photos, so she went back to editing. She chose her top three favorites for the cover and put them in a different folder to show the team later.

The one with Drake crouched down was her number-one pick. He was looking to the side, so you could only see half of his face. He didn't look as tense, and his shoulders relaxed. The next one, Drake wore a smug grin.

"Asshole," she muttered to herself.

Her laptop clicked as she shut the lid. Her eyes refusing to close, she stared at the ceiling as her thoughts wandered to her new friends. She was not supposed to make friends with this team. She couldn't help feeling connected to them though.

How was she supposed to watch them in The Championship? Getting roughed up and dodging other riders. She didn't want to watch any of them die, but she had lived through that before. She could do it again. Right? These three weren't her family. It would be easier to grieve. Right? She shook her head and wiped the stray tears that had escaped.

Halfway through the night, she woke up out of breath. That thick lake water traveled down her throat. She tried to swallow but choked. Coughing, she steadied herself on her bathroom counter. Inhale. Exhale. Cool water on her face and neck made her realize sweat coated her skin. Elle stripped down to shower, cursing herself for having nightmares at her age. A twenty-year-old shouldn't be having nightmares that wake her up in a sweat. Childish.

4:27 AM. Elle knew she wasn't going back to sleep. She packed her bag and headed to the coffee shop. A latte was exactly what she needed. She could get more editing done there.

Elle parked on the gravel road outside the garage. The truck wasn't there. The silence was chilling. Normally the tools and the revs of the engines echoed off the trees. With her camera in hand, she went around back to get photos of the white flowers in the middle of the track. She noticed a thin trail at the tree line and stopped. The camera strap was hot on her neck as she took a step toward the opening.

"It leads to an animal trap," Drake said.

Elle yelped and swiveled to see him standing behind her. "Why do you sneak up on me like that?"

"You didn't hear me pull in?" he asked, pointing over at his bike by the back door. He must have recently showered. His hair was still a little wet, and his arms weren't covered in grease or mud. He was the cleanest she'd ever seen him. "What are you looking at?"

"Nothing," she said. She pointed to the trees. "Can I see?"

"There's nothing in it. We have an alarm system for it."

"I want to see," she said, and he led her toward the trail. They walked for a few minutes. The leaves and twigs crunched under their every step. "What's the system?"

"There's a rock that swings above the trap to hit a trash can lid. It's loud as shit," Drake explained. "Vero did most of the work herself, but I helped."

"You dug the hole?"

He nodded. "Lex said I dug my own grave."

"I'm shocked Vero allowed you to do work for her. She seems like an independent, stubborn woman."

"She didn't know I was doing it. I did it overnight," he said. He peered over at her. "Never said I was smart."

"What kinds of animals do you trap?" she asked.

"Wildcats, coyotes, sometimes the occasional bobcat. Nothing crazy, but nothing I want them to deal with riding alone."

They walked another minute before Drake motioned to a clearing. There was a large hole with a net and boulders along the edge. Brown leaves covered the top, and hanging a few feet above was another net to cover. A metal trash can lid was in the tree next to a bucket on a rope.

"What's in the bucket?" Elle pointed up at it.

"Poison."

A shiver ripped through her. "Here I was thinking you jump in there and snap its neck."

"Could be the cover photo for the magazine," he suggested.

"Ready when you are," she said and held her camera up at him.

Drake stepped toward the hole and held the bottom of his shirt. "On or off?" He winked at her.

She laughed and took her eyes away from him. "How does it work?"

"Animal falls in, this comes down, rocks hold it in place, and the small rock swings from that tree to clap the trash can lid. I come down, kill whatever's in there, and move it, so the girls don't have to," Drake explained and used his hands a lot when he was speaking. He walked over to the rope with the trash can lid on it, and he undid it from the tree. It dropped to the ground, and he went to pick it up, but a piece was sticking out. Blood rushed out of his hand.

"Drake!"

"Oops." He chuckled and raised his hand, and the blood dripped down his arm.

"Come on," Elle said and led the way back to the garage.

"You're going to be my nurse?" he asked.

"You're such an ass." She sneered. She got to her car and rummaged through her bag for the tin of Blue Sludge.

He looked down at it with wide eyes, and she handed it to him. "Where did you get this?"

"Do you want it or not?"

He looked from the tin back to her before he smeared a dime-sized amount on his cut. The skin repaired itself before their eyes, and Elle shoved the tin back into her bag.

"Did you steal that?" he asked.

"No." She laughed and made sure her camera was around her neck before they walked into the garage.

"I've seen those around. Other teams get it off the street. Some trade it for drugs. Or sex." He glared at her. "I told you not to mess anything up for my team. That includes drug addicts coming after you for this shit. If Lex or Vero get in the crossfire—"

"Stop. It's not anything like that." She held her hands up. "Remember, you're not assuming anything about me?" Should not have shown him the tin.

"Could you get more?" he asked.

She scoffed. "Oh, so now you want some?"

"Knowing you didn't sell your body to get it, maybe."

"Screw you." She shoved him. Or tried to. He didn't budge.

Drake walked over to his bike, and Elle followed. He started to mess with the fireball launcher above his rear wheel. He loaded it up with the black lumps of coal. His focus was extraordinary. Never losing sight of his project or purpose.

The fireballs made her think of the research she'd done on The Championship. Each year they combine science with war and create beatable threats. Sometimes it's animals or monsters that they take ideas from. Like one year, they created lions that roared to send out a frequency that made the riders go deaf for a minute. One year they iced the entire track, so any bike that was on wheels had it harder than the ones that hovered.

Then they created Jelly Tunnels. Riders had to go through a dark tunnel with wires hanging down. If you hit them at the right angle and speed, they attach to your skin. Venom would slowly seep in and turn your organs into sapphire mush. The red wires were immediate. Venom that acted faster than acid. Instantly turning you into a pile of goo. The only way to prevent it was Blue Sludge or layers of protection.

Each year was more terrifying than the last. Another reason she stayed away so long. She never went to a race or watched any of them on television. If she wanted terror, all she had to do was close her eyes.

Drake began to shove coal into a bag, and Elle helped him load another to bring over to Vero's corner.

"Are you nervous?" Elle asked.

"For the race? No. Nothing I can do to change it." He looked at the pile of tools at his feet. He wiped his forehead of sweat and left a smear of grease. Elle chuckled at him. A questioning look dawned on him, and she handed over a clean rag and pointed at his head. He wiped it and sighed when he saw the black mark. "We prepare all year for it. So, why stress about it? All that's going to do is make my reaction time slower."

"What about the weather on the track? Or the terrain? One year it was tall grass, and one was like a desert."

"Yeah, it's tough. All I do is convince my body it's warmer than it is. And focus on the fact that I'll be out of it soon. Whether I'm dying there or getting out of the arena," he said and picked up a drill from the floor beside them.

"So before every race, you accept that you might die inside it?"

"Yeah."

His answer was so abrupt she almost couldn't believe it. She could never do that. Accept her fate without any hesitation or question. He didn't even seem to fear it.

"What happens if you win? What do you want to do with the prize money?"

"Move my family to Sunset Cove. That's where I was born."

He was born in Sunset Cove? Just like her. She hadn't seen that coming. "Excuse me?"

"Yeah, that was my reaction too." He smirked. He raised the drill to the bike and spoke before he used the tool. "We could have met on the other side."

"Impossible." She shook her head. "Everyone I knew from the other side is dead," she said and handed him the drill bit he needed next. He took it and double-checked it was the right one. Elle avoided covering her ears at the whirring sound it made. The tall ceilings made everything reverberate.

"You're not what I was expecting," he said.

"You mentioned that. So what? I'm more of a bitch?" she asked, and he chuckled.

"Definitely," he mocked her in a high tone.

She back-handed his shoulder. "Ass."

"Bitch."

The fire launcher ticked like a clock. Drake pushed her down as a ball of fire flew over her head. They sat up and stared at the three-inch round hole in the wall.

"Oops," he whispered. They glanced at each other before they started to chuckle. The door to the garage slammed, and Lex and Vero appeared. Drake's laugh erupted as they approached.

"What the hell is going on?" Vero asked.

"He tried to kill me!" Elle laughed harder. She pointed at the wall. Vero shook her head at him.

"Oh my goodness! Are you okay?" Lex asked. She bent down to check Elle for injuries.

"I obviously missed," Drake said, and Vero chuckled at that.

"You better work on your aim before tomorrow," Elle said.

seven

"I'm way more excited this year," Lex said and smiled at the riders unloading in the parking lot of the arena. There were dozens in black and brown leather. Only a handful of teams were in color and one in white.

Lex and Vero were in matching outfits. High boots, leather pants, a dark shirt, and their black team leather jacket. Their initials were on the lapel in white stitching. Team Evolution was in red lettering with a tree on fire under it on the back. Vero had her hair in a straight braid down her back while Lex had hers clipped on the sides to keep out of her eyes. She painted her eyes with a touch of an orange glow and glitter.

"Trust me, Lex, we can tell," Vero said.

"It's definitely busy," Elle mentioned.

She was finally able to see more ChaosMotors bikes. One hoverbike went past them with bright green and yellow stripes. It had a round wheel instead of handlebars. There were a few hoverbikes, but most of them weren't. She remembered what Drake had said. Most riders were not in a financial situation to purchase a new bike. They would create their own using scraps.

Some had large wheels in the front and small ones in the back. Others had two wheels, while some had six or seven. Handlebars varied in length. One even had two sticking straight up that the rider pushed on to accelerate. It reminded Elle of the elliptical Sarah used to have.

Elle carried Vero's helmet as she pushed her bike to the gate. Drake stepped beside Elle in his typical jeans and black T-shirt. His chunky black boots made clouds of dust as he walked. His jacket hugged every inch of his chest. He held his helmet under his arm and combed his hair to the side.

Lex stopped and hugged Elle, and then Vero pulled her in for a quick one. She handed Vero her helmet. Drake tensed when they made eye contact. Was he expecting a hug too?

"Don't die," she said.

"Try my best."

Elle walked to the other end of the lot. She spotted Nate to the side, searching for her. She turned back to look at the team, and Drake was staring at her. He pulled his helmet on, and she wondered why he put it on so early. That was strange. Wouldn't it be hot?

Elle felt the weight of the Sludge in her jacket even though she remembered to switch it to a less conspicuous tin. It looked like a tube of chapstick. Got through security without an issue. She ended up in the middle of the stands with Nate. He'd been to the last few races, so he knew where to sit and who to stay away from.

The track was all dirt. Elle took a sigh of relief. At least the terrain wouldn't be an issue this round. She pushed through the sea of people until he pulled her to sit.

"This is insane," she said.

Nate cracked his knuckles as he nodded. His unease started to rattle her. Elle turned her attention to the crowd. Hundreds of people stood with posters of their favorite teams. Teenagers held pink hearts with a contestant's name or picture on them. Others were in full leather outfits like their favorite rider. Some even wore helmets with a team logo on the side.

Elle looked through her camera lens to see more of the track. Hills and curves were throughout the arena, and a few wide tunnels with no light. There were large craters in the ground with metal spears sticking out from the bottom. The Guard surrounded the stands in full uniform and gear. They marched in pairs and held their firearms with two hands. Definitely seemed like robots today.

Elle stopped at Little Hearts that morning to get a mom hug from Sarah and a few of the kids wished her luck. Some told her not to get killed. Even the young ones understood the Guard were not to be messed with. When she turned to Samuel, he gave her a small rock. It was a dark shade of purple and smooth on one side. She wasn't sure what to do with it, so she slipped it into her front pocket. Sitting in the stands, she found herself rubbing it.

It was strange to see some of the mates in all bright colors like they were. The bikes matched their team colors, and some even had full-body suits with one zipper covered in their logo. Including their helmet. Team Halo, as usual, was all in white. A small golden ring wrapped around the top of their helmets. Elle rolled her eyes at that. If any of the rumors she'd heard were true, they were anything but angelic.

The race was about to begin. The riders were all lined up. Each row was a different team. The track was wide enough for roughly ten bikes, but no team had more than six. They had to complete three laps to go on to the next race.

"Breathe, Elle," she told herself, and Nate patted her back. "Hope you're not squeamish. I might puke."

"You'll be alright, kid."

"I'm only three years younger than you," she reminded him. She pursed her lips. He smiled at her and patted her head this time. She glared at him.

"I know."

Elle surveyed the crowd again until Nate cleared his throat.

"You'll be okay."

"Will you?" she asked.

"Sometimes I cry," he whispered and held up a small pack of tissues. This wasn't surprising to Elle. He wasn't the toughest guy on the block. Wasn't expecting him to be so open about it.

"Why come?" she asked.

"This year?" he said and motioned to her. "But before work, of course."

"You're here for me? You did not have to do that."

"Shut up. You know you're like my little sister. And I love you. Not like, ew, but," he shook his head, "but I'd worry if you came alone. So, just let me cry if I need to."

"No prob." She saluted him but then gave him an awkward side hug. "You know I love you too. Just not like, you know, ew."

"Yeah, yeah."

She tried not to think of the race. The worst possible scenarios flipped through her head. Any of them could happen today. She could leave having watched her friends die in the next hour.

The last teams lined up at the start. Elle waved to Lex, who blew her a kiss. Elle laughed. The team behind them looked over to see who was the recipient of such a gift, and Elle recognized one of them. The blue fan sticking out of his head stood out on the light background. He smiled and raised his hand up to Elle. She grinned back at Gage. Their team had all blue bikes, of course.

"You know other riders?" Nate asked.

"Only one couple from Blue Falcon. I met Gage the day I met Lex. He's very nice."

"I remember him from last year, actually."

He was hard to forget, considering even his helmet had a cutout for his hair.

The riders were ready on their battlefield. Ready for war. A team of five was at the start, followed by a team of four, and so on. Elle felt bad for the teams closer to the back. The placement didn't seem very fair.

Drake searched the stands, helmet on and ready to go. He faced forward and sat on his bike as the first gun went off. Elle jumped at the sound.

Inhale.

Exhale.

Everyone sat in the stands as Cyra came out of the box seat above them all. A microphone was set up in front of her.

"This is the one-hundred-seventy-fourth Covington ChaosMotors Championship!" she yelled. Her voice vibrated the bleachers. Everyone was silent until the confetti cannons exploded. White flakes came down on them, and the crowd erupted. The Guard were like statues hanging on her every word. "The first twenty teams that cross the finish line will go on to the next round. One member needs to cross in order for your entire team to advance." She gestured to a Guard on the track, and that was it.

Another gun went off, and the riders put their helmets on. They started to rev their engines. Dust began to rise in the arena. The third gun sounded. Elle held her breath as the riders launched forward.

An announcer started speaking from the same box seat. They spit facts about the teams, who were in the top twenty, and who lost their lives on the track.

Like a rocket, Drake went around the first bend. Elle stood to see until someone yelled at her from behind. Nate yanked her arm to sit back down.

"Sorry," she mumbled.

They were all moving so fast. She no longer felt the placements were unfair. Some from the last row were now in the first ten.

Lex and Vero stayed together for most of it. A red bike came up on Drake's left. They shot fireballs at him. He sped up and shot back. One hit the other rider's helmet. They swatted and rammed into the wall of the arena. The first death.

"Team Halfpipe, fatality. Team Quest, in the lead." The announcer was monotone, but Elle's heart raced.

Lex went over a hill and landed sideways. Missed the hole of spears by an inch. She gathered herself and got back in the game. Vero kicked a rider into the pit of coals. Elle could hear their shrill scream from the stands. Drake neared the end of his first lap when two walls slid open. The one closest to Elle released a metal ball the size of Drake's truck.

It rolled a foot from the edge. It began to open like a flower blooming. A tail came out with spikes running down the left side. Five paws came out next. Then they sprouted claws. Several inches in length. It growled at the fans in the front row. Three rows of razor blades sprang from its mouth. The crowd screamed.

They constructed the cat out of metal. Its body creaked and groaned with every movement. The eyes were too round and glossy to be anything but cameras. Elle wondered if someone controlled it that way or if they only wanted the instant replays.

The machine turned back to the track and sat down. It waited for a rider to pass by. A member of Team Quest was too close, and it swatted at them. They landed in the sand with a thump. Then they started to sink. Bit by bit, the quicksand swallowed them. They shouted for help the entire descent.

Their bike lay in the middle of the track, and the next rider crashed into it. They catapulted into the ramp. Their neck snapped, and they collapsed to the ground. Drake weaved around the bikes and hit the jump at an angle. He landed on the other side of the cat unscathed. Elle screamed with joy.

Two Guard members ran out and hauled the bikes and bodies to the side.

"Team Quest, fatality. Team Dread, fatality."

The machine had long pins coming out of its back. Like quills from a porcupine, but they were dark with a red tip. Elle wondered if there was venom inside. She didn't have to wait long. A rider impaled one and then started to melt. They pulled their helmet off before screaming. Their eyes turned to thick white liquid that dripped down their cheeks. Fatality.

Lex and Vero got around the cat with ease. A rider in all red leather got behind Lex. They started to shoot fireballs and spikes at Lex. Luckily she had shields. Two yellow sheets rose from the back of her bike to protect her. The balls and spikes ricocheted off. The coals snuffed out in the soil.

Lex shot a spear at them, but they dodged it. Wasting no time, she shot a spike at their back tire, and they faltered. Lex sped past. But the tire filled back up in seconds. Auto-fill. Elle squeezed Nate's hand when they stomped on their accelerator. Lex jerked to the right and rammed on her brake. The rider dove into the pit of spears. Elle cowered as their body was impaled.

"Team Fireball, fatality."

Elle pointed out each member of her team, and Nate smiled at her.

"You really are fond of them, huh?" he teased. "They're good, though."

Three teams got disqualified for using weapons not allowed in the arena. Immediate disqualification meant the announcer called your team name. And then the Guard picked you off one by one. Two options: follow them out or get shot down.

A team was being called over and over. The last rider on the team refused to leave. He flipped them off as the Guard pulled the trigger.

Drake was in fourth place as he approached the second opening in the wall. It opened, and short bursts of wind shot out. It was too late to avoid it. His bike fell on its side. Drake flipped onto his back and used the momentum to propel himself over again. He completed an entire roll and ended right side up again. His third lap had begun.

Elle's eyes watered as Vero got past the wind. Lex barely got through before it opened all the way. It wasn't short blasts anymore but a constant blow.

Drake stopped inches before he reached the monstrous feline. It was rubbing its back in the dirt. The rider behind him went past. Once the paw struck him, Drake hit the gas. Distraction. The cat swallowed him. Nate cheered for Drake, and Elle smiled wide at him. He hit her arm with his.

"Get with it," he told her.

Lex and Vero jumped over the cat together. The paw went right between them. Instead, it caught the rider behind them with its tail. It began to feast. Metal teeth crunched on bone. Elle tried not to gag. She fixed her eyes on the slim black bike at the front and reminded herself it was almost over.

Drake navigated around the patches of quicksand effortlessly. The riders that tried to pass him steered into the craters around them. When he focused, he was a machine.

Lex deflected a fireball as Vero pushed a rider off their bike in midair. He fell into the fire pit below. Instant fatality.

The wind shut off, and birds flew out of the door before it slammed shut. Each time they squawked, a fireball shot out of its beak. They had orange, red, and yellow wings. At least they were easy to spot.

One bird rapidly fired at Drake. He stood on his bike and slammed the bird into the stands with his hand. It ignited, and people screamed. The Guard extinguished it, and the crowd cheered.

Drake crossed the finish line in sixth place. He pulled over to watch Lex and Vero as he cradled his bloody hand to his chest.

Lex swerved between each fireball from the birds with ease. She was small. She would be fine, Elle told herself. It almost became a mantra in her head. She was small. She would be fine.

The door opened again, and a breeze went through the arena. It started getting heavier. Colder. Lex waited for the next rider and matched their speed. She rode beside them so they would get the worst of it. She got through to the other side. Two minutes later, she joined Drake. She'd completed the race. Eleventh place wasn't bad. Vero was the only one left.

She had four birds surrounding her. Pummeling her with coals. She started to drift left and right, so she was a more challenging target. Vero raised her fist and hit a lump of coal back at one of the birds. Struck it square in the eye. Its aim was off the rest of the race. The crowd exploded with cheers. She crossed the line and ran to Lex. She spun her around in a circle before giving Drake a pat on the back. They were all smiles.

Elle and Nate stood and hollered for her friends before the guy behind them complained again. She drummed her fingers on her thighs as she waited for the race to end. The contestant in last looked rough as he tried to make the final jump.

"He's not going to make it," Elle whispered.

He dropped into the pit. The stands went silent. He screamed as his leg caught on a spear. The right side of his body burned from the coals beneath him.

"Someone help him!" Elle shouted.

"How? Technically, he's still in the race." Nate put his hands on his head.

"When does the race end?"

"When you hear the last gunshot," Nate said.

The rider screamed again. The sound echoed in the deserted track. All the riders corralled through the gate to the parking lot. Half of the stands were empty already. People didn't want to stay for this.

Elle heard his scream on repeat. Over and over.

It began to muffle and fade.

Her family's van horn blasted.

The arena filled with water. Thick, murky, and dark.

Bubbles came out of Nate's mouth as he spoke and she couldn't hear him.

Everest spasmed in the bleachers beside her. His shriek echoed in her ears.

The gun sounded, and Elle took off. She could hear Nate's protests behind her. Disregarded him. Her legs had already carried her to the edge of the arena. She hopped the fence and landed on the packed earth hard.

eight

Elle ran for the pit, and the air shut off. The silence in the arena was resounding. The rider shrieked as she slid like she was trying to hit home plate. Elle lifted his torso and rested his head on her leg.

"Hey, can you hear me?" Elle asked.

He gripped her hand and looked up at her. Tears ran down his face. The right side of his body was black and bloody from the burn. Elle began to sweat from being so close to the hot coals. Spears surrounded the edge. One was clean through his thigh, holding him there like a stuffed pig over an open flame.

The burning flesh stank, but Elle kept her center. She hesitated as she reached for the tin in her pocket. Guard were watching. Waiting. Waiting for him to die. She slipped some on her finger inside her jacket pocket before applying it to his temple and cheek. The burn faded and his arm was half gone. Blood flowed from his wrist, what was left of it anyway.

"I'm stuck," he choked out. His eyes were bloodshot, and his hair was matted to his forehead. He couldn't be more than three years older than her. Maybe twenty-five.

Elle stifled a sob. "I know. Hang on."

"Robert!" someone yelled behind her. An older man sprinted toward them.

"Dad?" The rider's voice cracked as his eyes widened. "Dad, I'm stuck. I can't move."

The man got down beside Elle. He tried to pull him out of the hole before noticing his leg. The rider howled with pain, and his dad stopped.

Elle didn't apply more Sludge. His complexion started to gray. It was over. She held Robert's hand, and he looked up at her. His eyes became dull. Robert's father started to shift his leg but couldn't get the spear to budge.

"Rob, I can't—"

"Sir," Elle whispered, and he froze. He scrambled to look at his son. His face. His hand. He put his head down on his son's burnt chest and wailed.

An arm wrapped around Elle's waist and dragged her from the scene.

"Hey!" she screamed. The Guard had no right to touch her. But when she looked down at the arm around her, it was a human hand. Dirty, bloody, and bruised.

"What the hell are you doing?" Drake snarled into her ear.

"He was alive," she said and smacked his hand off of her. She hoped it hurt. He let go and left a bloody handprint on her favorite jacket. Rage boiled inside her.

"That is none of your concern. Do not put yourself in the spotlight. They will rip you to shreds!" Drake shouted at her.

"What? Who will?"

"The queen and her filthy bloodhounds," he said and grabbed her wrist to pull her to the parking lot. She turned back, and the man screamed at the Guard. They raised his son out of the pit. Limp and fragile.

"You mean Cyra and the Guard?" she asked.

He gritted his teeth. "Don't say her name." He tightened his hold on her and didn't let go until they arrived at the truck.

"What were you thinking?" Vero yelled at her. Blood and mud covered her entire right side. Bikes went past them in clusters of dirt clouds. Teams cheered together as they retired to the after-party at the manor.

"Elle, you can't save anyone here," Lex said softly.

Nate ran to her from the gate. "Elle!" He forced her into a hug. "What the hell were you thinking?"

"I know," she said. His eyes scanned the present company, and he let go.

"Fucking idiot," Drake muttered.

"She was trying to help." Nate tried to soften the blow. Elle appreciated him, but it was useless. She knew that.

"She didn't help him!" Drake snapped. "He's dead!"

"Hey! Wait!" Robert's father yelled from the gate. He came barreling toward them. Drake stood in front of Elle and puffed his chest, waiting for an attack. "I mean no harm. Please," he panted.

Drake took a cautious step to the side, and the man shoved his hand into Elle's. He closed his fingers around hers, and she could feel a small cold piece of metal. She opened her palm to a lapel pin covered in dust. She smoothed her thumb over it to reveal its shine. A gold leaf.

"He was a farmer. Loved plants and nature. He was my son." He paused to close his eyes tight before he continued. "You didn't know him, but in an arena full of thousands, you ran to him. The last thing he saw was your face instead of this prison."

He gave her a quick, tight hug. Releasing her, he sobbed as he walked away from them. Elle stared down at the pin in her hand. The group was silent. Tears brimmed in her eyes.

"Elle, are you okay?" Nate paused when Elle collapsed on her knees in the grass and vomited. Drake sat down beside her, and Nate handed her a tissue. She wiped her mouth and looked over at Drake before she started to snicker. He looked at Lex and furrowed his brow as the silence continued. Elle's laughter bubbled harder in her gut.

"Dude, she's lost it," Vero mumbled.

"Are you okay?" Lex repeated.

"Did you see when Vero hit that bird with its own fireball?" Elle asked, and Vero snorted. Drake hung his head before he concealed his face with his hands. He started to chuckle, and within a minute, they were all roaring with laughter. Lex started to cry. Elle had a couple of tears slip out but wiped them away fast. Nobody spoke for several minutes.

"We lived," Lex whispered.

"You were amazing," Elle said.

Nate handed Lex a tissue. She took it and thanked him quietly. His eyes stayed on hers too long. Elle wanted to smack the back of his head. Now was not the time.

Drake got up and offered a hand to Elle. She accepted it, and he hoisted her up with ease. Her hair swung and hit him in the chest before settling around her shoulders. She glanced down at her jacket and her eyes widened at the massive blood stain. It was her own fault.

"Drake, your helmet." Lex's eyes were wide. Fear flashed in them.

"I know." He crossed his arms in front of him.

Elle wasn't sure what the issue was but didn't want to press her luck.

Drake's hand was dark purple and swelling by the second. Elle dug in her jacket, and Drake jerked his head left. She dropped it back into the silk she loved so much.

"Not here," he murmured.

"I used it in there. Do you think anybody saw?" she asked.

"Let's hope not," he said.

"That was dumb, huh?" she said, biting her bottom lip. She couldn't believe her own stupidity. The Guard were so close.

"You were just being you." He gripped the back of his neck and sighed. "You care too much," he said venomously. "Dangerous game to play inside these walls." She hated that he spoke to her like that. But she couldn't help but agree.

Nate took a coworker home, so Elle rode with Evolution to the garage. Her car was there anyway. Lex let Vero sit up front in the truck. Elle caught Drake staring at her in the mirror every so often. This time didn't look away. She was curious. Maybe a near-death experience made him realize his asshole ways.

"Elle knows someone who makes Blue Sludge," Drake said.

Nope. Still an asshole.

"Really?" Lex asked.

"What?" Vero turned around to face her. "Is that true?"

"Yes, that is true." She handed the tube to Drake. He stopped at the last red light and put a tiny amount on his palm and the back of his hand. The skin became tan and smooth again. He wiped the blood on his jeans and handed them back to her.

"Dude, what the hell. Where can we get some?" Vero asked.

"I have another one in my car."

"I thought you only had one?" Drake raised a brow.

"I lied." Elle sneered at him. She was done with his bullshit. What an asshole. Should've never given him the Sludge in the first place.

"How do you know them?" Vero teased.

"What is up with you guys?" Elle chuckled. "It's my brother, alright?"

Vero gave her a confused look. "I thought you said—"

"Not by blood," Elle interrupted her. "The one who builds ramps for riders. Please don't ask more questions. I'm risking his life by telling you."

"You can trust us," Lex said.

"You two, yes. Him, no," she glared at Drake.

"What did I do?" he snapped as they climbed out of the truck at the garage. The sun was beginning to set and fireflies were hovering over the track around the side and back of the building. Elle wished she was with her family catching them now. Not arguing with the captain of the team. Would this be it? Would he tell her to leave now?

"You told them. I trusted you with it, and that was only yesterday!"

"You expected me to keep it from my teammates when it could help them? Fuck off, Elle. You're even more of an idiot than I thought," Drake said, and Vero stopped walking to turn toward him. Lex stood by the truck and crossed her ankles as she leaned on the side.

"If they needed it, I would have given it to them. I should have never told you. I shouldn't have let you take me into the woods. And I definitely should have let your hand heal on its own. Screw you, Drake."

"You took her into the woods?" Vero asked him.

"Not like that!" He looked repulsed. Which angered Elle even more.

"Whoa, dude, I didn't do anything." Vero pointed at her own chest.

"You're not helping either."

"Dude, you got yourself into this mess. She trusted you, and the next day you blab about it. She's right. You had no reason to tell us. Maybe, for once, you'll think about apologizing for something you've done," Vero said.

The quiet of the clearing made her words echo off the garage in front of them. Lex stepped towards Elle and had the key in her hand when Drake punched the side of his truck.

"I'm not apologizing for shit!"

Lex put her hand on Elle's shoulder to pull her into the garage. She shook her head.

"I'm going home," Elle said.

"No, don't. Come to the party with us!" Lex pouted. "Drake doesn't go anyways."

"Shocker, you don't go out with your team to celebrate," Elle said.

Drake crossed his arms in front of him. "Going to get drunk in a house with a hundred people fucking each other isn't my way of celebrating."

"Funny. That is exactly what I picture you doing to celebrate," Elle said, and he huffed at her. "Tough guy like you can't win a girl in a room full of other men?"

"Is that why you go to parties? To watch all the other girls get picked?" His eyes narrowed on her as he spoke.

"Drake," Lex gasped. She looked at her friend before covering her mouth. Elle wasn't surprised. He was punishing her.

"You're such an asshole," Elle breathed.

"And you're a bitch," Drake stepped to her.

Vero pushed him, and he stumbled back. "What is wrong with you!" she yelled, and everyone froze. Lex pulled Elle toward the car to get her out of the way.

"What are you doing?" Drake said, and she slapped his arm.

"Pull yourself together!" Vero screamed at him. "Can't you see what you're doing? Stop it!" She slapped him harder. Again and again.

"Veronica, stop," Drake said, and Lex put herself between them and pushed Vero further away from him.

"You're acting exactly like him! When we all know you're not! I'm so tired of it!" Vero screamed at him. She took another step back from him. Taking deep breaths. Elle watched from the side, unsure if she should jump in her car and leave or not.

"What the hell are you talking about?" Drake groaned.

"Sebastian!"

He lowered his voice. "I'm nothing like him."

"Then prove it," Vero muttered. Her eyes trained on him.

Lex went back to stand with Elle. Her boot dipped into a puddle of mud. "Guys, we've had a rough day."

Vero held her hand up. "I'm not moving until Drake apologizes to her."

Elle sighed. "Seriously, it's fine."

"I'm not moving," Vero repeated louder and glared at Drake. Elle opened her mouth to respond but stopped herself. She put her hand on Vero's shoulder and pushed her to the side. Now she was face-to-face with him.

"Drake." Elle paused. Drake hung his head for a second before he straightened himself back up. "We clearly butt heads. I have come to terms with it. But it's upsetting your friends. So can we come to an understanding at least?"

"Sure," he mumbled.

"Great. I'm good with that. Everyone else good?" Elle said.

"No." Vero shook her head at him.

Drake let out a deep groan. "Elle, I apologize for being a dick. It was not my intention to break your trust. I'm sorry for upsetting you and also my friends."

"Elle?" Vero said.

"Breathe," she whispered, and Drake tilted his head. He heard her. She forgot not to say it out loud. "I forgive you. Thank you for apologizing."

"Are we good now?" Drake asked Vero.

"Yeah. See you later," Vero said. She gave him a fist bump.

"Now, can we please go to this party?" Lex asked. She turned to Elle pleading with her. She began to pout, and Elle sighed.

"Alright. Just gotta grab my bag," Elle said, and Drake chuckled. "What?"

"You think you're wearing that?" Lex scowled at her. "You can borrow a dress! I wear one every year."

"Lex, seriously, I'm comfortable in this. Please do not try to doll me up."

"You'll wear a dress." She grinned, and Elle shook her head.

"No." Elle shook her head again and again. "No, I will not."

nine

Elle got out of Drake's truck in a dark green dress. It was tight to her chest and flowed out and down to the floor. She convinced Lex to let her keep her tennis shoes on. The dress was long enough to hide them anyway. Elle thanked the stars that Lex's mom was her size. Most of the clothes in Graves Valley were thrifted or handed down. Lex saved dozens of dresses in her closet.

The manor was lit up, and a hundred people crowded the front lawn. Lights flickered around them. Everyone wore suits and gowns. Elle wished Lex had let her wear her stained jacket, if only for that square of silk. At least she had her camera.

Elle watched Nate rake his fingers through his hair twice before she caught his eye and waved him over. She knew exactly why he had come to the party. Considering all he looked at walking toward them was the short blonde beside her. He wore a dark brown suit that she'd seen him wear a handful of times. He still looked nice, though.

Elle caught a glimpse of herself in the reflection of a window. She didn't recognize herself like this. It was rare that she got dressed up. It was rare for anyone inside the Valley. Her hair surrounded her face in big curls. A strap fell off her shoulder again, and she groaned.

"Stop looking so tense. It'll come out in the photos," Lex teased, and they laughed. Vero fixed the strap for her before Nate took her camera. He snapped a picture of the three girls.

Lex wore a short gold dress. Vero had a coral suit that went well against her dark skin. She had a white button-down under the jacket and had the top three buttons undone. She allowed Elle to do her hair, so it came down her shoulder in three waves.

Elle took photos of the girls before Vero split from the group. Elle nudged Nate, and he glared at her before turning to Lex and asking if she'd dance with him. She smiled big and took his hand. Elle ended up alone. But she wasn't mad. She had some exploring to do.

Loud music floated through the manor. Mobs of people danced in front of the stage where Cyra made her first speech. A live band played, and red lights flickered around the room.

On the loft, she spotted a group of blue-haired men. Josh noticed her first as she ran up the steps. He tapped Gage on the shoulder.

Gage screamed with his hands in the air. "Elle! You look gorgeous, darling! Come give me a kiss!" He was clearly inebriated. He pulled her in to kiss her cheek. She wiped off the slobber he had left behind. Josh bent down and gracefully kissed her other cheek and introduced himself properly.

She turned and introduced herself to the other member she hadn't met yet; Rafael. He was quiet. He seemed to be one of the oldest riders. Gray hairs lined his short beard. But the hair on top of his head was, of course, blue. He shook Elle's hand and then headed down the steps a minute later. Gage pulled her into a room off to the side. At least she could hear better.

Elle congratulated them with a smile.

"I can't believe you came to the race," Gage said.

"I wasn't going to miss it."

Elle spun around to take in the room. It was red. Very red. The curtains made it seem like blood had poured from the ceiling. Only to fill the carpet beneath her feet. There was a plush loveseat in the corner.

Chandeliers made of rubies hung above them. Each gem reflected the light around the room.

Gage grabbed a thin glass from the table by the doorway and downed the purple liquid. "Do you like Evolution? I remember rooting for Drake when he first started racing. I was so young."

"You know him?" Elle didn't curb her surprise.

"Yeah, we go way back." Gage giggled. His breath smelled of peppermint, and Elle had to hold back a gag. "He used to come visit me when I was a kid. Not anymore."

"What do you mean?" Elle asked.

Gage didn't look much younger than her. If he was at all. She wasn't sure how they'd run into each other before The Championship.

"I don't know why he doesn't come see me now! You should ask him." Gage stuck out his bottom lip before finding another tray of beverages beside the loveseat.

The door opened, and a tall thin woman walked in. She had a strong jaw and a shaved head, but the hair left was bright pink.

"Find her?" Josh asked, and she shook her head. "This is Elle." He motioned toward her.

"Oh, hey, I'm Aster. Josh's cousin," she said, and Elle smiled at her. Her shirt was pulled off her shoulder so Elle could see the deep scar. It ran from her left ear, down across her neck, and ended at her right shoulder.

"Nice to meet you," Elle said. Her jaw tensed when she noticed Aster's outfit. Baggy jeans and a long sleeve shirt. "And now I'm furious. My team said I had to wear this." She grabbed her dress and pulled its fabric to show her disdain.

"You're a rider?" she asked. Aster pushed her sleeve up to reveal her forearm. It was at least twice the size of Elle's.

Elle laughed. "Hell no." She thought Elle could be in The Championship? "No, I'm a journalist. I'm writing an article on Team Evolution."

"Oh." Aster blushed. Her shoulders slumped, and she looked away from Elle.

"You know them?"

"Just in passing," Aster blurted. "I've seen them around, I mean."

Aster grabbed a milky emerald glass and took a sip. She coughed into her fist and set it back down. A crimson knife in a dark sheath poked out from her waistband. Elle wondered how many people she threatened with that. It reminded her of Vero.

"Love your hair," Elle said. "Has it ever been purple?"

Aster was about to respond when Gage screamed in the doorway and grabbed their attention. He started to dance to the new song that blasted from downstairs.

"How many has he had?" Elle whispered in Josh's ear.

He laughed. "You don't want to know."

The three of them chatted and talked about the race together. While Gage sashayed around the room and hummed along to the music. Elle got to know Josh a little more as the night went on. She took a few photos of them before deciding to head back to the party.

"You should swing by this week. We can show you around our garage," Josh said.

Elle smiled. She almost turned him down but thought better of it. This wouldn't be for work or the article. Strictly for fun. What could be the harm?

"Definitely." She handed him her phone, and they exchanged numbers. She chuckled to herself. She really was making friends. With riders.

Elle said her goodbyes and turned to get photos of them taking a shot together. She stopped when Gage found Josh's face with his lips and wouldn't stop attacking him.

Elle went back down to the main entry. Riders took shots off of each other's bodies and sucked limes out of their mouths. A team stood on the ledge of the railing above the stage and belted out the song the band played from below. Elle got photos of the wannabe pop stars and hoped somebody pulled them back. She figured riders had acclimated to seeing blood and guts, but she hadn't.

Another loop around the house had her end up on the back deck. It looked out onto the yard, and the manor was so large it swung around so she could see the other side of it. The grass was cut in perfect lines going east to west. It was nothing like Little Hearts. No broken floorboards or creaking steps.

A group of riders made a semi-circle on the lawn with lit candles for the fallen. She took a deep breath and put her arms on the cool rails in front of her. The wind drifted around her and swayed the tree branches beyond the fire pits. Riders danced and ran around carefree. Vero sat around one of the fires and talked to a couple of guys her age. They were in flashy orange suits with red ties.

Elle found herself searching the crowd for a man in black with blue eyes. He wasn't coming. She wasn't even sure why she was looking for him. Other than that, it seemed he was the only person not there.

Elle wondered where Cyra hid on days like today when people overtook her home to party. She saw pairs of Guard at every exit and entrance and six of them stood near a door on the other side of the manor.

She watched and didn't have to wait long. They parted, and Cyra stepped out from the entry into the lawn. Glorious as ever in a white gown that floated behind her as she walked. She slowly paced around the party and ended up coming onto the deck. Elle followed a few paces behind her as she headed inside. Cyra went down the first hall and entered another room.

Elle waited a moment and then went through the same door. It was empty. The room was a small kitchen. Clearly not used very often. Dark cabinets lined the walls from the floor to the ceiling. No other way out of the room meant there must be a secret door nearby. Making haste, she grazed each cabinet with her fingers until she felt a cool draft. She opened the door, and it creaked in response. A wide long dark hall was in place of shelving. She poked her head inside and checked over her shoulder before stepping through. No cameras had been back here in decades. The cobwebs in every corner made that clear.

She held her breath and tiptoed to the end of the hall until she heard Cyra's voice. She stopped and hugged the wall next to a large armchair. Her eyes quickly found pockets of light in the darkness. Furniture seemed to be randomly placed inside. Was it to muffle the echoing?

"Don't be foolish," Cyra's voice came from the room. Elle crouched down behind the back of the chair to hide in case any Guard came by. "I killed them all for a reason. This year won't be any different than the last."

"Just thought I'd bring it to your attention, ma'am." Even with the voice changer, she could tell the Guard had a deep voice. She peeked inside the room from the cracked entry beside her.

Elle wanted them to take their helmet off so she could see who was speaking. But that would never happen. A Guard without a helmet faced instant execution in the Valley. Elle would face the same fate if they found her in here. She didn't dare move. She was already inside the hornet's nest.

"Bring me Salvador. He's up for review."

"Ma'am," the deep voice said. Footsteps left the room, and new ones appeared a moment later.

"Ma'am?" a thick southern accent echoed through the hall.

"You've been Guard for how long now? How many missions have I sent you on?"

"Six years, ma'am. Hundreds."

The voices began to muffle, and Elle heard the Guard coming down the hall from the room. She tucked herself smaller on the floor and kept her head down. Three more Guard entered the kitchen, and there was a gunshot from the room beside her. Elle flinched but didn't flee. She bit her tongue. Was it the man? Salvador? Or Cyra?

"Jeffries, clean this up." Cyra's voice was loud as she walked by Elle in a hurry. Elle stiffened as her heels clicked past.

Muffled voices came through the kitchen, and she didn't move until the coast was clear. She poked her head into the other door first. Seemed like some sort of office. Green curtains and a large oak desk in the center. Windows surrounded the room. A man lay dead in the middle of the floor. But not any man. Guard. His helmet lay next to him. His dark beard covered an inch or so of his neck. His hair wrapped up on top of his head in a knot. His eyes were open and empty.

Elle quickly snapped a few photos with her phone before a group of Guard came into the room. They entered through the door inside the manor, and Elle crept back into the shadows.

One Guard put his palm to the man's chest and mumbled a prayer.

"Another debt paid," the Guard said, and Elle scrunched her nose at that. This was what happened when Cyra let them pay off their debt as being Guard? Once they got close to the end, she killed them? Instead of letting them go. Elle's hands became fists.

She listened at the secret door before walking through to head back to the party. One second after she closed the cabinet door, a woman in all gray entered the kitchen.

"Sorry, I got lost." Elle played a fool and the woman pointed through the hall. Her face was covered by her hood. Another Cyra soldier. Elle joined the party again and wiped the bottom of her dress of webs and dust.

Lex and Nate danced by the stage as the live band played. Elle squeezed through the crowd to get shots of them having fun. Even the lead singer didn't seem to mind being in the frame. She eventually trailed to the side of the room. A couple came out great from the sidelines. She lifted her lens again when a guy swayed in front of her and blocked her view.

"Do you mind?" She scowled at him.

He ran his hand through his wavy blond hair. "You are the most beautiful girl I've ever seen," he stammered. He wore a white three-piece suit. With gold accents and chains around his neck. Must be on Team Halo. She cringed from being near the man.

Elle couldn't help but compare him to Drake. This guy was all muscle. Way bigger than Drake. Shoulders and chest. Even his legs. Was there such a thing as too muscular? If so, she'd found it.

"And you're the most idiotic. Never compliment a woman by telling her she's a girl," she said and pushed him aside. He grabbed her arm, and she shoved him off of her. "Don't touch me," she warned and bolted out the front door. He followed her, and she groaned.

"Just one kiss," he said, and she tried to get more distance between them. She went down the steps and toward the fire where she assumed Vero was.

"Fuck off!" she yelled, but he grabbed her arm again and, this time, wouldn't let go.

"Just one kiss, baby."

She punched his forearm, but he didn't budge.

His fingers dug deeper into her arm. She slammed her fist into his chest.

Nothing.

His eyes burned into hers, and he tugged her toward him. She tried to push him away. She heard the sound from his nose before she saw it. Vero was at her elbow. He released his hold on her, and Vero hit him again. Blood spurted out of his nostril.

"Don't ever touch her again!" Vero yelled. Spit flew from her mouth as she spoke. Her eyes blazed with anger.

Elle pulled Vero away from the creep. The rider staggered away as blood poured down his chin onto his pristine suit. At least Vero got him good. Elle turned to see Josh, Rafael, Aster, and Gage walk out of the back door.

"Get me out of here," Elle begged Vero.

Vero ran around the front of the manor to grab Lex and Nate. She came back fast to try and comfort Elle in the car. It didn't work. She should have been able to handle herself.

She convinced Nate to let the girls take her home. He seemed to understand her silent internal turmoil. He gave her a small hug and waved goodbye to the three of them.

"Elle, don't blame yourself. He was a drunk jerk," Lex said when they entered the elevator. Elle pressed the number four, and it lit up.

Vero scoffed. "He's a bastard, and I'm glad I broke his nose. He's lucky I didn't kill him." She should have hit harder or punched him like Vero had. Right in the face. "His name is Seth. His whole team is assholes and alcoholics."

"What team?" Elle asked. She had to be sure.

"Halo. Don't worry, we'll take care of him on the track," Vero guaranteed.

They let her get some rest with the promise of picking her up tomorrow afternoon. All she wanted was to be alone. Elle sat on her bed and didn't bother to change out of her dress. She rolled over and covered herself in her blanket.

Hours went by, and she woke up in a sweat again. Another failed attempt at washing her worries down the drain in the shower. Elle pulled jeans and her favorite black T-shirt on. A sob slipped out when she noticed how purple her arm was. Her skin was sore and it hurt to twist her arm a certain way.

She could hop the fence at the arena to help Robert but couldn't fight for her own life? Should have socked him in the jaw. Instead, she had to be saved. Always had to be saved.

Elle was past exhaustion. Tired of watching her friends train to be beaten. Tired of watching her friends be badasses, yet she couldn't even get a creep to leave her alone.

She was pathetic. Fragile. This whole experience was to get that photographer position. She was going to their homes and now parties. Clearly, she had lost her focus.

Sleep evaded her. Elle reviewed the photos from the party to keep her mind off the rider from Halo. Most of the pictures came out great. Even the ones of Blue Falcon. She finished editing her favorites when there was a knock on her door. It was too early for it to be Lex or Vero. Probably her neighbor, Mrs. Francine, asking for milk or eggs.

Elle opened the door and immediately slammed it shut.

Two soft knocks came, and she opened it again.

"Why'd you do that?" Drake asked. His hair brushed back. No dirt or grease on him. His shirt didn't have any wrinkles yet.

"I wasn't expecting it to be you." She opened it further for him to walk in. "What are you doing here?" she asked and closed the door behind him.

Drake was inside her apartment. Drake was inside her home. Drake.

"Your car was still at the garage this morning. I didn't hear what happened until Vero and Lex got there." Drake looked around her small kitchen. The magnets on her fridge caught his attention. He didn't look away from them until she sighed.

"Great, so you heard how pathetic I am too?" She flopped down on her bed face first.

He chuckled at her. His eyes danced on the photos that hung by the door as she sat up. He looked at each one before he sat beside her. Considering she didn't have a sofa, she wasn't sure where else he should sit. He was so close. She put her head in her hands. He smelled of lavender and pine. Strange scent for a man, let alone a rider.

"Elle, you're a lot of things, but pathetic is not one of them. That guy was an asshole. That's all." Drake intertwined his hands in front of him and leaned on his knees.

"I couldn't get him off," she whispered. "He wouldn't let go."

Drake released an exhale. He fixated on her bruise. "It doesn't mean you're weak. Those parties get wild."

"It seemed like everyone was there except for you," she said.

He stood up and walked over to her door. Of course, he would leave. He stopped beside the door. Her jacket hung on the hook. Drake reached into her pocket and came back with the small tube of Sludge. "You wish I had gone?"

"Yes." The word slipped out. He dabbed his finger to the top and rubbed her purple skin. "For Lex, I mean," she added.

"Lex?" he asked. The bruise disappeared, and he put the lid on before he rested it on her nightstand.

"She wanted more photos."

"I see." He nodded. There was another knock. He sat up straight. "Expecting someone?"

She wanted to laugh at him. He was such a jerk to her, yet he still wanted her safe. He was hard to figure out.

"Most likely my neighbor," she said and sighed. Drake got up and answered the door before she could even stand.

"Elle, oh. Hello there." Mrs. Francine grinned.

"Hey, Mrs. F, you need eggs?" Elle asked. She headed to the fridge as the older woman stepped inside the kitchen.

"And sugar." She adjusted her attention back to Drake. "You must be Elle's boyfriend."

"He's n—"

"Drake," he interrupted. "Pleasure to meet you, ma'am."

Mrs. Francine was a small plump woman with a cotton top and beady eyes. Like usual, her old house slippers, the shade of cotton candy, poked out from under her soft dress.

"What a gentleman." Her hands clasped in front of her. A thin-lipped smile.

"He sure is something," Elle said through her teeth. "Tell Mr. Pat I said hello." A half carton of eggs and a full bag of sugar went into Fran's hands.

"I will, dear. See you soon," she said to them, and Elle locked the door behind her.

She stomped over to Drake and smacked his arm. "Why did you let her think you were my boyfriend? Now she's going to tell the entire building."

He glared at her. "Maybe I want her to tell everyone."

"Why would you want that?" He was insane. Definitely insane.

"So maybe word will get out not to fuck with you." He lowered his voice and dipped his head toward her. "Maybe, next time some asshole wants to grab your arm, he won't because he'll know people have your back."

Was he saying he had her back? She didn't exactly hate that. "You're so annoying." She rolled her eyes at him and crossed the room to grab her laptop.

Drake stopped her from closing it. "Are these the pictures you took?"

"You can't look at them yet."

"Why not?" he said and pointed at the screen. "These look edited."

"Well, actually, I did finish them. Alright." She pulled the chair out for him to sit. She set it up for him and opened the first album. His jaw dropped.

"You don't like it? We can redo it if it's not hiding you enough," she said and gulped. "I thought it was pretty good. Lex looks amazing. Vero is badass." Then she focused on Drake in the photo. "You look serious, but you can't really see your face. I figured that's what you would want. I mean, the tree is a great backdrop, and you're relaxed, which is shocking considering how straight your posture normally is. It's because you're always so guarded. If you let yourself relax, it wouldn't be so bad all the time. Well, I guess good posture isn't a bad thing, so never mind. Be tense, I guess. But it might..." She stopped herself when she realized she was yammering. She blushed. "Sorry. You should stop me, or I'll go on forever."

"I don't mind it," he said and clicked to see more.

He complimented her. Well, kind of. Not really.

He clicked to see the next one and then the next. He stopped on the photo that he had taken where she was laughing with Lex and Vero.

"You know," he leaned back in the chair, "I never did ask what upset you that day."

Everest, Evelyn, and Ezra filled her thoughts. The red balloon. The fountain. Her mother's jacket. Her father's laugh. Elle eased into her answer. "I rarely see myself like this," she said. "Happy, I mean. I wasn't expecting to make friends doing this dumb article."

He stared at her. Most likely didn't expect her to be honest. "Sounds like you don't like your job," he said and clicked again.

"I want to be a photographer. Only a photographer. But I have steps to take. I'm on a path. And this might be my last stop before getting there." She bit her lip.

He stopped at the last one. The photo she had taken of him on the balcony above Cyra. He dropped his jaw. "I knew I saw you." She laughed as he pointed at the screen. "You lied."

"Excuse me?" She drummed her fingers on her thigh.

He closed the laptop and packed it in her bag for her. "You said it was Vero that caught your attention. But you didn't take her photo." He winked at her.

"I didn't mean to take that!"

"Yet you didn't delete it." He smirked.

"Asshole."

"Bitch," he said, and she laughed.

Elle went to the door and pulled on her jacket. She yanked it off when she remembered the blood stain. Drake stopped her as she grabbed the door handle.

"Yes?" She turned, and he crossed his arms and then rubbed his hands on his jeans. Then moved his arms to cross them again. "You look like me," she said, and he chuckled.

He opened his mouth to speak and nothing came out. He wiped his palms and tried again. "I'm not good at this kind of thing," he whispered. "I wanted to apologize. I know we keep butting heads like you said, but I really don't think you're a bitch. I know we joke, but I guess I don't mind you being around."

"Oh. Um, alright?" Unexpected. Something was up with him today. "I guess I don't hate you as much as I originally did. Kind of."

"Fair." He exhaled.

"Alright, good chat." She smiled, and he opened the door.

They walked together to the elevator and out to his truck. She got in the passenger seat for the first time. It was strange to sit there. She couldn't watch him in the rearview mirror this time.

"Do you have everything you need for the article?" he asked.

"I need to edit my words a bit, but mostly, I need help choosing which photos to send. Of course, I will allow the three of you to pick which ones I send to my boss. And read the article. As promised."

"You can't use my first name," he said abruptly. Almost a shout. Upset, but not at her. For once. She eyed him. He took a breath when she nodded at him. Had he been expecting her to be angry?

"Alright." She shrugged. "Last name is fine?" she asked.

"Yeah." He rested his arm on the open window and his other hand on top of the wheel. He seemed calm.

Elle opened her phone and went into her version of the article and edited some words to make sure it fits his name issue. Questions began to pile up, but she didn't ask. Maybe one day, he'd trust her enough to spill. That wouldn't be today.

"The photos were fine," he added.

"You liked them?" He hadn't said otherwise, but he had yet to voice a positive opinion. "Wow. Team Evolution Captain, one-hundred-time racer, hitman Drake liked my artistic ability to capture a scene." She grinned at him. He gave her a half smile in return. Today seemed like a new day for them. She didn't mind this Drake.

When they arrived at the garage, Elle made them sit down together to review the photos and her article before sending it to Randy.

"Now what?" Lex asked.

"We wait for his response." Elle shrugged. "If he likes it and the direction I went with it, he'll print it as is. Though normally, he has something for me to fix. So hopefully, it's not the photos of Drake."

"What if it is?" Vero asked.

"Then I tell him that Drake doesn't want to be in any photos at all and what I've sent him is the best he's going to get. Can't have a Championship team cover photo with only two members."

They worked on their bikes to prepare for the race that was in two days. Vero went out to the track, and Elle followed with her camera. Drake waved goodbye to them as he headed to his truck. He sped out of the driveway, and Lex came to join Elle as her phone chirped.

"Is it him? Did he like the photos?" Lex asked, too excited not to yell. Elle grabbed her phone and opened the email.

Elliot,

I'll send you a rough edit. Get it back to me by morning. Promotion is yours. Send me photos like these of the next race, and your debut as a photographer will be a cover page too.

Randy, ChaosMotors Magazine

Elle read the email aloud, and Lex screamed. Vero jumped off her bike and ran over.

Vero smacked her on the shoulder. "Nice job, Vanilla!"

"Don't you want to call your mom?" Lex asked.

"I should, right?" she asked.

The girls laughed at her. Lex pushed her toward the garage to make the call.

Elle strolled over to the back door and called Sarah. She tried not to cry when she spoke, but she couldn't help it. It's all she's wanted for years. Since she was a kid watching her mom photograph everything she walked by.

"Oh, honey! Congratulations! You're amazing! Now everyone will know it," Sarah shouted. Elle had to hold the phone away from her face so she wouldn't be deaf for three days. Sarah was proud.

Elle paraded around the outside of the garage as she spoke. She filled her in on the events of the last few days with the team. Told her about the angle she took on Drake. He was more like a mystery. It was intriguing, and she hoped it would pull some readers in. By the end of the second race, they'll be dying to know who he is. Fans will root for Team Evolution, and she hoped the team would be able to handle it. Sarah wished her luck, and she hung up with a smile.

She did it.

ten

Elliot woke up and decided she deserved another latte. She made sure she packed her bag for a full day and headed to Bernie's. Her shoes hit the sidewalk with ease as she strolled inside.

Bernie handed her a small cup, and they chatted at the counter. Her coffee was gone by the end of the conversation. She savored every drop and headed out the door with a grin.

A whip-like crack sounded from across the street. Elle froze. She'd know that sound anywhere. A Guard gunshot. The sound of the reload. Another shot.

Another.

She stepped back, and the Guard across the street pulled the trigger again but aimed at the sky. Six of them surrounded three dead bodies and had three men pinned to the pavement.

"Stay down, mate, or you'll get the rod!" A man writhed under the Guard's boot.

The man in the middle tried to stand. The Guard shot him between the eyes. Blood splattered behind him. His body went limp, and the other two men stiffened under the Guard's hold.

A hand clamped over Elle's mouth from behind. An arm wrapped around her waist. This time she didn't scream. The scent of grease came from Drake's hand. He pulled her back to the alley beside Bernie's. Her back pressed against his chest, and he loosened his grip on her. She grabbed his hand from her mouth and held it at her side. Tears in her eyes, she couldn't look away from the horror scene.

"What did you steal, mate?" the Guard asked. The voice changer inside the helmet made his words crackle. The man trembled. Elle could only imagine the fear that coursed through him. Much more than her own.

"Nothing, sir! It w-was all Henry. Henry stole from the shop. Y-You killed him already. S-Sir. I didn't take anything!" he cried and begged.

The Guard poked him with the black rod. He screamed into the gravel. The Guard bashed his head. Again and again. His skull beat until his face was unrecognizable.

The venom from the rod would've killed him in minutes, but that wasn't fast enough for the Guard. He strolled to the next man, who started to squirm. Once the rod hit him, he stopped moving. He struck him in the back. Elle knew the venom had entered his body when he started to shake. She spun into Drake and hid her face in his chest. That's what Everest looked like. Everest spasmed just like that.

Drake pulled her deeper into the alley.

"What happened?" She kept her voice soft and pulled away from him to look into his eyes. He kept his attention on the street.

"They caught them stealing a block away. I followed them here." His voice quiet yet steady. He was used to seeing things like this. Especially on the track. Riders had a saying; death is just a side effect. Elle agreed after seeing the first race.

Guard would often beat or kill people for small crimes inside the walls. Easier than taking them to Cyra for her to decide their fate. Only two options; death or adding to their dues.

"Why would you do that?" Elle didn't understand why he would risk it. Why follow the Guard back here? He was definitely insane.

"I knew you were at Bernie's," he said, and she blushed. How did he know that? He dropped her hand. "They're gone."

"How did you know I was here?" she asked, and he looked down at her. They were standing so close. She took a step away from him. He took another.

"I noticed your car on my way to town. When I saw the Guard, I turned back. It would've brought too much attention if I had gone inside to get you," he said. His eyes on hers were too much. She forced herself to look away.

"Where were you going?"

"Work," he said.

It hadn't occurred to Elle that riders in The Championship would work normal jobs. Although, the race was only one month out of the year. What if they didn't win? They couldn't afford to not pay their bills. Cyra would always get what was due. They all knew that.

She looked down at his pants. Covered in grease and dirt. What job didn't mind if you showed up filthy? Elle wanted to ask but figured with Drake, it was better not to. He would've told her if he wanted to give the specifics.

"Let's get you out of here," Drake said. He walked her to the car, scanning the street the whole way. He opened the door and shut it when she sat down. He got on his bike a few spots behind her.

She sat in silence and studied the bloodbath on the sidewalk. So close. Too close. Drake rode past her and headed up the hill. She did her breathing exercises to calm down before she grabbed her phone.

Elle wanted to call Sarah until her phone started to ring. Josh.

Elle reached Blue Falcon's garage and parked next to a small green car that looked about a hundred years old. The handles were rusted, and the side mirrors were nowhere in sight. Dents and scratches covered the left side. It was worse than her own car. A deep blue helmet lay on the passenger seat in pristine condition. Must be new.

A brick driveway was strange to have in the Valley. You could tell they had done it themselves. Amateur placing and cracks throughout. She grabbed her camera from the back seat and locked her car. The white building was twice the size of Evolutions from the outside alone. She could hear them talking inside and the echoes of tools hitting metal. There were three giant windows on the opposite side of the building.

She was about to knock when she thought better of it. She walked in and smiled at Gage. He yelled and ran over to her.

"Elle! I'm so glad you came! Josh said you might swing by. Come on, I'll give you the tour."

Gage was great to be around. High energy and all smiles. He spoke with his hands, and when he thought of things he didn't like, he reacted with his whole body. Sticking his tongue out or shaking his arms. She enjoyed the tour of the garage as he guided her around the tools and extra bike pieces and scraps. The large windows gave an extra dose of sunlight that Evolution's garage didn't have.

Gage led her out the back door, and she gasped at their practice track. High hills and holes in the ground dug to mimic the race itself. Most of it was paved with wide turns and sharp throughout. She couldn't even see the entire thing from where she stood.

Josh found them out there and gave Elle a small hug.

"Good to see you. Keep him busy so we can fix his damn bike, would you?" he said. His belly shook when he laughed, and Elle nodded.

"No problem. Come on, show me the other side." Elle dragged him to the far side of the track, and Gage pointed out his least favorite spots.

They talked for a while before he brought up team Halo. He went straight to the point, which Elle appreciated.

"Ran into the captain. If you ask me, it was on purpose. He asked me if I knew someone at the magazine. Says he wants to talk about getting on the cover. Listen, I'd go see what they want, but I wouldn't do it."

"Why's that?"

Gage shrugged. "Full honestly? Because they're assholes. Only look out for themselves. And they probably want something else from you that they're not saying. I'd figure out what that is. To be in the know. Understand?" he said. Elle nodded. He handed her a business card from his back pocket.

TEAM HALO CAPTAIN

KANNON WALKER

7346-3842-9387

Elle would definitely call. Wouldn't take the job, like he warned, but she thought of Nate. Depending on the situation, if the money was good, she'd pass it along. She thanked him again, and Aster came running over to them. She waved at Elle flashing her white teeth at her.

"What's up?"

Aster wore dark green pants with big chunky black work boots and a long sleeve red shirt. The contrast between the red and her pink hair made Elle cringe. Instead, she looked at her scar. So interesting. She would expect a woman to hide such an intense mark. Not Aster. She wore it with pride.

"It's not a secret," Aster said, and Elle winced. She'd been staring.

"I'm so sorry," Elle started, but Aster stopped her.

"I was in the Cove when it happened. Guard came to take my father to Ashbury Valley. Ever been hit with a lightning zap?"

The man writhing in the street came to her mind. She shook her head. "What's that?"

"Like the rods the Guard use here, except instead of venom, it's a lightning bolt." Aster raised her fingers to trace her scar. "My mother tried to stop them. Almost killed her. I saved her and they punished me. Knocked me right on my ass."

"How long ago?" Elle asked softly.

"Been almost four years now. We sent him letters sometimes, but over there, it's different. More," she shrugged, "advanced."

"What do you mean?" Elle asked. Gage seemed to already know everything she was saying. He swayed beside her patiently.

"The weapons they use and the races even. You know some of the creatures they test over there before they're sent here?" she asked, and Elle dropped her jaw. "Graves Valley might've been first, but Ashbury is brutal. All the stories I've heard," she whistled, "it's mad."

"How did you get letters to him?"

"Different rules over there," Aster explained. Elle let that information sink in as her mind raced with questions. Aster was ready to drop the conversation, though. "So, ready to watch us ride?"

"You're going to ride right now? This?" Elle asked, pointing at the track.

"I need to practice. I'm on the bench. Rules of The Championship say you have to be inside for a minimum of six months before you can enter as a team. But that rule doesn't apply if you're back up." She winked at Elle.

Elle watched Aster and Gage ride around the track one full lap. They swerved around and played with each other. The dynamic was so different yet so similar to Evolution that she almost couldn't believe it.

Josh joined her again and brought Rafael out with him. The man grinned at Elle as he put his helmet on to join the riders.

"I'm glad you called me," Elle told Josh. His eyes were covered in blue eyeshadow, and a small clear gem dangled from his left ear. His nails were chipped in black paint.

Josh didn't respond with words. He just smiled at her.

She left them with a promise of returning soon. Gage made sure to give her his phone number too. Aster waved from the track, not stopping to say goodbye. Too focused. Elle knew she'd see her soon anyway.

Elle called the number on the business card Gage handed her. Might as well get it over with. Kannon answered after the first ring, and she made plans to meet up in the town square. Public place. If anything happened, she could get away faster there. She wasn't sure what to expect, but she knew he wasn't one to trust.

Elle sat at a table in the middle of town and watched as people walked by chatting. A small cafe had its windows open and she could smell the fresh coffee. Guard marched by with guns on their hips. She thought of Aster and her experience with the Guard and a lightning bolt. She'd been through a lot. All to end up here.

A man in all white came around the corner and smiled at Elle. He was tall, with thick brown curls touching his shoulders and dark chocolate eyes. His white pants made him stick out more than his white T-shirt. His ego radiated off of him in giant waves.

He sat down across from her and sized her up twice before he spoke.

"You must be Elle. I'm Kannon, Captain of Halo."

He looked at her like a tiger scanned a doe. Elle wasn't stupid. He was much bigger than her. According to her research, this year was his sixth race. She knew he could snap her in two in less than a second. But she instantly didn't like him. She'd keep the meeting short. "I heard you wanted to get some photos done for the magazine? Make it onto the cover."

"Right you are." He grinned. "Here's the deal, we're trying to win this year. And a part of winning is getting people to know you. Better chances out on that track. If you get what I'm saying." He twined his fingers together on top of the table between them. His elbows rested on the wood.

"You believe Cyra, the Superior, will move things around so a team with more fans will win versus a team with zero?" she asked him.

"That's exactly what I'm saying." He leaned on the table, moving closer to her. Elle stayed sitting upright. Very still. He reminded her of a snake in the grass. Maybe if she didn't move, he wouldn't strike. "Word is you're doing an article on Evolution." He scoffed at her.

"Yes. I am. And?"

"Elle." He tsked his tongue at her. "That's not the team you want to work with."

"Oh? Why's that?"

"They're low on the pole. Nobodies. People don't care about them. They're the team that comes every year, so teams like mine can beat them. Somebody has to be in last in order for us to be first. Get what I'm saying? We're willing to pay you. Whatever you want, if we win." He flashed her his pearly whites.

She didn't respond for a minute. "I think I'm done here. Thanks for your time, I guess." She started to stand, but Kannon slammed his palm on the table.

"Sit." His voice was stern. The word came from his throat. His eyes were slits as he stared at her.

Now, this is the man she expected. The man behind the mask.

"Mr. Walker." Elle looked around at the people passing by looking over at them. "It would be wise for someone interested in making fans to not threaten me out in public. You've also got the wrong idea. Article is already done and sent. And no team is better than another. You're all fighting for the same prize."

"That's where you're wrong." He smiled at her. "You think we're all trying to get out of here? Some of us like it inside."

"What?" Drake might be insane, but this guy? Certifiable.

"I want to win. For the money. The prizes. I want to win every year. Not just this year. I want the best bikes and shields to take down every team who thinks they're better than us. Team Halo will go down in history. Maybe one day they'll call it the Halo Championship."

"Might want to win first before you start spreading that around. In case you forgot, as many times as my friends haven't won, neither have you. Excuse me," Elle said and got up from the table.

Kannon laughed as he stood across from her. "Friends? Do you hear yourself? They're not your friends. They are riders. They want fame. It's all part of the game."

"You have no idea what you're talking about." He didn't know Evolution like she did. They weren't like all the other riders.

"I know a lot of teams. I know over a hundred riders. You've met what? Two?" Kannon scoffed. "They're using you. When they're done with you, they will throw you to the dogs. It's an opportunity. You're just going to walk away from working with the best team in the Valley... for Evolution?" He shook his head at her. Then sneered, "They better watch their backs at the next race."

"Go near my friends because of our conversation. I'll fucking kill you," Elle warned and was proud of the weight she put in her words.

"Don't make promises you can't keep, sugar." He chuckled at her.

"I'm done here." Elle started heading to her car. She'd never threatened someone before, and damn, did it feel good. Fuck that guy. And the rest of his team too. She wasn't about to let anyone threaten her or her friends. Her heart was beating out of her chest as she was about to round the corner.

"You're making a mistake!" he yelled after her.

She thought of Vero as she flipped him the bird.

eleven

Elle knew it was a slim chance someone would be at the garage. Couldn't stare at her computer screen anymore. She tried to edit the last of the photos for Lex, but all she could think about was Kannon. His face when he said they were using her.

The door creaked as she walked inside. The girls were nowhere in sight. Drake spread out on the floor in the corner next to his bike. A tool she'd never seen before in his right hand. It looked like a mix between a screwdriver and a pair of pliers. His shirt had ridden up to show his lean torso. It wasn't until she got closer that she realized he was asleep. She stopped to laugh into her hand.

With her back against the wall beside him, she began editing again. The empty and silent garage was eerie. She kept looking up at the door expecting someone to walk in. But nobody did. Elle closed the lid of her laptop when she finished an hour later. She put her fingers to the bridge of her nose and took a breath. Drake bolted up. He raised the tool like a throwing knife aimed at Elle's head. She yelped. His breath came out hard and raspy as he calmed. He came out of his daze. Finally, his eyes settled on Elle.

The tool clattered on the floor next to his bike. "Must've dozed off."

"Sorry, I didn't want to wake you," Elle said, her words coming out harsh as she tried to calm herself down too.

Drake wiped his hands on his jeans and looked around his corner. Most likely trying to remember what he had been doing before he fell asleep.

"Thank you," Elle said. Drake's eyes snapped to hers. "For earlier. I didn't thank you before."

"Sure," he said. Guess he didn't want to talk about the murders they'd witnessed. "How'd you know I was here?"

"I didn't. I couldn't sit at the coffee shop after—you know. And I didn't want to be home." She wasn't sure how he'd feel about her hanging around Blue Falcon and then having a meeting with Kannon. So she kept quiet about her day. Elle rested her laptop beside her.

"I thought you sent in the article already?" he questioned with a raised brow.

"I did. I was editing photos for Lex." She paused and looked down at her computer. "You want to see?" He nodded, and she handed it over to him. "I did this last. Do you think Lex will like it? I thought it was cute. Maybe she'll like it. I don't know. Sorry. Rambling." Elle bit her lip.

Drake looked at the screen. Lex and Vero, all dressed up outside of the manor. Lex's head on her shoulder and their back to the camera.

Drake chuckled at the photo. "Feels like they're an old married couple. She'll love it."

Elle smiled at him. Her laptop dinged with an incoming message. Randy responded to her edits of the article.

Looking great, Elliot. Printing tomorrow.

"Randy liked the story. Perfect timing for the race tomorrow." Elle took the laptop back to respond. Drake was quiet. His eyes fixed on the office door across the room.

"Elle is short for Elliot?" His voice wavered. "Not common for a girl. I assumed your name started with the letter L." He stood and scrunched his nose. He pointed over his shoulder with his thumb. "I gotta go."

"Uh, alright. See you."

The door slammed shut.

Elle waved at him, but he didn't see. He definitely recognized her name, though she wasn't sure how. Didn't think it would matter what she wrote in the magazine. That was the only way he'd know her. She rolled her eyes as she grabbed her stuff. Then she realized he had left the garage unlocked with her inside. Elle searched for a key or another solution but gave up. Lex answered on the third ring.

Vero and Lex came to the rescue and locked up the garage. Lex invited her out to get a slice of pie with them. She was about to decline, then thought, it's just pie.

Elle explained what happened in the garage with Drake as they drove to the diner across town. They all agreed it was strange, but Vero made sure to tell her that Drake himself was strange.

"Don't worry about it," Lex said as they sat down in a booth at Moonlight Diner. The only good pie in town. Especially after seven o'clock. "I invited him, but he didn't respond. He could be spending time with his parents."

Clearly, Lex wasn't worried about it. So she shouldn't be.

Guard stood at the entrance as they walked inside. Elle tried not to pay any mind to them. One incident was enough for today.

Elle sat beside Vero when the server came to the table in a short blue dress and a small black apron. Her gum smacked in her mouth, and Elle could see a pink lipstick smudge on her teeth. Her strawberry blonde hair was pushed back with a thick headband and an entire bottle of hairspray. Or so Elle guessed, simply by the smell of her. She placed three water cups in front of them before she checked on her other tables. Lex kept her eyes on the menu the entire time the woman was at the table.

"You know her?" Elle asked, and Lex nodded once.

"Story is, she went to school with them." Vero filled her in. "She was in love with Drake and used Lex to get close to him. Bitch. But we all grow up, right? Well, some of us, anyway." Vero eyed Lex as she blew the long part of her straw wrapper at her.

"So, the solution is to ignore her?" Elle asked. Vero shrugged. Guess so.

"Big day tomorrow," Lex tried to sway the conversation. She plucked a fuzz off her dark brown dress. It had short sleeves and a scoop neck that showed off her simple silver string necklace. The race was in a few hours. Elle was glad to sit beside Nate again. Still wasn't ready. Wasn't sure she would ever be. "What do you think the track will be like?"

"I'm going to guess that it's scorching hot. Maybe a beach umbrella turns in circles and cuts our heads off one by one," Vero said. Elle shuddered.

"My parents might come tomorrow," Lex said. Elle wasn't sure if she should offer to sit with them or not. She went with the latter.

"They support you racing?" Elle asked.

Lex laughed. "Not really, no."

"So how do you not hate yourself riding when you know they hate it?" She regretted her words immediately and tried to backtrack but Lex waved her hand at her to stop.

"Once I quit allowing others to control me, I became who you see today." Lex raised her glass to her lips and took a sip. "I want to race, so I'm going to. Even if my family doesn't like it. Because I don't live for them. I wake up on the day of The Championship, and I can hear the first gun go off, feel the wind rushing past, and smell gas in the air. It's dangerous, but everything is. I could die walking down the street later today. You know?"

Elle smiled at her despite the flashback of her morning outside Bernie's. Yes, she knew.

Lex continued. "If I die doing what I love, so be it. I'm having fun, and my friends cheer for me in the stands."

"Inspiring," Vero moaned.

"I thought so," Elle said. "Sometimes I think I chose journalism out of fear. I've been writing articles for years at the magazine. I could have been getting more experience behind the lens. I could've created a Valley Blog. Should've jumped right in. Sounds stupid now." Elle shook her head and looked up when a big family sat two tables away from them.

Four young girls were across from their parents. A familiar hollow formed in her chest. She remembered meals like that when she was a kid. Countless tea parties in the kitchen with Evelyn and Ezra.

"It's not stupid, Elle," Lex snapped her back to reality. "Sometimes it takes time to get there. And some courage. I can help. I'll teach you my ways." Lex grinned at her from across the table.

"Yeah, do what she does. Run around in dresses and talk like you just swallowed a balloon," Vero teased, and Lex glared at her. Elle laughed.

"So, after that whole speech, you're going to let our server get to you?" Elle said. She crossed her arms, and Vero clicked her tongue.

"Shit," Vero whispered. "She's got you there."

Lex whined. "It was embarrassing. I didn't know she was using me. And Drake certainly didn't either." Some of her hair hung in her eyes as she looked down at her lap. Today she wore a pink hairpin to hold the rest back. Vero lifted her knee and rest her boot on the booth. She bit her thumbnail and looked around the diner. Her eyes stayed on the Guard longer than anyone else. They made everyone nervous. Elle strangely felt comfort in that.

"What did Drake do?" Elle asked. She moved her glass around in circles. The condensation from the cup darkened the wood grain of the table.

Vero laughed. "Lost his shit. The usual." She took her thumb out of her mouth and smoothed her black crop top under her team jacket. The stains were hard to notice under the dim lighting.

The server came back, and Elle read her name tag. Annaleise. She raised her notepad and looked at Vero. She ordered first, then Lex.

"Apple, please, no ice cream," Lex mumbled. Elle couldn't stand to see her look so defeated.

"And for you?" Annaleise faced Elle. She was still focused on Lex. "Hello?"

"Oh, yes. My apologies," Elle said and glanced back at the menu. This girl made Lex so uncomfortable. Messed with her. Embarrassed her. To hell with it. "Let me have the same as Alexandra, please." She handed her the menu. The girls looked over at her. Probably wondering why she used her full name. "Since you're here, may I ask you a question?"

"Sure," she muttered. Her pen clicked, and she popped her gum as she glanced at Elle.

"I hear you knew Alexandra before she was famous. Would you be willing to sit for an interview? I'd love to ask you some questions. I want to know what she was like before all the spotlight."

"Huh?" Her posture straightened. Her eyes squinted. Elle had her attention now.

"Elle." Lex kicked her under the table.

"Oh, you haven't seen all the press? The Championship? Their team is doing well. They'll probably win this year. They have an article coming out in ChaosMotors Magazine. Could I leave my card with you?" Elle dug into her wallet to pull out a business card. "I'd love to know what she was like as a child."

Annaleise stumbled on her words. "Uh, sure."

Elle smiled wide as she walked away from the table. Stunned would put it lightly. Vero put her hands over her mouth to stifle her laughter.

"Elle," Lex whined. Her cheeks reddened.

"Fuck that bitch," Vero said as she gave Elle a fist bump.

twelve

Nate picked Elle up in the morning to take her to The Championship. When they pulled into the parking lot, her stomach was in knots.

Girls stood in groups and held signs with Team Evolution written in black sharpie. Some of them held Drake's photo and screamed at any rider that rode by who might be him. Some even glued his picture onto poster boards with red hearts, and a few wrote, 'marry me?' Nate pointed each one out to her.

"Whoa, I hope that captain of yours loves this because I would hate it," Nate murmured.

"I just hope he doesn't hate me," Elle sighed.

"You told him this could happen. You warned him."

They circled the lot in search of a parking spot. Elle cleared her throat before she spoke again. "Thanks for coming today. I have to take photos of the race, but you could've stayed home. Instead, you're here. It means a lot." Elle focused on the cars in front of them.

"Couldn't let you come alone. Plus, it seems like you keep getting opportunities thrown at you. Halo might know other teams looking for a cover photo."

"You think I should've taken him up on his offer?" She whipped around.

He was smiling at her. She relaxed. "I'm just messing with you, kid. You did the right thing. I don't trust any rider. Especially that Halo guy. What'd you say his name was? Casey?"

"Kannon," Elle corrected.

"Christian?"

"Kannon," she spoke louder.

"Oh, Carter, got it."

They smiled at each other before he found a spot in the last row.

She grabbed her bag and made sure the tin of Sludge was where she had put it last night. After pie, she went home to make a new batch just in case. She wanted to leave with a full one. However, it was unlikely. Elle reminded herself what Lex had said last night. They wanted to race. Nobody could change their minds. It was their happiness, their purpose. Their lives. She would support them.

They got out and started to head toward the main gate. Elle looked around for Drake's truck but didn't see it yet. The girls screamed at each rider dressed in all black. As if Drake was multiple people. Elle rolled her eyes at the stupidity. She remembered Evelyn screaming about some boy band when she was about twelve. People in the Valley didn't have that. They had the ChaosMotors Championship.

Elle spotted the truck and pointed so Nate would see. Drake had his head down behind the open driver-side door. He tried his best to hide from the crowd.

"It's going to be alright," Elle said behind him. He whirled around.

"Fuck," he choked, and she pulled him back down.

"Sorry, didn't mean to startle you." She rubbed his back twice before she let her hand fall back to her side.

"You're here," he said, surprised. He wasn't smiling, but he didn't look mad about it.

"Of course," she said. Lex and Vero stood on the other side of the truck.

"She can't leave now, Drake. We got our hooks in her," Vero said, and Lex laughed.

"Yeah! Our hooks!" Lex raised her fist in the air. Elle laughed at them. Lex helped Vero with the bikes while Drake stayed put.

Nate went over to the girls to chat as Elle tried to comfort Drake. Elle watched Nate sway back and forth before fixing his glasses on his nose twice. He made eye contact with her and she motioned with her hands to snap out of it. He listened and offered to help Lex with her bike. She gladly took him up on it.

Drake pulled her attention back to him. "This is way more than a group of girls with a crush." Drake peered over the truck and pointed to a few groups that stood out.

"You have fans. So, play it up. Wave at them. Wink if you get close without a helmet on. They'll go insane. Then in the next race, you'll have more. Because one girl will tell her friend, and that friend will tell six more. You get what I'm saying?"

"You turned me into a celebrity overnight. A fucking craze for tweens." He stood up straight. His broad shoulders strained against his T-shirt. Elle looked away so he wouldn't catch her staring.

"At least they fell for it. They don't have your face with a big red X over it. Not yet anyway," she said, and he nodded once.

"Let's get you in there, big boy," Vero said and slapped his ass. He pointed his finger at her and glared. They all laughed. That's when Elle realized he wasn't wearing his jacket. Vero and Lex were in their gear like last time. And he was in a T-shirt. A T-shirt.

"You're wearing a T-shirt," Elle spoke out loud this time.

"I forgot my jacket this morning. I was in a rush." Drake grabbed his helmet from the front seat and locked his truck. He handed his key to Vero and went to get his bike from the trailer.

"Your arms won't be protected," she said. He wasn't worried. Why wasn't he worried?

"I've done this damn thing in less," Drake said.

Elle dropped it. Even though the feeling in the pit of her stomach wouldn't go away.

Elle hugged Lex and Vero. When she turned to find Drake, he was already several feet away. He pulled his helmet on and tried to stay hidden from the group of girls.

Nate walked with her into the stands and found seats closer to the starting point. Elle took a breath before looking out at the track covered in trees. Puddles spread throughout. Vines crawled up the sides of the arena. Waterfalls in the center. Clouds hung around the top. Would it rain on them this time? She looked at the other end, but it was hard to see. She grabbed her camera to use the zoom. It was covered with heavy greenery, but that's when she saw it.

A tunnel.

Thin ropes hung down through it. Like wires but with a small bulb at the end of each one. Blue and red. She gulped. She grabbed Nate's hand to steady herself.

"What? What do you see?" Nate asked and stood. He searched the track as he fixed his glasses on the bridge of his nose.

"A jelly tunnel," she whispered. Frantically, she threw her bag on the bench and set her camera down. She slipped the inconspicuous tin into her pocket. "He doesn't have sleeves."

Nate froze. Confusion turned to fear.

"I can jump down there before the gun goes off, right?" she asked as the riders began to fill the spots behind the starting line. Nate went wide-eyed behind his frames. "Will they shoot me if I hop the fence!" she yelled at him.

"No," he said.

Before he could speak another word, Elle jumped over the two rows of seats in front of theirs. The people sitting yelled at her. She ran for the fence. Like last time, she hopped over and rolled into her landing. It was a farther drop. She righted herself and started to sprint. Drake and Vero were in sight. Lex was too small to see yet. She waved her arms over her head to get their attention. She screamed. Panted. Her shoes hit the dirt harder. Faster.

Vero finally locked eyes with her, and her jaw dropped. She smacked Lex's arm. Drake turned to see her. They still couldn't hear her. Elle skidded to a stop in front of them and ripped open the tin breathing hard. She grabbed Lex and started to rub the space between her gloves and the sleeve on her wrist.

"Elle, what the fuck are you doing?" Drake seethed. He flipped open the shield on his helmet to see her better.

"Tunnel," she wheezed and turned Lex around to get the back of her neck. Vero was next. Then she turned to Drake.

"I don't know what you're talking about," he said and she started to apply the Sludge to his hand.

"Help!" she yelled at him, and he dipped his finger into the blue substance. He started on his neck, and she sighed.

The Guard watched her, but they didn't stop her. She suspected that meant they didn't realize what she was using. Either way, she didn't stop.

"What's the tunnel?" Vero asked as Lex got the back of Drake's other arm. He closed his eyes for a second.

"Sorry, Drake," Lex mumbled.

Both of them touching him must be his worst nightmare. This was life or death, though. He'd have to get over it.

"Jelly tunnel. They had them eight or nine years ago," Elle explained and started to rub up to his shoulder.

"Fuck," he whispered. His shoulders slumped and his fist tightened.

"Sludge will help. It won't come off if it gets wet. If a hook touches you, it's more likely to rub off than sink into your skin. If the stem latches on, don't try and yank it out. It's around the second bend. Don't die," Elle said and finished his left arm. Her eyes locked on his. Fear danced in them until they hardened and turned to determination.

"Thanks for the rub down." He winked, and she chuckled. Only he could make her laugh in a time like this. Asshole.

She ran back to the fence and warned Gage as she ran past him. His entire team was covered. Nate helped her climb back up the fence before the first gun went off.

"You're absolutely nuts, kid." Nate shook his head at her. They sat back down together, and Elle's heartbeat was in her throat. Ba-bum. Ba-bum. She couldn't hear anything else.

Inhale.

Exhale.

Ba-bum.

Cyra stepped out of the box and waved at the screaming crowd. The stands were fuller this time around. Nate asked about the tunnel, and she repeated what she had told the team. Others leaned in to listen too. This crowd didn't know what they were in for.

"It's the same technology as the rods the Guard use. Electrical currents and microchips pass venom into your system. Different venoms have different effects, but the most common is a slow death. Your organs start to turn blue before they melt from the inside out. If you're lucky, you have a couple hours before it's fatal."

Elle hoped she had enough Sludge after the race if any of them were injured or stung. Cyra made a speech, but this time, Elle didn't hear a single word of it. Her eyes were on her team.

The third gun went off. Elle grabbed Nate's hand and squeezed tight.

"It's going to be alright," she lied.

There were only twenty teams on the track this time. More room for them to not ram into each other. Drake went around the first turn. The rider in first was wearing a T-shirt, jeans, and boots that came up past his ankles. His bike was large and red and hovered above the ground. The wheel in the front rotated so fast that it didn't look like it was there at all. The front one was normal looking to Elle, big and black, while the two back wheels were on their sides. Rotating like helicopter blades. They lifted him off the ground while the front wheel steadied him after jumps. He disappeared from their view for about ten seconds when he entered the tunnel.

When he came out on the other side, his left arm was blue. And his right was completely gone. The bike went sideways, and he slammed into a vine-covered wall. They started to move. Slithered down like snakes. They wrapped around his body and suffocated him.

That's when a family of monkeys came down from the trees. Maybe lemurs? They started to gnaw on his body. They were metal, too, of course, so each shift made a creak Elle never wanted to hear. The riders' cries were deafening as one of the monkeys bit off a finger. Then the vines finished him off. The first death of the second race.

"Team Tilt, fatality."

Drake entered the tunnel. Elle held her breath and felt tears form in her eyes. Seemed like years of waiting for him to resurface. Sweat formed on her brow from waiting. He would make it out. He had to make it out.

Drake came out the other side unscathed. He raised his fist high in the air. Elle sighed in relief and let herself exhale. Lex entered the tunnel and then Vero. They came out side by side. They were okay. Nate squeezed her hand again, and she put her free hand on top.

Drake slipped into a patch of rain. The track became more mud than dirt. His tires slid more and more. The bike itself was covered in muck, and his legs were soaked. She prayed mud wouldn't take Blue Sludge off easier than water. She hadn't thought of that.

Lex swerved out of the forest of trees, and a group of lemurs jumped out from the vines. She ducked down and escaped without a scratch. The rider behind her wasn't so lucky. One of the vines smacked her in the head and knocked her off the bike. The three-wheeler she was on slammed into the tree and blew up. The explosion splattered her innards onto the line of trees beside the track. The lemurs' eyes went red, and they all dove for the fresh blood. They licked it off the bark viciously. And shrieked at each other for more.

Vero had to fight off five lemurs before she got to the next section of the race. The rain became rougher. Pounded her shoulders in buckets. She avoided the fireballs a rider shot from a maroon bike. Vero tried to ditch them, but they were too good at missing the deep puddles. They shot a spike at her and missed. Vero eased up on the gas and slammed into their back tire. It faltered them enough to let her get away.

In fifth place, Drake was being shot at. Spikes came out of a rider in plum. They weren't letting up. Shot after shot. One ripped a hole in Drake's T-shirt. Blood pooled on his lower right side. Elle let out a shrill cry. An arrow grazed him. At least it wasn't stuck in him. But now his bare skin was visible.

What about the tunnel?

"He'll make it," she whispered. "He has to."

Nate pushed to stand at the edge of the fence. Elle joined him. Girls screamed at Drake as he rode past.

"It's only a scratch! Don't be a pussy!"

"Marry me!"

"Don't let a little cut get to you!"

The rider in purple got on Drake's right. They released another arrow past him. Drake leaned toward the other rider, grabbed his arm, and twisted it. He released, and the rider fell off his bike. Mud splattered both of them. The rider's bike slammed into a wall of vines. It squeezed the bike until it popped. The vines broke it in two. The rider rolled to the side, but Lex came up next to him and shoved him into the wall. Vines wrapped around his body instantly. A lemur came and stole his helmet, and the rider's eyes bulged out of his head. Then the monkey took his boot. The vines did the rest.

Elle held her breath as Drake entered the tunnel again. Her shoulders sank when he came out. He was holding his side, and blood covered his hand.

thirteen

"He was stung," Elle said.

Nate was wide-eyed. He knew how much she cared about her friends.

"Doesn't mean he'll die. He can live through a sting," she reminded him, but it was more to remind herself.

"He'll make it," Nate repeated the words she'd said.

Drake went around a couple of bends and turns. The next six jumps were flawless. He held his side between, but his speed doubled.

Lex arrived outside the tunnel and raised her fist in the air; safe. The rider behind her was on a large blue bike and passed by her smoothly. Josh. Elle smiled to herself. He was okay.

Vero got through the tunnel and caught up to Lex. They rode side by side before Vero sped past. Surrounded by trees again, the rain was like bullets. The mud became sticky like glue. A rider got stuck and tried to pull his way out with the vines when a lemur grabbed him. Ripped him limb from limb in a tree above. Lex dodged the monkeys and pummeled one in the face when it tried to lift her helmet off.

Drake moved slower as he entered his third lap. A rider was right behind him on a black bike with red handles. He kept revving his engine and popping up on one wheel to get the crowd roaring. Drake went inside the tunnel with the rider behind him. When the other rider came out first, Elle's heart sank. Where was Drake? A full minute passed before he came out. Elle put her hand to her chest. Drake bent his head in toward his chest, and his wound dripped blood. It was blue.

"Is that bad?" Nate asked.

"It's not good." Elle bit her tongue. She knew what that meant. Time was ticking. His organs would be liquid in... an hour? Two? They might have updated the technology from the last time they used the tunnel. She held her breath.

Vero ran over the line and started her third lap. Now only two behind Drake. The rider between them on a gold bike was about to kick Drake off. The rider behind Vero sped up, got between them, and swerved into the gold bike. They rammed into a tree head-first. Elle had to squint to see who had helped Drake. Blue bike. Hair sticking up from the helmet. Gage. Elle screamed in the stands and clapped for her friends.

Lex punched her fireball launcher, but nothing happened. Nothing came out. The rider beside her underestimated her. Lex pushed them off their bike into the pit beside them. Everyone cheered behind Elle.

Another rider targeted Drake, but Gage blocked it. Drake backed off and got behind Gage. Every swerve the rider made, Gage followed. He rode his ass. The three of them stayed single file until they finished the race. Drake took fourth place. Vero and Lex weren't far behind.

She waited for the rider's gate to open before she clawed her way through. Nate carried her bag and raced after her. Her camera slapped her side as she ran. She found Drake lying in the dirt on the side of the track. Lex and Vero stood over him. Lex sobbed as Vero tried to get him up.

"Move!" Elle yelled at them. She pulled Drake's shirt up and wanted to vomit. His wound was deep. His blood was neon. She grabbed the tin and dipped her finger into it.

"Squeeze," she said and yanked his hand into hers. He screamed inside his helmet as she dug her finger into his wound. He crushed her hand as he slammed his head into the dirt.

"Lex, get the truck! Vero, get the bikes onto the trailer. Nate, help me move him. Come on!" Elle shoved the tin back into her pocket and stood. Vero tossed the keys to Lex, and they took off.

Nate got on the opposite side of Drake and helped raise him to his feet. He slumped into Elle and hung his head.

"We got you," she whispered, and they walked him out to the parking lot.

Nate helped pull him into the truck bed. Drake pushed himself up and took his helmet off. He flung it into the corner with a grunt.

"Let's go!" Elle screamed and pulled the tailgate shut. Lex climbed into the passenger seat, and Nate got behind the wheel. Vero got in the back seat and opened the window to keep an open line of communication.

Lex directed Nate as he sped through the lot and the streets of the town. Each turn made Elle's hair fly toward Drake's bloody mass. She handed Vero her camera to put inside the truck so she wouldn't damage the lens.

"Drake, don't you dare die. I'll fucking kill you." Elle opened the tin again. She could hardly see through her tears. Felt him tense beneath her. Blood flowed out of his wound. He grabbed her hand as she rubbed more Sludge into him. Drake wailed into his other hand. She stopped for a minute so he could breathe. Elle wiped her face. He looked up at her and started to laugh.

"What the hell are you laughing about right now?" she snapped.

"Irony," he said, and she put her head on his chest for a second. He was delirious. Loss of blood. Elle ripped a piece of her shirt off and shoved it into his side to stop the bleeding.

Nate pulled into a driveway of a small yellow duplex. White shutters and front door. Daisies lined the front walk, and a large maple was in the yard. Lex honked the horn twice, and a man ran outside to help. He was built like Drake but with lighter hair. Must be his father.

"Drake!" he yelled.

"Fuckin' hell," Drake mumbled.

"Howard, he was stung!" Vero yelled.

The man got into the bed of the truck, and Elle helped him pull Drake out. He bit his lip and winced as they walked him toward the door. Howard led him to the living room couch and Elle stopped him.

"No, bathtub. We need a tub."

His dad looked at Drake. "I trust her," Drake groaned. Howard looked over at her. His big dark eyes scanned her. He nodded.

They lowered him into the tub, and Elle turned both knobs all the way to fill it fast. Once it covered his wound, she stopped the water and took a breath. The bathroom had a light green tile on the floor and the tub was the same shade. The walls were a crisp white. It was clean but definitely the most used. A small clump of hair was in the far corner next to a yellow rubber duck. She imagined Drake playing with it as a child.

"You must be Elle," Howard said, and she looked back at him. Getting a closer look, he definitely had Drake's build, but he dressed more like Nate. Khakis and a sweater.

"Yes," she answered softly and lowered herself next to Drake on the cool floor. Vero, Lex, and Nate sat in the hall to give them space.

"Elle," Drake said. He was covered in blue blood and mud. Sweat and tears smeared his face. His eyes were on hers. Solid and still. "Why am I in the tub?"

"The wound needs to be submerged. Use Elastaderm and then let it soak. After ten minutes, empty the tub and repeat." She still tried to catch her breath.

"Elastaderm?" his dad asked.

"Blue Sludge," Vero said.

He gaped. "Where did you get that?"

"Her friend gave her some. It's a long story."

"Do you have more?" he asked. He pointed at Drake in the water. A worried look on his face. She couldn't imagine what his father must be thinking about all this.

"Some. I can get more, though." Elle bit her lip. She'd think of an explanation later. She had at least three in her safe at home. She might have more in her car.

"Elle," Drake repeated. She faced him. His eyes burned on hers. So blue she wasn't sure how she hadn't noticed the first time she saw him. "You saved me."

She felt the blood drain from her face.

"You saved us all," Vero corrected.

Elle turned to Vero. "Look at him. I didn't save anyone."

"If you hadn't rubbed that shit all over me, I'd be dead. What are you talking about?" Drake seethed. Elle started to retort until he snapped at her. "Shut up."

"I don't know how you knew about this stuff Elle, but thank you," Lex said and started to cry again. She got up and leaned over Elle to hug Drake. He groaned before he pushed her off.

"Lex, I'm fine."

"Move over. It's my turn," Vero whined. They traded places, and Drake winced as she hugged him too. Nate stayed in the hall, probably feeling so out of place here.

"Quit crying over me." Drake punched the wall beside him with the side of his fist. "And stop touching me. Please."

"No," Vero said and kissed the top of Drake's head. Howard laughed. Lex went back to the hallway and sat down with Nate. Howard came next to hug Drake too.

"Worst day of my life. Please stop touching me. I said please. Twice," Drake grumbled before he started to mumble to himself. Howard walked out and suggested the girls use the hose in the backyard to wash off the mud. Nate followed to assist them. Howard went to the kitchen to make them a quick dinner. He seemed like a decent father.

Elle drained the tub. She pulled the tin out and looked at the dime-size left. Drake closed his eyes. He ripped his soaked shirt over his head and chucked it into the sink next to them. Elle turned red. This was not how she wanted to see him half-naked for the first time. Not that she thought about that, of course. She looked down at his chiseled chest. His blue wound pulsed hard under his abs.

Elle dipped her fingers into the Sludge, and Drake's fists clenched at his sides. She bit her lip but decided to ask anyway. "Do you—"

"Yeah," he spat and grabbed her free hand on the side of the tub.

"Alright, on three," she said, and he nodded. Sweat dripped down the side of his face. "One," he took a deep breath, "two," she said and shoved the Blue Sludge into him. He squeezed her hand, but she was too focused on the way his body was turning back to a normal color to care. She smiled as she cried into the side of the tub. She let her sobs out for once.

He let go of her hand and sat up. Drake pulled her into the tub. Tucked her head under his chin and wrapped his arms around her. She couldn't stop the flood of tears. Drake held her close as she calmed down. Ran his fingers through her hair.

"It's over, Elle," he whispered. She tried to count her breaths. Dr. Gordon taught her well. Drake's heart beat beneath her. He rubbed her back. "Breathe," he said, and his chest rose and fell. She tried to match him. His wound looked like a scrape now. The skin already back together. She'd need more Sludge to finish the job. She wiped her face and looked up at him. His expression was unreadable.

The back door creaked. Lex and Vero came inside. Elle jumped out of the tub and sat down where she had been before. She leaned over to fill the tub again. Lex poked her head in, and Drake covered his face with his hands. She was in underwear and a bra.

"No! Out!" he yelled at her. Elle laughed.

"We need towels. Stop being so dramatic." Vero rolled her eyes at him, following Lex in her underwear. "We were covered in mud. And by the way, so are you."

"I'm in the tub." Drake pointed at his chest as they wrapped towels around themselves.

"Better start rubbing him down again, Elle," Vero teased. "He seemed to like it earlier."

"Out! Go away!" Drake yelled at his friends. Elle stood and looked down at her ripped shirt. "You didn't have to do that," he said.

"Here, Elle." Vero handed her a shirt from the hall. Vero and Lex headed back to the kitchen to help Howard.

Elle raised the shirt she had on over her head and threw it in the trash can. She pulled on the black T-shirt from Vero and could smell Drake on it. It was two sizes too big, but she didn't mind. Drake had his eyes glued to the wall.

"You looked away? You know, bras cover the parts I don't want you to see." Elle chuckled.

He smirked at her. "You look good in lace."

She smacked his arm. He was back to his normal self.

Elle stopped the faucet, and Nate came to join them. Lex and Vero plopped down a few minutes later. They all looked at his wound and decided Elle should be the official doctor of the group. She shook her head at them. She did not want the responsibility of that title.

"This might be a bad time, but I need to ask," Lex said softly. Everyone turned their attention to her. "Another team heard a rumor. And that rumor started a chain of messages to all teams."

"Spit it out, Lex," Vero groaned.

"Did Halc contact you, Elle?" Lex asked.

Elle held her breath. She turned wide-eyed to Nate.

"I didn't say shit." Nate held his hands up.

"Elle?" Vero asked.

"Well." She slumped. She kept her eyes down. "Yes. I met Kannon yesterday. He wanted me to stop giving so much attention to you and give it to his team. He was—is an asshole. And so I told him to fuck off."

"What?" Drake said. They locked eyes for a second and she looked away. She should've told him when she had the chance. She bit her lip.

"You did more than that," Nate mumbled. The air left her lungs as she prepared herself to explain further. Would they be angry? Would they understand? She closed her eyes for a brief moment. Don't let this be the end. Don't let this be it.

"Elle," Vero snapped at her.

She looked at all of them. Her friends. And Nate, her best friend. He nodded to her to keep going. Explain, he mouthed. Elle took a deep breath.

"He tried to blackmail me into giving his team the cover page. He told me you were using me to get famous. He said he'd try to," She paused to take another breath, realizing she was about to babble. "Kannon said you'd better watch your backs at the races. I told him I'd fucking kill him if he tried to get near you. He was an asshole. Did I mention that?"

Vero put her arms around her. Elle froze.

"Thank you," Vero whispered to her and let go.

"You chose us," Lex said, grinning at her.

"Of course, you're my friends," Elle said. The words came out so confidently she wasn't even sure it was her own voice.

"We definitely got our hooks in you." Lex snickered.

"It's official, Vanilla, you're one of us," Vero said.

Elle chuckled at her nickname and turned to Drake. He nodded once at her. He agreed? She couldn't help but smile at him. Howard knocked a few pots together in the kitchen and Nate offered to go help. Lex's eyes lingered on him as he walked down the hall. Elle nodded to her and she blushed as she looked away.

"And I guess Nate is alright," Vero added, and they all laughed. Drake included.

"Know what this means?" Lex said. Drake objected immediately. "It's time for a celebration!"

Elle groaned with Drake that time. "Another party? Do we have to?"

"Yes!"

"Drake's coming this time. If he can stand." Lex looked down at his wound. There would be a scar left behind. Considering the alternative, she figured he would be happy with that.

"Suddenly, my legs aren't working," Drake said. He grabbed his thigh under the water. At least his sense of humor never left.

Elle pointed at him. "Oh, no, no, no. You're coming if I'm being forced to go."

"Remember last time?" Vero looked at Drake and motioned to Elle.

"Hey!" Elle yelled.

"I'll go," Drake said.

fourteen

Elle assisted Lex in her room as she zipped into a short burgundy dress. Vero grumbled in the doorway as she waited for them to be ready. The guys left a while ago to sort out the car situation and went in search of a suit for Drake. They agreed to meet at the manor. She hoped Nate got along with Drake.

Lex persuaded Elle into a long black gown with a deep V cut. It was a little tight around her chest. Sleek and shiny but not sparkly. The skirt cascaded to the ground. Which thrilled Elle. It meant she could hide her tennis shoes again.

As they piled into Elle's car, she ran back inside to grab her camera. She put the strap over her shoulder and nearly fainted.

The cover photo.

She didn't take a single photo at the race. Her camera was beside her the entire time. Her mind had been on the team. Her mother would have a mouthful to say right now. Not to mention Randy. Disappointed. Atrocious. Unprofessional.

Elle clamped her eyes shut. She worked so hard to get to this place. All for nothing. Her throat dried. Turns out her fear of Drake pushing her away was pointless, she would cause her own demise. Years of work. Years of dealing with Randy. Yelling. Complaining. Convincing her she'd never be good enough on her own. Randy would certainly yell now. But she could work herself back up to this moment again. She would have to.

Elle took a deep breath. Think about the team. They survived another race. That's more important than a promotion. They survived. Until she could be alone, she'd force a smile. After she collected herself, she walked back out to her friends.

Once they arrived at the manor, Lex swayed Elle to take a photo with her. Vero stood in front of them in a deep cobalt suit. She clicked the shutter before Lex was ready. She complained and whined until Vero agreed to take more.

Behind Vero, groups of riders walked toward them. Elle spotted Josh, Aster, and Gage. Aster smiled at her first. She sported a yellow blazer with baggy dark pants and combat boots.

Elle waved her over. Vero turned to see the girl with pink hair. The camera flashed, and she jerked. Elle couldn't help her chuckle. She'd done the same thing to Drake. But that was different. Totally different.

"Elle!" Gage squealed and ran to kiss her cheek.

He introduced himself to Vero and Lex. And then kissed their cheeks. Josh laughed and introduced himself to them with a handshake. Glitter coated his lips while a bold navy covered his eyelids.

"How's Drake doing?" Gage asked Elle. "I was going to call him but didn't think he'd answer."

A cloud of silence hovered over the group.

Lex glanced at Vero. Then gawked at Gage. "You know Drake?"

"Since I was a child." Gage glanced between them. "He didn't mention that?"

"No," Lex said. Her posture sank. Her eyes glossed over. That must sting. Drake was in the business of keeping secrets.

"Doesn't surprise me, baby." Gage shrugged it off. He took Josh's hand in his. Aster stood beside Elle but stayed quiet. She rubbed her head with her palm.

"That was a great hit in the first race with that bird," Josh said to Vero. Elle was glad about the subject change. "Caught it on the replay."

Elle wasn't sure if she should walk away from the riders. She felt out of place. They had more in common. They fought for their lives on that track. She just sat in the stands.

Aster smiled. "I saw that. Good shot."

"Thanks," Vero mumbled.

Elle grabbed her camera out of Vero's hands. She flinched and released the camera with a shy smile. Elle gave a comforting squeeze before she let go.

"Are you joining The Championship next year, Aster?" Lex asked.

"This year, if they need me. Been in the Valley three months, and these bitches already got me signed up." Aster rolled her eyes.

"First race is always the hardest. Don't focus so much on the track. The pussies out there are what makes it worse," Vero said, and Aster nodded.

"Aster's used to watching out for pussies." Josh chuckled and hit his cousin's shoulder with the back of his hand.

Aster snatched his arm and twisted until he squealed. Her glower hardened. Vero laughed as she released him.

"Crazy ass," Josh complained. Shaking his arm out. Gage pulled him toward the door, and Lex followed. She wanted to find the dance floor.

"I'm off to take photos. Go dance, guys." Elle shooed the two girls left inside.

Vero's eyes went wide, but Aster took charge. She grabbed Vero's hand and pulled her up the steps of the manor. Vero's glee sparkled from her.

Elle made her rounds. This time, she avoided drunk people. And prepared herself to deliver a punch if necessary. There was a group in white on the front lawn lobbing a bottle of whiskey back and forth. A moment later, Kannon joined the group. Then that other asshole, Seth, from the first party. She gritted her teeth and turned her heel. Don't make eye contact. No drama at a race party. It's a celebration for the riders. They survived. She wished a few hadn't.

She headed inside and explored the manor. Murals covered the walls in the upstairs hallway. Red and gold flecks danced among the lines of the abstract piece. Her camera flash disturbed a team at the end of the hall. They growled at her as they stomped past. Elle took the steps down and found Nate and Lex.

"Lookin' good, kid." Nate waved at her.

He was in a deep chestnut suit she'd never seen before. It was tight to his chest, and she could tell he had help. She smiled at the thought of Drake helping him with the tie.

Lex had her hands locked around a glass of champagne, and Nate pulled her to the back room for food. Elle tagged along until she realized Drake had come with Nate. She started to search for him.

Drake strolled in from the back door. A suit made perfectly for him. All black. Even his tie. His hair combed to the side. It made his eyes more visible. People ran past, and he dodged them better than he would in the race. He teetered on his heels to avoid them. Their eyes met, and he stopped in his tracks. His famous smirk appeared.

"Did you find her?" Lex yelled at him as she turned and pointed at Elle. "Hey! There she is!" Lex wobbled, and Nate helped keep her steady.

Elle turned to Drake. "Looking for me?"

"I have no idea what she's talking about," he said.

Drake surveyed the crowd around them. Then rubbed his palms on his jacket. He opened his mouth when his gaze locked on her. "You look—"

"Elle!" Gage yelled from behind her. "We're going to the fire pit down by the lake. Find us later!" She nodded at him. Then he saw Drake. "Hey, great job today! Glad you're okay." He raised his fist. Drake tapped it with his own.

Josh waved as Gage pulled him out the back door. Aster and Vero followed. Drake whirled around to see them leave. He scrunched his nose and looked over at Lex.

"She dyed her hair! Now it's pink!" Lex shouted.

"So that's purple hair girl," he said and wiped his hands on his jacket again. He exhaled hard. Another. And another. His eyes went around the room. Sweat formed on his forehead. Someone bumped into him, and he gripped his fist. His eyes burned on the culprit.

"Alright, come on." Elle grabbed his hand and dragged him out the back door.

Elle didn't stop until they were halfway to the trees. About to step into the grass, Drake pulled her back. He pointed at the bottom of her dress. She lifted the skirt an inch to show him her shoes. He chuckled at her. They sat on a log at the closest fire pit. The trees at their back. Lights from the manor glowed before them.

Elle pointed her camera at the fire to get a shot of the manor behind it. She went around to the other side and took one of Drake. Shocked he didn't object. The fire in front of him made his eyes shine. She sat down beside him again.

"I'm ready to get out of this dress," Elle confessed, and he lifted his eyebrow at her. She realized her phrasing and laughed. "That is not what I meant."

Drake chuckled at her.

Vero ran up to them. "Hey, can I borrow your camera for two seconds?" Elle hesitated but agreed. She handed it over and turned back to Drake when she heard the shutter behind her a second later. "Thanks!" Vero yelled and gave the camera back. She ran off with Aster behind her, giggling like fools.

"Bitch," Elle grumbled and picked up the camera again.

"You'll get used to that." He grabbed the camera out of her hands and opened the photo. Drake looked right at her in the picture. "You are beautiful, Elle," he said softly. Like she wasn't supposed to hear. She had to look away from him. "You can take all my bullshit but can't take a compliment?"

Elle tried to read him. "It's not what I was expecting you to say."

She looked different in this dress. Like a lady. Like Evelyn. She didn't feel like herself. This wasn't her. Him saying that now only meant he liked her when she wasn't really her.

He rested the camera between them. The log creaked as he leaned forward to rest his elbows on his knees. "Why did you bring me outside, Elle?"

"I could see you." She pointed at his hand. "I do it too. When I start to freak out. I didn't realize you were claustrophobic."

He looked at the fire before he smiled to himself. Ran his fingers through his hair. He sat up. "You're not what I expected. I know I've said that." he stopped and lowered his voice to just above a whisper. "I've been claustrophobic almost my entire life. And not a single person knows."

"That's ridiculous. Why wouldn't you tell your friends that?" Elle asked. Another secret. What a surprise. "Everybody is afraid of something."

"Telling someone means trusting them to not use it against me," he said.

"You don't trust them?" Elle scoffed. Now that was ridiculous.

Drake shrugged. "It's more complicated than that. One wrong move messes everything up for me on the track. The wrong person finds out, and all they'd have to do is put in a smaller tunnel. Then we're all fucked."

Elle could tell this bothered him. He didn't want to keep secrets. Felt he had to. But if it meant he couldn't race...

"Does this mean you trust me now?" she asked.

"I don't know," he said. She appreciated the honesty even when it burned.

"I won't tell anyone." Elle tucked her hair behind her ear. He kept quiet, but she expected he knew she'd never tell.

"I wouldn't blame you. I haven't been very nice to you."

Elle sighed. "Agreed. You've been alright the past few hours. Maybe it's because I saved your life or whatever." She brushed her shoulder on his and smiled.

His eyes were glued on something behind her. They might have looked dark before, but now they were a black hole. Sucking everything in to destroy.

Elle followed his gaze to the rider, who grabbed her arm. Seth. Team Halo. His black eye prominent on his face. He had on a white suit with a gold bowtie.

"Do you know him?" she asked. She turned back and Drake was no longer there. He was halfway to the rider. Elle bolted up.

"Drake! Stop!" she yelled, but his hand was around the rider's throat already.

He slammed the rider into the nearest tree. Blood splattered out the back of his head. Bark hit the ground at Drake's shoes. The glossy finish now tainted with a layer of crimson. His jaw tight as he ground his teeth.

The rider laughed. Scarlet bubbled between his teeth. "Now I understand. She yours?"

Drake squeezed tighter. His lips pursed. The rider's face turned red before starting to go blue. "Don't touch her again. Or I'll crush your skull with my bare hands." He spoke through his teeth.

"Matthews," he choked. "We've known each other for years. You gonna let some slut get between us?"

"Stop!" Elle yelled. "Let him go!"

Lex and Vero ran toward them. Gage and Nate on their tail. Groups of riders started to crowd around to watch the scene.

"Drake!" Vero cried and tried to pull him off the rider. "You can't do this!"

Drake grunted and shoved the rider's head into the tree one more time before he dropped him. He slumped to the dirt as Drake walked away from him.

Nate bent down to check on the rider and he shoved him away. Nate lifted his hands up and stepped back. "Back off!" the rider screamed at him. Blood sprayed as he spoke.

Four guys in white picked up their teammate. Two walked him inside, and the other two eyed Drake the whole time as they followed. Elle chased Drake back to the fire pit. He paced back and forth.

"Drake," Lex started.

"You can't do that," Vero finished for her.

"You gave him a black eye, V!" Drake yelled.

"Yeah, to get the guy off of her. Tonight he walked by. You can't attack for no reason."

"No reason?" he repeated. His chest puffed out.

"I made you a celebrity, remember?" Elle chimed in. "Everyone is watching you."

Drake glanced around at the riders staring at them. "And listening."

Gage put his hand on Elle's shoulder. He looked her up and down. "You okay? Josh saw from the lake." He pointed behind them.

"I'm fine. Drake is the one who went berserk." Elle turned to Drake. He went after him the second his eyes locked on him. "Do you know him?"

"He's always been a dick, Drake," Gage said. "Bobby forced Seth out, remember?"

Drake glared at Gage. Fists at his sides. He stood between the log they were sitting on and the tree line. Elle expected him to take off running. She sent Gage a questioning look.

"Bobby's Home for Boys," Gage explained.

Elle knew Bobby. Sarah worked with him from time to time. Elle gave him tins of Sludge for the boys. The rider grew up there with Gage? How did Drake fit into that?

"People are listening," Drake mumbled.

"That doesn't answer my question. How do you know him?" Elle asked Drake.

Gage dropped his jaw. "Drake."

"Shut up, Gage," Drake spat.

"Hey!" Elle scolded.

Gage held his hand up. "It's fine. I'll see you guys later." He kissed Elle's cheek. "Glad you're okay. You look stunning."

"Thank you," she said.

They were silent as Gage joined his friends on the back deck. The team went inside, and Elle turned back to Drake. "What the hell is wrong with you?" She crossed her arms in front of her. Rage boiled inside her.

"Dude, I thought you were going to kill him," Vero said.

"I was," Drake said matter-of-factly.

"You can't go around throwing fists at every asshole here. People are counting on you to be in the next race," Elle said.

"So you'd rather he grab someone else?" He sneered.

Elle sighed. "No. I'm saying let The Championship do the work. Have someone else take him out. Someone who doesn't have friends that watched him almost die a few hours ago. What if he hurt you?"

"I'd deal with the consequences," Drake mumbled.

"You're absurd," Lex groaned, grabbed Nate's arm, and pulled him to the front. He waved at Elle. Vero followed behind them. Nobody knew what to say to him.

The two of them were quiet as the crowd thinned out.

"You're so reckless. Can't you see that you're hurting the people around you?" Elle asked. "I get that you don't care what happens to you, but we all do. You dying wouldn't be nothing to them."

"It doesn't matter."

"Lex and Vero aren't that girl from Beehive," Elle snapped at him. That shut him up. "You care about them. Realize and accept it. For fucks sake. You're infuriating." She felt her eyes fill up. "I'd die to have a family again. And you sit there and act like it doesn't matter." She cursed herself for allowing him to affect her this much.

"Elle."

"Lex and Vero are your family. So act like it."

She left him standing alone by the fire.

fifteen

Elle collapsed into her bed in pajamas. Commotion in the hall kept her up. One of her neighbors stomped back and forth from the elevator. There were seven other apartments on her floor, but she only knew two of them. Opening the door to tell them to stop pacing was out of the question.

Luckily somebody down the hall did it for her. A few grumbles and stomps later, it was quiet again.

She stared at the ceiling. Drake looked her up and down in that dress. Elle bit her lip. Closed her eyes. Tried not to imagine it as Drake biting her lip. She used her pillow to muffle her groan. He drove her up a wall. She couldn't want him that way. That would be insane. They were all her family now. Why couldn't he just talk to his friends like a normal person? Why couldn't he—

She sat up.

People are listening. That's what he had said. Did that mean something?

The clock flashed four. Under her pillow, she found Drake's shirt she had hidden. A strange floral scent crowded her senses as she scrunched it under her head.

Her thoughts traveled to Evelyn and the trail they used to take. Lessons on types of flowers and wildlife were her favorite. She would make up songs for Elle to remember it all. Evelyn was the smart one of the four of them. The one everyone thought would go to college. Have a family. A full career. A full life. Now Elle was the only one left.

When the clock read five, she rolled out of bed. Sleep wouldn't happen tonight. Might as well go to the field of flowers. She needed those calendula blooms anyway. She used a bundle for each batch of Blue Sludge. The flowers were great for healing and reducing inflammation.

She drove out to the lot and parked before grabbing her camera bag. She always needed an excuse to be out there in case Guard showed up. The sun was beginning to rise as she started up the hill. Memories came of Evelyn dragging her up and down slopes in the Cove. They wandered for hours to get to an empty field for a patch of white daisies or honeysuckle. She missed her sister. Her carefree spirit and her smile.

Camera in hand, she captured the landscape in front of her. She took her time getting the sun rising through the trees beyond and the green weeds at her feet.

Elle sat down in front of the marigolds and began to pluck them. Carefully digging to get most of the roots. She looked around at the plants. Not a lot of these left. She'd have to start searching for a new area again soon. Elle shoved the bundles into her bag. Three more batches would last her a few months. Weather permitting, she could come back and plant more next week.

Next week her life could be different, though. Her friends could be dead. Living in the Valley, couldn't anyone be dead tomorrow?

Not a cloud in sight, she drove to Little Hearts. Sarah served breakfast at eight. She could help cut strawberries and bananas for the kids. What she really needed was a Sarah talk. Randy hadn't called yet. Eventually, he would. She hadn't even told her about Halo yet. Let alone the whole Drake situation.

Elle arrived in time to wake some of the older children and tell them pancakes were ready. Their faces lit up when they heard the menu. Pancakes were a special treat. Only once in a blue moon.

The children clambered about and hurled objects and yelled. She didn't mind the noise. Needed it. This was home. Sarah sat down with her at the table and let her ramble. Halo was the first topic. Sarah clenched her jaw.

"This is what I'm talking about. You need to watch yourself around riders."

Elle's phone started to ring in her bag by the front door. One of the teenagers grabbed it and ran to her, screaming she had a call. She took it from him, and Lex's name was on the screen.

"Hello?"

"You answered!" Lex yelled. It wasn't a happy yell. "Have you seen it? You haven't seen it. Oh, Elle." She sighed heavily.

"What are you talking about?" Elle chuckled.

"Racer Magazine. You're on the cover."

Elle blinked twice. "Huh?" Was this a prank? She must be joking. Elle hadn't done anything to warrant a cover photo. The only one she'd posed for was with the team by the willow tree.

"You and Drake are on the cover of Racer magazine."

Elle laughed. "What are you talking about?" She's not in The Championship. She put her phone to her chest to ask Sarah if she got that edition at the house.

"Might be on Pedro's bed. He gets the mail for me." Sarah ran up the stairs. She came back down a minute later with wide eyes. Elle dropped the phone when she saw it.

Drake sitting beside her on the log at the party last night. Elle rubbing Drake's arms on the track. Six photos of them with the caption: *Bachelor?*

We don't think so! Evolution's Hottie has a girl! Sorry, ladies! Evolution liars!

The teen magazine blasted fake stories about their love, marriage, and happy life together. You couldn't see Elle's face in any photo, so people were guessing who she was in the story. Rider from the previous year? Daughter of a celebrity?

Sarah looked it up on her phone. Most comments were negative. *They lied! Evolution is full of lies! Liars!* Elle picked up her phone to Vero, shouting.

"We're coming. Send the address."

Twenty minutes later, the girls knocked on the door. Elle was nervous about letting Sarah meet riders and have them in her house so soon after that conversation. She always assumed Sarah hated riders. But like anyone else who came to the house, she let them in with a smile and a handshake.

Sarah led them into the kitchen. Kids ran around, and Elle shouted at them to slow down. Lex sat at the table with Sarah as she sipped on a glass of her tea. Vero looked at the magazine and read the story again.

"What's the point of this?" Elle asked and sat down next to Sarah.

"Is it possible they don't want Drake to have the attention he's been getting from all those girls?" Vero suggested.

"Why would that matter?" Lex asked. "Don't they want The Championship to get all the press?"

Sarah cleared her throat. Her red locks trapped on top of her head in a bandana. "The Championship runs off celebrity status and the who's hot or not list. If Drake is at the top and they don't want him to be...this is stage one. Pushing him down a level. They have to do it gradually. Or else people will get suspicious. I remember about thirty years ago, there was a rider. Young girl, pretty, full of joy. This place hadn't broken her yet. She was getting all the male attention, even some female. And they tried to knock her down too fast. Told everyone she cheated and that she lied in an interview, but the fans brushed it aside. Nobody believed it." Sarah raised the magazine to show Drake and Elle together. "This is believable."

"You think Drake and I look like a couple?" Elle snorted. Lex giggled.

"Yeah," Vero said. "Look at this." She pointed at the photos.

"What did Drake say?" Sarah asked.

"He hasn't answered his phone," Lex sighed. "Hopefully, he'll come to the garage later. He needs to fix his bike before the next race. We only have three days. And I still need his help with my fireball launcher."

"Who do you think sent the photos in?" Vero asked.

Elle felt the knot in her stomach. She didn't want it to be true. But she knew. Certain she knew. "Kannon," she mumbled.

Sarah nodded. "I agree. With everything you told me, honey, sounds like he's got his hands in the cookie jar."

"Maybe we should call him. Make sure. What if it's not him, and we have a bigger problem on our hands?" Vero suggested as she bit her thumbnail.

Lex nodded. "Yeah, we should make sure."

"Alright," Elle said. She didn't want to. However, they made a point.

"I'll do it. So you're not involved." Vero got her phone out, and Elle gave her the number. She placed it on the counter, on speaker, so everyone could hear.

"Evolution, I'm assuming? I was wondering when you'd call," Kannon's voice echoed in the kitchen.

"Did you print that cover?" Vero asked. Straight to the point. One thing she liked about Vero.

"Elliot made the wrong choice. Now she'll pay for her actions."

"What do you gain from doing this to Drake, you psycho?" Vero snapped at him.

He laughed through the phone. "Halo is going to skyrocket to the top. See you at the arena."

Kannon hung up, and they collectively sighed. Sarah put her hands on her head.

"Well, I think we should just let it go," Elle said. "Nothing we can do. Halo will print their stories and hopefully nothing else on Drake."

A group of kids ran through the kitchen, and two of them stopped to whisper in Sarah's ear. One boy stared at Vero until she flung her fist in the air, and he screamed. Lex rolled her eyes at her while Elle laughed. She liked messing with them too.

"If you don't do something, it'll get worse." Sarah went to the fridge and grabbed an apple sauce for the boy whining with his hands up. "Okay, grabby. Here." She put it in his little hand and gave him a spoon. He ran out the back door and jumped off the steps into the yard.

"What do you suggest we do?" Vero asked Sarah.

Elle was glad her friends trusted Sarah enough to talk about this. She thought of Drake meeting Sarah at this moment. How closed off he would be.

"Turn the story. Elle is a photographer at a magazine, for crying out loud. Use it," Sarah said.

Shit. She never told her about Randy.

"So... about that." Elle stopped and looked at Sarah. "I didn't take any photos at the second race."

"What do you mean?" Lex asked. Her posture straightened, and her eyes widened.

"I was so worried about you guys and then everything happened with Drake, and—I—"

"What happened with Drake?" Sarah interrupted. Elle bit her tongue.

"Elle saved him," Vero said.

Sarah glanced at Elle and smiled. "You didn't tell me that."

"I don't know if Randy will let me send him any photos to print. I might get knocked back down to journalist." She wanted to cry but refused. There were more important things right now than her job.

"Couldn't we send them in anonymously?" Vero suggested.

"Great idea!" Lex said.

"See, you've got these two to help you out." Sarah grinned.

Lex smiled at Sarah. "I like you."

"I like you too." Sarah's wrinkles closed in around her eyes. "So glad my Elle has friends to come to her rescue." Sarah put her arm around Elle and squeezed her to her side. "She hasn't had friends since she was in the Cove."

"Alright." Elle winced. "Thanks, Ma."

"We knew you were a loser already, dude. No secret," Vero teased.

Elle let the girls leave before her. She sat in her car a minute before she pulled out of the driveway. At the first red light, she heard a familiar sound. A bike. Not just any. A ChaosMotors bike. Drake flew past her toward the outskirts of town. That's odd. Where could he be going? The car behind her honked, and she jerked to press the gas.

Elle helped Vero fix up her bike before moving Drake's to his normal spot. That way, it would be ready for him when he got there. Vero walked back to her corner when Elle realized something was off about Drake's area.

She looked across the room. Lex had photos up and letters from her family. Vero had sticky notes and old family photos, and a recent one of her and Lex. Drake didn't have a single thing here. Nothing. Didn't he have anything from his parents to hang? Just dirty rags and a pile of scraps at her feet. The floor was scuffed and scratched and grease-stained sections of the center.

Elle looked at the empty wall and thought back to when she first got to Little Hearts. She didn't want to own a single shirt yet. All of her things were in the Cove. She wanted to go back there so bad she didn't want a single dust bunny in her possession. It wasn't where she belonged. She knew someone would come and take her back any second. Believed it. Her reality settled in eventually. Sarah and Dr. Gordon helped with that.

The door creaked open, and Elle rushed back to Vero's side. She didn't want Drake to catch her in his space alone. Vero asked for a tool, and Elle handed it to her. Drake's heavy boots stopped beside her.

"I'm sorry I was a dick," he said. Unexpected. She turned toward him. He looked—well, like shit. Dark circles under his eyes. Dirt smeared his jaw. His arms splotched in grease. "I'm not sorry I roughed him up, though."

"Fair." Elle smiled at him. She could tell he was expecting her to be mad. She wasn't, though. "Forgiven," she added.

"I need to tell you something." His voice lowered. Elle furrowed her brow at his serious tone. He already apologized. What else was there to say? Vero got closer and he leaned in to Elle. "Later." She nodded.

"So, you guys are married and in love, huh?" Vero put her hands on their shoulders and laughed before walking back to her bike with a different tool in her hand. Drake huffed at her touch.

"It better be big, Drake," Elle whispered.

He went rigid. "What?"

"The ring." She winked at him and held up her empty left hand. He laughed. An actual laugh with a full tooth display. He ran his hand through his hair.

"What the hell have you been doing? You look disgusting." Lex motioned to his attire, and he flipped her off. Elle hadn't noticed the rips in his shirt or pants. His boots had dirt caked on them.

"I need to go shower. So, I'll come back." Drake took out his keys. He flipped them in the air and caught them.

Vero raised her hand at him to stop. "Wait, what are we going to do about the magazine?"

"Nothing. What can we do?" he said.

Vero sat back down and slid under her bike. Lex handed her another tool she needed and wiped off a table beside them.

"Elle's mom thinks we should put out our own story," Lex said.

Drake took a rag from Lex and started to wipe the grease off his arms. "What would we change it to?"

Elle laughed. Put her hands on her head and sighed. Finally, she got an idea. She was insane. But it could work. "I think we should lean into it." Elle crossed her arms and glanced at Drake.

"You want people to think we're in love?" Drake raised a brow at her.

"Know what sells better than a bachelor?"

"Sex!" Lex yelled.

"Shut the hell up, Lex," Drake snapped.

"Dude, she might be onto something," Vero said. "People will root for you as a couple. Because you're the hot guy in love. That guy deserves to win the race to move to the Cove with his family."

"How do we do that, though? Take some photos and send them to your magazine?" Drake asked and threw the rag into a bin behind him.

"Pretty much. But, like this," Elle said. She took her phone out and showed Drake some examples. He turned a shade of pink.

"You want to take photos like this? Me and you?" he asked. He cleared his throat.

"Yes." She chuckled. "Scared?"

"Scared of getting a boner!" Vero yelled, and Drake flipped her off. Vero laughed.

"Let me see." Lex grabbed Elle's phone and gasped. "Sexy!"

Vero stood and took the phone from Lex to see for herself. "Damn, Elle, how are you going to get Drake to look this good?"

Drake hit her arm with the back of his hand.

"I'm thinking in the field, on his bike. I'll ask Nate to come take the photos. Lex can help. I'll edit and send them in tonight. Before they can get another photo of you to use." Elle looked out the door at the sun. They would lose light fast. It was almost noon.

"Fine. Before I second guess it," Drake groaned. "You want me dirty or clean for this?" He looked down at his clothes.

"Clean. Definitely clean." She scrunched her nose at him. "I need a shower too. So we'll meet back here."

"Shower at mine. It's closer," Drake said. He was going to allow her into his personal space? His bedroom? Her curiosity got the better of her wondering if it was just as empty there as it was here.

"Alright," she paused to throw her keys at Lex, "go to my place and grab the gray bag in my closet. No snooping." She pointed her finger at her. Vero followed Lex to the car. Elle was suddenly very aware that she was alone with Drake again.

sixteen

Drake was quiet on the drive to his house. The window was down, and his arm rested on the frame. His fingers drummed on the steering wheel to the music. It was playing softly, but she could make out the songs.

"Where'd you go last night?" Elle asked.

His fingers stopped tapping. His posture straightened. "A friend's place."

"You have two friends. And they live together. I know you keep a lot of secrets. You don't have to lie. All you have to do is say you don't want to tell me."

"It's not that I don't want to."

"You can't tell me. I understand. So, in the future, just say that." Drake was speechless. "You said people were listening. I heard you." She stared out the windshield as he pulled into his driveway. He rolled the window up but locked the doors.

"Don't go looking into this. You can't." His eyes were hard on hers. "I'm serious. You could get killed."

"Killed?" By who? Was he serious? Death was always a possibility in the Valley. Why was this even more of a threat than the Guard?

"Swear," he snapped at her.

"Alright, I swear," she whispered. He was serious. He grabbed the door handle and she reached for his hand between them. Drake stopped and looked at her. "Could *you* get killed?"

He scoffed. "I'm a rider. The second I entered my name in that first race, I put a target on my back. Now, unfortunately, it's on yours too. So, let's change that," he said, and they got out.

"Hey, Drake," Howard said as they walked inside. His eyes widened and mouth gaped. "Elle. Hi." Clearly not expecting her.

"Howard, did you see the magazine?" Drake asked as he closed the door behind Elle and locked it. Howard?

"Sure did." He chuckled. "Good luck with that."

"Elle has a plan. I'll let you know how it goes," Drake said and led the way to his room at the end of the hall. They passed the bathroom they had spent the most time in yesterday, and Elle felt a bit nervous. She hadn't spent this much time with Drake alone before. And now she was about to be in his bedroom. And take a shower. Naked. Alone. With him. Well, not shower with him. Well. Was her face red?

Drake opened his mouth to speak and stopped when he turned around. "What's wrong?"

Of course, he'd seen right through her. "Why do you call your dad Howard?" she asked.

He crossed his arms in front of his chest. "Why do you call your mom Sarah?"

"She's not my real mom." She squinted at him. Obviously. Was he being a jerk on purpose?

"Right," he said and opened the door to his bathroom. What did that mean?

He grabbed some towels and told her he would go first. That way, the girls would be back with her clothes by the time she finished. She agreed that was for the best. Plus, he smelled.

Elle sat down at the edge of his bed and looked around. Dark comforter and pillows on his large bed. Dresser and two nightstands and a closet. The door was open, so she could see the leather jacket hanging and two helmets on the shelf. One shoe box in the corner. Nothing else. No extra hangers. No extra clothes. His walls were clear. Not a photo or personal touch anywhere. Her guess had been right earlier. Just as bare here as the garage. She desperately wanted to open his dresser to see if it was empty but didn't dare move from the spot she was in.

There was a knock on the front door, and she could hear the girls talking with Howard in the living room. So he wasn't his dad. Stepdad? Her curiosity itched at her insides.

Drake opened the bathroom door and stood in jeans and his boots. He was pulling his shirt on as he stepped into the room. She gulped at the sight of his bare stomach.

"Your turn." He grabbed the rest of his stuff out of there, and she looked in his bathroom. Barren. Two gray towels hung on the rail. A simple black bath mat on the floor. One toothbrush in the cup by the sink.

"Do you live here?" she asked.

He chuckled at her. "What?"

"It's just." She trailed off as she turned around in the small room and swayed before looking back at him. "You don't have anything around."

"I don't need anything else," he said. "You want me to decorate my room?"

She laughed. "Would be nice."

"I'll think about it. If you'd like to use the other bathroom, feel free." He pointed over his shoulder but took a step toward her to lean on the door frame.

"No, I'd rather use yours." She said it too fast. It came out weird. She realized she was about to ramble. She looked down at the tile floor. No need to tell him all of the thoughts rattling around in her brain about using his shower. Her naked. Him naked. Drake naked. She locked eyes with him again.

He smirked at her. "No, go on."

She bit her lip to make sure she didn't speak. She shook her head. His eyes drifted to her mouth. Was he looking at her mouth? She released her lip, and he took a step back from her.

"Hurry up, we're losing sunlight," he said.

She shut the door and let out a sigh of relief. She quickly stepped into the hot water. A familiar scent overwhelmed her. A clear bottle with green liquid was on the shelf. Elle brought it to her nose. That floral scent from his shirt. Interesting. Why on earth did he use this? It was very feminine.

Oh. Could be someone else's. Did he have a girlfriend? She could be the friend he was with last night. She could live on the other side of town near Sarah. He said it was dangerous to look into it. Maybe she was a rider too.

Elle let the water soak into her soul. Stop thinking about him.

She got out of the shower and wrapped the towel around her.

Vero knocked on the door. "Yo, open up."

Elle opened it to Lex, holding up one of her tins.

Shit.

"Start talking." Vero glared at her.

"Where'd you find that?" Elle sighed. She remembered putting three in the safe under her bed, but she couldn't place the other two. She had forgotten to bring them inside with her the day she went to Bernie's.

"Your trunk." Vero crossed her arms in front of her.

Drake walked in and eyed the group. "What's up?"

"Elle had two of these in her car. I don't care what she told us before. No way her brother makes it. Too many laying around." Vero tossed him the tin. "So she has two seconds to explain."

"You're right. I lied," Elle said. Might as well come clean. She was screwed.

Drake opened the tin to look at it.

"Your brother doesn't make it?" Lex asked.

Drake threw the tin at Elle. She caught it. "She does," he said.

Lex giggled into her hand.

Elle froze. How did he figure her out? "How'd you know?"

"You're serious?" Lex gaped.

Vero stared at her. Her dark eyes scanned her up and down.

"Please." He rolled his eyes. "I knew when I found you at Bernie's."

"What?" Elle was even more confused. That didn't make sense. Because she went to a coffee shop, she made Blue Sludge?

"Only two people I know get this exact tin of Sludge. Bobby and Bernie. Wouldn't surprise me if Sarah had the same. Lucky for you, nobody else knows you like we do," Drake said. "Secret's safe another day."

Elle let out her breath slowly. They would keep her secret. So why didn't he trust them with his own?

"Elle, why would you lie?" Lex asked.

"They will kill her if they find out. They'd kill us for knowing," Drake explained. She was thankful he stepped in. She couldn't put that in words right now. "What I want to know is how you know the recipe."

Elle considered lying again. Thought better of it. She was in this deep anyway. And his blue eyes were staring into her. "I snuck into a lab. I watched them make it. Then I found replacements for their fancy, bullshit ingredients. If it weren't for me, people out here wouldn't have any."

"I can't handle any more drama, Elle." Lex put her head on Elle's shoulder.

Elle stepped back into the bathroom and changed into the outfit Lex had brought. Black jean shorts and a white tank top. It would go well with her black bra. Drake stood at his dresser when she finished in the bathroom. Lex whistled when she came out.

"Shut it." She pointed her finger at her. Drake crossed his arms in front of him. "So, for you." She paused, and he opened the dresser drawer. "Hm, what I expected. This black T-shirt or this black T-shirt," he grunted. The shirt he had on would have to do.

They all got in the truck and headed to the garage. Nate met them there and smiled wide at Lex. She helped him carry his camera bag to the track. Elle watched from a distance as her friend crushed on the small blonde. Nate had on a sweater vest and khakis, and Vero made fun of him so much he took off the vest to reveal a plain white T-shirt. Elle laughed at him, and he rolled his eyes at her.

Nate showed Lex how to assist with Elle's camera. With two of them shooting, they were bound to get a few decent shots. He walked her through his process, and Elle went to Drake on his bike.

"This doesn't feel real," Drake mumbled to her, watching Nate and Lex get ready. "It already looks fake." He motioned to her outfit.

Elle looked down at herself. Shorts and a tank top. "You think I should wear jeans and a stained shirt for a cover photo?"

"I think you should be comfortable," Drake countered.

Elle stepped away from the group. Comfortable. The red trees swayed in the slight breeze. Birds flew overhead. The bike was ready in the middle of the track. Little white flowers surrounded it. A light sweet scent in the air.

Vero stood several feet from Nate. No. No, that would not do. She turned to Lex. Definitely not. Comfortable? Not fake. Natural. Then she looked at Drake. That was it.

"Give me your shirt," she said to him.

"What?" he asked.

"You're right, give it up," Elle said and pulled her tank top off. Drake blocked her from Nate's view. She blushed at that.

"What are you doing?" he said and peeled his shirt off, and handed it to her. She pulled it off her right shoulder and combed her fingers through her hair one more time.

"Better," she said and walked over to the bike. Drake stood behind her, and she pulled him over to the other side. Told him how to sit and then went over everything with the group again. Okay. She held her breath. About to get on the bike in front of him, she stopped.

Wait.

"Oh." She turned to Drake. Her eyes widened as she stared at him. "Oh no."

Lex looked her up and down. "What? What did we forget?"

"I'm an asshole," she whispered. Drake looked up at her. "Drake."

"It's fine. Get on the fucking bike Elle," he grumbled, and she flushed.

Lex looked at each of them before Nate called her over to start teaching her where to begin.

Elle lowered herself onto the bike. Drake held her steady and had his right leg planted to hold the bike. She put her hands on his shoulders and looked into his eyes. She started to laugh.

"You look terrified," she said.

"I don't want you to do this. You're putting yourself in the crossfire," he spoke softly. Barely moving his lips. His eyes locked on hers.

"A near-death experience is good every once in a while," she said, and he chuckled at her. "I'm sorry I didn't think about how I had to touch you during this. I'm an ass."

"Elle, we are in an open field. I don't feel like you're suffocating me. I'm not in a car. There are no chains. I don't feel like you're going to crush me. Can we please take these damn pictures so I don't get a damn boner and make Vero or Nate point and laugh?" he rambled. Like she normally did. He went quiet again. He was getting used to her. She smiled at him.

"So you think I'm hot?" she mocked him, and he chuckled.

She moved his leg and tilted his head. Put one hand on her waist and the other on her neck. He tensed but let her move him wherever she needed to and eased his posture. She held her breath as his fingers pressed into her skin. His bare chest brushed her arm, and she prayed he couldn't feel her pulse quicken. She put her forehead on his and heard his shallow breath.

"You think they're actually taking these?" Drake asked, and she laughed. The whole bike started to tilt, and he grabbed her so she wouldn't fall. "Okay, no laughing," he said, and she laughed harder. She put her forehead on his shoulder.

"Alright, sorry, sorry, focusing," she said.

"This is the weirdest thing I've ever done," he whispered.

"Not me," she said, and he questioned her silently. "I hopped the fence at the arena twice, tried to save a stranger with Sludge, rubbed you down before a race. I could go on."

"Your life has been quite full since you met us. Can't deny that." Drake moved again without her assistance. He was a quick learner. She pictured taking his photo with only the two of them. Don't blush. Don't blush.

"Definitely," she choked out.

"Is that what you want?" he asked.

She stifled a laugh. "You think I want my life to be boring?"

Drake shrugged. "Boring is safe."

"I'd rather have an adventure," she whispered. His arms around her tightened, and the bike beneath her shifted.

Drake parted his lips to speak when Vero reprimanded them. "Quit talking! It's making your mouths look weird!"

Elle smiled at him, and he rolled his eyes at his friends. Nate moved them several times before he asked them to get off the bike. This time she sat sideways and had him stand in front of her. Then they traded spots. She leaned in and chuckled.

"Sorry, it's funny, you smell like that soap. I kept smelling it on you before but couldn't figure it out until today."

"What soap?" he asked.

"That green stuff in your shower," she said. She kept him on the bike and moved around him in several places. The camera faced Drake's back and Elle looked at the camera over his shoulder. She slowly turned his head to face over the same shoulder and leaned towards him. She knew that was the shot she needed.

"Oh, Jane makes it. I have to use it," he said.

Jane. So he did have a girl. Elle directed him again and he moved smoother this time.

"She said if I didn't, I wouldn't be a supportive son."

"What?" Elle didn't understand.

"My mom, Jane, makes her own soap for the convenience store. She owns it, and Howard helps when he can," Drake explained.

"Your mom makes soap." Elle was still stuck on that. She needed to stop assuming anything about this guy. Needed to eat her own words.

Drake chuckled. "If you like it, I can get you a bottle."

"So I can smell like you?"

"In case I—" he stopped talking. His shoulders slumped. Eyes fell away from her.

In case he died. She knew what he was going to say. He could have said it. It was true.

"So I can think about you when I shower? Drake, I thought we went over this already." She sighed as she pulled him off the bike. "It's always been Vero."

They laughed, and this time, Lex yelled at them for talking.

"I'm sorry to be the one to tell you this then, but she's got her eye on someone else," Drake whispered. Elle chuckled as she posed for another photo.

"I wish we could get some height." Elle yelped as he lifted her up in one swoop. She wrapped her legs around his torso and laughed into his shoulder. "Warn me next time! That was terrifying."

"Next time, huh?" he said. He was playing with her. She bit her tongue.

His blue eyes were electrifying today. She traced her fingertips from his jaw to his chin. He shut his eyes, and she felt his hands tighten around her. His body on hers. Wearing his shirt. She took a deep breath to savor the moment.

But this was all fake.

She didn't want to admit it to herself, but she wanted that. Wanted him to hold her. Wanted him to be close. For real. Not whatever this was. She needed to get out of there. She started to tense, and he sensed it. Gently put her down.

"Elle?" he said.

But she had put up her wall already. "We should be good. I need time to edit them," she said and walked over to Lex and Nate.

"You okay?" Lex asked as she handed over the camera.

"I'm alright. This should be enough. Thanks for being a great photographer." She smiled at her. It was a fake smile. Like this was all fake.

Nate started to pack up and handed her the chip from his camera.

"I'll give it back tomorrow," she promised. He nodded.

"You got it, kid. Good luck," he said and waved as he left them all. Lex watched him walk away. Maybe she did like him back. Elle wasn't really sure yet.

Vero lay flat in the grass and looked up at the sun. Her jacket in the grass next to her. She crushed a beer can in her hands and tossed it at Lex. She caught it and threw it back at her. Vero swatted it towards the garage.

"I'm going to head home to edit," Elle said.

Lex eyed her. "You want me to drive you?"

"It's fine, I'll take her. I have to get my shirt back anyway." Drake stood and started walking to the truck. Elle followed him. Breathe, she told herself. Breathe.

She got in the passenger side and shut the door. Drake backed out of the driveway. One good thing about Drake was that he was quiet.

"So, want to tell me what that was about?"

Guess not today.

"You gonna tell me all your secrets?" she snapped.

He smirked. "Touche."

"How come Lex and Vero don't know? Whatever it is you got going on."

He sighed and shook his head at her. "They know enough. And because it's dangerous."

"Like the race isn't? You're the one who said once you put your name in, it puts a target on your back. So there's a target on their back too." She was angry. Angry at herself. She allowed herself to have feelings for a guy she didn't know. A guy who was always moody and unpredictable. She crossed her arms over her chest. He pulled off on the side of the road. "What are you doing?"

Drake put the truck in park and leaned toward her over the console. His face was so close to hers that she could practically taste him. "My real family tried to kill me," he said. "They think they succeeded, but they failed. I'm assuming they don't know what I look like because I haven't gotten killed. The second they figure it out, if they ever do, everyone I care about will die. That's the kind of target I'm talking about." His jaw tightened as he looked away from her.

She pulled him back to her. Grazed his jaw like she had earlier. But this was real. "Stop hiding so much of yourself. What if they can help protect you? What if I can?" she asked, and he leaned back in his seat. His eyes softened as he stared into hers.

Drake shook his head from side to side. "You can't."

"So you're going to hide forever? Never put a picture up in your room or your corner of the garage? You're fine with not having anything to leave them when you die? Whether that's at the hands of your family or another rider on the track."

"You don't need items to hold onto someone. Memories are enough," he said and put the truck in drive.

"More like fuel for nightmares," she mumbled.

seventeen

Drake got out of the truck and walked Elle inside her apartment building. He waited beside her at the elevator, and they got in together. He pressed the fourth floor, and the doors shut.

They were silent on the way up. Elle kept her eyes on the floor and not on his bare chest. The doors opened, and someone was banging on her door. Brown waves swayed over his white leather jacket as he pounded his fist.

Drake stiffened next to her. "Is that—"

"Don't hit him," Elle said under her breath and casually approached Kannon. "What the hell are you doing?"

Kannon gripped a manila envelope in his hand and paused his banging. He took one look at Drake. Still shirtless. And then at Elle, wearing his shirt. He laughed and pointed at Drake but kept his stare on Elle.

"Really, Elle? Seth was right about you. Just another race whore taking any cock she—"

Elle punched him in the nose.

Blood came gushing out. He smacked the ground with his hands as he tried to steady himself. The envelope dropped. Drake leaned down and spoke in his ear. Kannon glared at him. Elle couldn't hear, however, she could imagine. He picked up the envelope and ushered Elle inside. He locked the door as Kannon yelled from the hallway.

"You broke my nose! Crazy bitch!"

They heard his moans and groans until the elevator doors shut at the end of the hall.

Elle put her hand on her head and closed her eyes. "I hit him. No hesitation," she said. "I punched someone!"

"Elle, he was being a dick." Drake bit the inside of his cheek. His fist clenched at his side. Knuckles white. She took the envelope from him and ripped it open. The cover for the magazine Halo would print tomorrow. Photos of their team. How great their team captain is. How great they are. Great. Great. No mention of Drake or Elle at all. She smiled up at him.

"This might work. As long as I get these to the magazine tonight," she said and held up her camera. Drake took the folder and looked for himself.

Elle went to her dresser and pulled out a shirt and jeans. Drake sat down on her side of the bed. She could see his shirt peeking from under her pillow. Don't spot it. Don't.

Elle came out of the bathroom. Drake flopped back on her bed. His jeans pulled his boxers down to show more of his torso. She sat down on the opposite side of the bed and leaned back to put her head beside his. He locked eyes with her.

"What about elevators?" she asked, and he smiled at her.

"Usually, I'm fine, unless they're full."

"Cars are worse?"

"Yeah," he said. His eyes danced around the room. The photos around her bed. Her stacks and stacks of books on her shelves and floor. Her desk was full of photos she wanted to frame but hadn't gotten around to. "It smells like a printing press here. So much paper around, it would be easy to start a fire."

She winced. Ouch. "Don't tell me that. Now I need to get an air freshener."

"I like it." He smirked. "Smells like you."

"I smell like a printer?" She laughed at that. "I'll be getting some perfume later."

"Don't," he said. He liked that she smelled like paper?

"What about rooms without windows?" she asked, looking out the small one above her kitchen sink.

"Not great. Same with tunnels."

"Are hugs worse or better than tunnels?" she asked.

"Depends on the person, I guess. People, in general, are worse. More common to run into a person than a tunnel."

"Is it easier if you touch someone first? Like today, you picked me up. What if I had tried to hug you? Better or worse?"

"Situational," he said and looked up at the ceiling. "Depends on the person. If I know it's them. Where we are. Am I prepared? I've given hugs before, just not taken many. I don't fucking like it when Lex tries to hug me." He shuddered. "She's a damn snake. Squeezing too tight, and then she's squirmy. Then she asks too many questions and tries again. And again. I can't stand it," he ranted, and she laughed. "What?"

"Again, you should tell her. You trust them every day with your life. Especially during a race. You think you can't tell them this? When I flipped out over you telling them about the Sludge, I was pissed. But I trust you all to not blab. Same thing," she said with a shrug.

He turned his head to look at her again. He let out a heavy sigh. "Elle, I need to tell you something."

She waited for him to speak, but no words came out. He looked back to the ceiling. "Good chat," she said. He put his hands on his head and stood up.

"I need to fix my bike," he groaned. He started for the door.

"Wait, your shirt." She held it up from the end of the bed.

He waved her off. "Keep it. Put it with the other one under your pillow." He winked and left her apartment. She was thankful he did so she could hide her flaming embarrassment in his shirt.

Elle called Nate later when she realized she had left her car parked at Drake's house. She didn't want to bother Sarah and figured she could vent to Nate about the photoshoot on the way. He was more than willing. She figured he'd want to spill about his obvious feelings for Lex, but when she got in the car, she wasn't expecting the nervous air around him. The intensity of his eyes. Something was wrong.

"Spit it out, Nate," Elle finally snapped at him when he didn't come clean immediately.

Normally he would've laughed at that. Not today. "You know how I've been hired by Cyra the last few years? Photo shoots for magazines and newspapers, Guard, Cyra, different spots around the Valley."

"Yes." Elle nodded.

Nate dug into his pocket. He set his jaw. His lips pursed tight. He hesitated before handing her a copy of his camera chip. "Listen, this is... illegal."

Elle turned to him. "Excuse me?"

"I'm trusting you," he spoke in hushed tones. Even though they were alone. Even though they weren't being watched.

"What's on here?" Elle put it in her jeans pocket. Close to her. Like he had it.

"Guard." His voice wavered. He fixed his glasses on his nose and took a deep breath. "Superior."

"Doing what?" she asked.

He cleared his throat and straightened in his seat. He didn't respond.

"Alright, I understand," Elle said. "Why give it to me?"

"Because I believe you can use it. More than me."

She nodded. She wasn't sure how to take that. Did he know she'd been sneaking around and digging into things she shouldn't be? If he did, he wasn't opposed if he was giving her this.

Once Elle was alone and at home again, she ran to her laptop and plugged in Nate's chip.

Hundreds of photos of Guard killing mates in awful ways. Cyra slitting mate necks as well as Guard. Shooting them. Pushing them off cliffs. In a couple of them she was smiling as she did it. Her gowns glittered in every shot.

Elle took the chip and hid it in the safe with the Sludge. She took a moment and sat in silence as she thought over her next move. She already knew what she was going to do with the rest of her night.

She tied her hair up and jumped in the car. The manor was a short distance from her apartment. Elle pulled off and parked in town, and headed into the woods on foot. Zipped up her black hooded jacket and kept her head down. The manor had to be in this direction. She hadn't taken this path in a long time, but she'd eventually get there.

Once it was in view, she hid in the shadows on the edge of the forest. She watched as Guard approached the front door, knocked in the same way every time, and pressed their thumbs to a scanner before being allowed to enter.

A car pulled up, and a Guard stepped out from the driver's seat and used the scanner. He waited outside a minute in a ready pose. Hands behind his back and his head held high. The light reflected off the glass on his helmet and shined toward Elle, observing from the trees.

Cyra stepped out. A dress made for a Queen. Wisps of light fabric draped from her hips and hit the grass as she sashayed. Guard in toe.

Then a man came from the back seat of the car. Dressed in a white suit. He bowed to her and kissed the top of her hand. Cyra smiled at him as he did it.

Elle recognized him. He was at the first meeting she'd been to. She remembered thinking of his relation to Cyra, but now she couldn't help her thoughts leading to Kannon. Was he on Team Halo? She was about to head to her car to try and follow them when a twig snapped behind her.

"Thought that was you."

"Whatthehell." Elle covered her mouth as she jumped. Lex crossed her arms and smirked at her in the dark. How the hell was she here? Lex had shorts and a long sleeve blue shirt that had rips all the way up on both arms. A thin headband wrapped around her head to keep her hair back. A small red leaf stuck out from the very top. Elle reached up and plucked it from the elastic.

"What are you doing out here?" Lex whispered.

"I could ask you the same." Elle glared.

Lex chuckled and pointed at the manor. "Same as you, it would seem. Who is that?"

"No idea. I'm about to find out."

Cyra got into the car beside the man, and a Guard drove. The car pulled out of the driveway, and Lex yanked Elle through the trees and hopped on her yellow bike. Elle held on tight as she weaved through the branches and ended up three cars behind them in town. They made a turn and headed toward the checkpoint.

Lex parked near a cafe and sat down at an empty table. Elle sat across from her so they could watch from a distance. Cyra slowly led the man into the small Guard station in front of the checkpoint.

"C'mon," Elle said. Lex went wide-eyed.

Elle pulled her toward the vent she'd crawled through in the past. Knowing her way around, she guided Lex, and they slid side by side toward the voices. Lex stayed silent.

Cyra stood with the man in white as a Guard lay bleeding at their feet. It wasn't until they spoke that Elle realized the man was dead.

"Thought he could outplay me. Last person who thought that was my own child. Everyone believed I wouldn't kill him because he was my blood. Fools. I killed him for that reason. You think I want someone to replace me whenever they feel like it? I couldn't live with that hanging over my head everywhere. No. Arlo, no. I made sure he died so I could stay where I belong. In charge. Superior Covington will be my legacy to pass to you, and only you, when the time comes," Cyra's voice echoed through the vent.

Her sparkling gown was so out of place inside the station. All the walls were gray. The entire place felt stale. The air thick.

"And when that time eventually comes, my dearest Superior, I will work hard night and day trying to make you proud." He put his fist to his chest, just like Guard did when speaking to her. Who the hell was this guy?

"You already do, my friend."

Arlo smiled as he brushed the tip of his white boot to slide the man's leg. He bent down and picked up the Guard gun.

"Think I could get the Dragon to reprogram the weapon?"

"I'll send Superior Ashbury a message. I'm sure it won't be an issue."

"I'll let Kannon know. He could use a backup." He bowed his head to her.

So he did know that scumbag. Elle locked eyes with Lex, and she nodded with the same realization.

"And how is your son doing? His team seems to be doing well this year."

Son? Elle mouthed to Lex. She rolled her eyes in response. Elle pulled out her phone and took photos of the three of them in the dull room through the vent slats. They weren't great, but you could tell who it was. Plus, you could see the dead man beneath them.

"Yes, ma'am." The man grinned. "Thank you again. I'll meet with you soon."

Cyra patted his shoulder and headed out.

The girls stayed put for a while before attempting to leave. Elle led the way out, and neither spoke until they were near Lex's bike in the trees.

"I've never seen that man before. Have you?" Lex asked, pulling on her helmet in the dark.

"Just at the first meeting. He was there."

"I didn't see him." Lex shrugged.

"Too focused on bouncing balloons." Elle chuckled.

Lex drove her back to her car by the manor. Elle knew they'd probably never speak of this. What else was there to say? But she felt closer to Lex now. They had secrets to share. Even more than they already did.

eighteen

Elle woke up late. She decided to get a latte from Bernie anyway and sat in the shop for a minute. The magazine had been printed, and people were all over the ChaosMotors mag website asking who the mystery girl was. She chose seven photos. They showed Drake the most but still hid both of their faces. She was strategic. The main one was her favorite. His back to the camera and her looking at him while he looked out into the distance. It was beautiful. His tan skin shined in the sun and her eyes popped off the page.

"This you?" Bernie held up a magazine from behind the counter. She chuckled and nodded. She didn't want the fame, but it was a strange feeling when people she knew could spot her on a cover page. That was for celebrities. For Superior. Not her.

Elle said her goodbyes and headed home. An idea popped into her head, and she needed to get it done fast. She printed out all the photos she needed before heading to her favorite tree.

Elle rearranged the photo album for Lex in two hours. She called Sarah to tell her about the photo shoot while she worked. She slid the finished album into her bag before she laid back in the grass. Sarah squealed when Elle confessed she might have a slight crush. Elle shot it down fast.

"Ma, it's not going to go anywhere. I can't let it. He's a rider, first of all, and second, he's out of my league." Elle chuckled to herself. "You should see the guy."

"I've seen him. Tall, dark, handsome, mysterious." Sarah giggled on the other end of the phone.

"Ma, I'm serious, he's the complete opposite of me."

"Which is probably why you like him so much, honey. So are you going to tell him?"

Elle laughed. "No way. They'll win the Championship, move to the Cove, and then I'll never see them ever again."

"Right." Sarah scoffed.

Elle didn't want to hear it, but she knew Sarah. She'd hear it anyway. "What? Spit it out."

"You've convinced yourself that you mean nothing to them. That they're going to forget about you when they leave. What happens if they want to bring you to the Cove? What happens if they don't win? What about the other possibilities, honey? You get so stuck on one ending, you forget there's a million possible outcomes."

Elle was going to respond when she heard Drake's truck coming down the path. "Ma, let me call you back." She hung up and watched as Lex and Vero hung their heads out the back window.

"Well, what are you waiting for?" Drake said as he approached her. He was in his typical black shirt and chunky boots. His hair was ruffled from the wind blowing in the truck. "Let's go."

"What the hell is going on?" She laughed. "How did you find me?"

"Please." He rolled his eyes at her. "You done talking to the tree or what?"

"I guess so." She took his hand to help her stand up. "Where are we going?"

"The lookout. It's Light Up Night at the Cove. We have to hurry. I got done with my bike early to come fucking find you. You don't answer your phone."

"You called?" She looked down at her blinking phone. "I was talking to my mom. What's Light Up Night?"

Elle hopped into the back of the truck, and Vero turned to her to explain.

"Every year, they light up the whole town for a week starting on the day it was founded. It's dumb. But it looks cool from the lookout."

"You'll drop me off later to get my car?" Elle asked. She didn't want to call Nate twice in one week to grab it for her.

Lex laughed. "Of course, silly. We have to hurry! Step on it, Drake!"

They pulled into a small parking lot, and the girls ran to the cliff. It wasn't a big drop. Rocky though. Lex sat down on the very edge, and Vero joined her. Elle stood behind them. Drake didn't run, so he walked up behind her. She flinched when he put his hand on her shoulder. He shifted her to the left and pointed at a tall building in the distance.

"That's town hall," he whispered and dropped his hand. Then the building lit up. A rainbow of bright colors flashed before it stayed constant. Then the rest of the town came on in spurts. Elle gasped. She'd never seen anything like it. Nothing ever happened in the Valley. Nothing like that.

"Whoa," Elle said. She grabbed Drake's arm and smiled up at him. "How did you know about this?"

"I remembered from when I was a child, I come every year." He smiled at her, and she realized she was still holding onto him. She took a step from him and crossed her arms. Something must be wrong with her. She's never been handsy with anyone. So why was she starting to be with the one guy who didn't like to be touched?

The buildings were still lighting up, and Lex pointed out her favorites. Of course, her number one was the all-yellow one. Elle pointed at one that had a bunch of stars on the top.

"What's the point?" Elle asked.

"It's pretty," Lex said. It was but Elle didn't understand it. So much went into it for only one week.

"There is no point," Drake answered. "It's rare to see things for entertainment in the Valley. Everything has a purpose."

"Even the mates." Elle nodded.

"Elle!" Lex yelled at her use of the word.

"She's not wrong," Vero added.

The air up there was thicker. Closer to the clouds. The soil was thin and more like sand. It had a red tint and Elle wished she had come sooner to take photos in the sunlight. Vero ran back to the truck and came back with a six pack. She gave a can to Lex and held one up to Drake but he turned it down. She held it out to Elle and she shrugged. She took the can and opened it. She sniffed it before looking over at Drake. It had an unexpected apple scent. He raised a brow as she took a sip. The beer was harsh on her throat and the taste was a mix between a sour apple candy and a cinnamon stick of gum. She scrunched her nose and stuck her tongue out, which reminded her of Gage.

Drake laughed at her and took the can. He took a long sip and shook his head before handing it back to Vero. Lex tapped hers to the side of Vero's and they shared a silent conversation.

Elle turned to Drake. "How do you remember the date of this every year?"

"My birthday," Drake mumbled. He didn't look at her. His eyes focused on the lights.

"Twenty-five is a big one," Vero said.

"You could be Superior." Elle laughed. Nobody else laughed.

"Can I give you a hug for your birthday?" Lex yelled and came at him with her arms raised.

"Don't touch me, Lex," he snapped. "I don't like hugs."

Lex started to pout. She opened her mouth when Drake interrupted.

"I'm claustrophobic," he blurted. He took a step back from them, and Elle smiled into her hand. Finally.

Vero was silent.

Lex gaped before she looked over at Elle. "You knew?"

Elle wasn't sure what to say that wouldn't hurt her feelings. Lex's best friend didn't tell her about himself for fear of being the reason they either died or didn't win the Championship. Both were valid. Elle didn't agree with keeping it to himself but she could see his logic.

Drake stepped in. "She figured it out at the party."

"So, when I hug you, and you push me away, it's not because you don't like me?" Lex asked. Her pale cheeks turned rosy.

"What? Lex." Drake put his hand on his head.

"You don't let us take pictures of you. All we ever get is time with you. That's it. I'm not saying it's not enough. Why wouldn't you tell us?" Tears pricked her eyes. Drake looked at Elle. She shook her head at him. He did this to himself. Lex calmed herself again. "You don't trust us?"

"It's dangerous," he said.

"Isn't everything we do here?" Lex asked. They were quiet. Everyone agreed.

"I'm sorry, Lex. I do trust you." Drake spoke so clearly. Elle knew Lex would forgive him and she did.

"Well, time with Drake is more than enough for me. I don't need any photos of his ugly mug," Vero said, and they all laughed.

"Elle! Take a photo!" Lex suggested. Elle looked at the group. This team standing on the ledge. Her friends. It was hard to imagine that she'd only met them a few days ago.

She directed them on where to stand and stepped back before hitting a large boulder.

"Rest it on the rock and get in it!" Lex whined. Elle set the self-timer on and then ran over to stand with them. Lex squeezed her, and they all smiled as the flash went off.

"Wait, I'll see if it's good!" Lex yelled and went over to the camera to check.

Elle turned to look at the lights again. The buildings in the distance. She could see the fountain she had always thought about. Ezra's balloon. Her dad's laugh. She kicked a pebble over the ledge.

"Get ready!" Lex yelled and ran over for the second photo.

Vero shoved Drake into Elle, and she tripped. She landed on her ass in the dirt. She laughed, but Drake was at her side.

"Elle!" He grabbed her arm. She couldn't stop laughing. "I'm sorry, Vero pushed me." He stopped when his hand came back bloody.

"I'm alright," Elle promised and looked at her roughed-up elbow. "I've lived through worse."

"Do you have any Sludge with you?" he asked.

"What are you guys doing?" Lex whined as she looked at the camera again.

"I fell down, you ass," Elle said, and they laughed. "I have some in my car, remember?"

"Okay, let's go," Drake said and helped her stand.

"But! The lights!" Lex pointed with both her hands.

"We'll go later," Elle said, and Drake looked at the scrape again.

He sighed. "Does it hurt?"

"If I was twelve, sure. I scratched my elbow. Calm down." Elle chuckled at him. Was he worried about her? Now she was reading into things.

Vero sat down again and waved for Lex to join. Lex took their photo, and they started messing around together. Vero held a beer can over Lex's head and pretended to pour it on her. Elle no longer had that sinking feeling in her gut over them touching her precious baby. Actually, she smiled watching them.

Elle hung her legs over the side, and Drake sat between her and Vero. They looked out at the town she'd probably never be back to. But they most likely would. She believed that. Believed in them.

"What was it like over there?" Lex asked.

Elle brought her knees up to her chest and wrapped her arms around them. "I was too young to remember much, honestly. I remember my family. What about you?" She turned to Drake beside her.

"I remember everything," he said. "I remember waking up to watch cartoons and eat cereal. My mom teaching me how to ride a bike in the street. My dad yelling at me to mow the lawn."

"Howard made you mow?" Vero laughed.

Drake sighed and looked at his friends. "Elle knows he's not my real dad."

Lex's jaw dropped. She locked eyes with Elle. She blushed as she turned away. Feeling self-conscious. He should not have told them she knew. Then Lex smiled at her.

"So," Vero broke the silence, "you two really are getting married, huh?"

nineteen

Drake dropped Lex and Vero off before he drove Elle to her car. They were silent on the way to the tree. He kept the windows down, so by the time they got there, Elle's hair was a mess. She pulled it up on top of her head, but her bangs stuck to her forehead.

She jumped out of the truck and looked around at the dark water and the fireflies floating around the edge. Frogs croaked, and crickets chirped. A slight breeze kept her cool enough to not need her jacket, even though she missed it terribly.

"Damn, I forgot." Elle cursed herself when she got to her car. She put her bag in the backseat and turned around. Drake was so close she jumped back. He chuckled.

"Sorry," he mumbled. "What did you forget?"

"I made an album for Lex. I forgot to give it to her." Elle pulled it out of her bag and handed it to him. He sat down in the grass and put his back to her tire. She joined him and pointed out her favorites. He flipped through it, stopping to look at each one. Sometimes he had to hold the book up to use the light coming from her backseat. She pointed at the one she'd shown him before.

"I'm glad you didn't give it to her. You can add the ones from tonight," he said. She smiled and grabbed her camera. Drake flipped through the album again as she clicked to see the photos from the lookout.

Lex and Vero smiled at the camera with Elle, but Drake had his eyes on her. She went to the next one, and Elle was on the ground. Drake was halfway to her at that point, so he was blurry. The girls stood smiling. Elle chuckled at that. The last one, Drake smiled. An actual smile. Right at the camera. She covered her mouth with her hand. Drake closed the album and tried to look at the screen, but she turned it off.

"Let me see." He reached for it, but she slid it onto her backseat and shut the car door. He chuckled. "That bad?"

"If you see it, you'll delete it. Not an option," she said. They sat side by side on the ground. The light shut off, and Drake smiled at her in the dark.

"I won't delete it."

"I don't trust you."

"Yeah, you do." He brushed his shoulder on hers. "Or else you wouldn't be out here with me right now." He motioned to the empty field and dock in the distance.

Elle looked over at him, and their eyes locked. He licked his lip. She was suddenly very aware of their proximity.

Drake's phone started to ring. He cursed before he answered.

"Riley, I'm sorry. I'll be home soon. Swear." Riley? Another secret. Elle sighed as she stood up. He put his phone in his pocket.

"Elle." His voice was thick with annoyance. He opened her car door for her. She eyed him before sitting down behind the wheel. "Sludge?"

"Oh yes," she said and opened her glove compartment, and grabbed a tin. Before she could react, Drake yanked it from her hand and opened it. He lifted her arm and rubbed it on her elbow. He wiped the dried blood on his jeans.

"How come you never think to take care of yourself?" he asked.

"Growing up at Little Hearts it was all about the group. I guess I learned early on to think of everyone as a whole. Makes the most sense to me," Elle explained. That was when it clicked. The home. Howard. Jane. Gage. Bobby. "You grew up at Bobby's home for boys."

"What?" he said and wavered in front of her. "What did you say?"

"Now I understand. You didn't want anyone to hear because then they would've known Jane and Howard weren't your parents," Elle said. "Gage knew, though, because he was there, right? Is that why you hate him?"

"What? I don't hate Gage." Drake chuckled.

"You were an ass to him."

"I'm an ass to everyone." He paused and let out a sigh. "Listen, I used to be close to him when we were kids. I'd go see him all the time, and then…he got into some things I wasn't okay with."

"What the hell is that supposed to mean?" Elle was fuming. So because he was gay, Drake didn't like him? What about Vero and Aster? Or was that fine because they were women?

He took another step back. "It's nothing."

"Don't give me that bullshit. What?" She smacked her steering wheel.

"Drugs, Elle, I'm talking about drugs." Drake looked out at the water before he turned back to her. "He started using and then selling. Got his hands on some Corzantine and Thylopan. Two drugs you can only get from Ashbury Valley. It was awful. He almost died. Twice. He only stopped about two years ago. That's when he joined Blue Falcon. He's been better off since."

"Oh," Elle said. "Ohh." Her mind was reeling. Whoops.

"What the hell did you think I meant?" Drake asked.

"Nothing," she mumbled. "I apologize." Just that he was homophobic and more of an ass.

The silence overpowered her. The frogs nearby croaked louder. She put the key in the ignition, and the field in front of her lit up. A few pairs of eyes stared back at her before running toward the trees beyond.

"See you tomorrow?" he asked.

Elle rolled her window down before he shut the door. She leaned her chin on her arm and rested it on the opening. "Yes."

She didn't want to leave yet. He stood a few inches from her in the grass. The crickets around them competed with the frogs. She was about to pull away when he raised his hand to her cheek. The back of his fingers brushed her face. Her cheeks blushed at his light touch. He tucked a strand of hair behind her ear and took a step back.

She finally had to look away before she did something stupid. Elle took the gravel road out of there. He seemed so distant in the rearview mirror. His hands were on top of his head as he spun toward the lake. He had touched her. Voluntarily.

Again.

twenty

Elle set an alarm to wake up early. She headed to the office. It was a mistake. The second she walked inside, she was bombarded.

"Elliot!" he yelled. "In here, now!"

Elle walked in to find Randy behind his desk. Mounds of papers covered every corner of his desk. A cup of pens lays sideways on the ground beside him. His monitor flashed at him with unread messages. He stroked his mustache twice before looking up at her.

"I believe I assigned you to bring me a front-page photo of the second race in the ChaosMotors Championship. You did not deliver," Randy grunted at her. "You have made a fool out of me, Elliot."

"No, no, you don't understand."

"No, I assure you. You do not understand. I gave you this job out of the goodness of my heart, and since that day, you've been nothing but mediocre. I finally gave you a shot of a lifetime, and it backfired in my face in a matter of minutes. You're done. Pack your things." Randy picked up his cup of pens and put it back on his desk.

"What? No, Randy, don't do this. Please, I can take photos of the third race. I promise. You don't understand. My team was injured."

"Your team?" Randy laughed at her. "Oh dear, you've gotten yourself into a mess. Riders are not ones to make friends. You're not on their team. You're nothing to them. Get your head out of the clouds. Realize that in the Valley, you have two options; kill or be killed."

"What?" Her dream job. He was pulling her away from her dream.

"This was your career. Your way to pay your dues. You decided not to fight for it. Goodbye." Randy waved his hand at her. Like she was a gnat flying around his face. An annoyance.

She didn't know what to say. Elle had worked so hard for this. For so long. Couldn't be fired. Over one cover page. Because she helped Drake, she missed a deadline. Other media pass holders stayed after the race to take photos but not her. She was too busy shoving Blue Sludge into Drake's wound. She couldn't watch him die, though.

Placed her badge on his desk and walked out of his office. With her head down, she walked to her little chestnut desk and grabbed her three items sitting there. Elle tucked in her brown chair on the light beige tile floor. At least she could keep the camera. Sarah had gotten it for her.

Elle shuffled out of there and sat in her car. Stared out the windshield in a daze. All her work went down the drain. It was all for nothing. Her dream, gone. Her passion, gone.

Now what?

Shouldn't have made friends with this team. Elle should have done what she always did and kept her head down. Had to go running around like they were her friends. Her family. She would never have a family again. Randy was right. Her head was in the clouds.

Elle drove to the lookout. It was the only place she could think of where nobody would find her. Just wanted to be alone. Wanted to scream from the top of a mountain, and this was the highest point in the Valley. So it would have to do.

She wasn't expecting Lex to be sitting there when she pulled up. Lex came to her door and opened it carefully with worried eyes.

"What's wrong?" she asked. Elle shook her head, and the tears began. "Oh, no, what happened?"

She hugged Lex for a minute before telling her the whole story. Randy was a horrible boss, but it was all she ever knew. Her dream: gone.

"Oh, Elle, you'll figure it out. You don't need him. Your work is amazing. Someone else is bound to pick you up. What if you did something else with photography?"

"Like what?" Elle asked.

"I don't know. I don't know about that kind of thing. Maybe V does, though. She's an artist, right? Hey, we will figure it out." Lex smiled at her.

"I hate how optimistic you are. It's annoying," Elle groaned.

"I know." Lex laughed. "You want to be alone for a while?" she asked, and Elle nodded.

"I'll call you later, promise," Elle said. Lex nodded and gave her another hug before she left. Lex really was like a sister to her. It was strange how normal that felt. Not upset as if she was replacing Evelyn. But happy she had someone to share her excitement or sadness with. As she calmed down, she knew she had made the right choice. And she'd do it all over again.

Elle looked out at the lit-up Cove until the sun started to set. She realized it had been a few hours. Didn't want to move. Not yet. Not until she had a new plan. What was she going to do? How would she pay rent next month? Or make payments on her dues?

Heard Drake's bike coming up the hill and sighed to herself. Elle didn't want him to see her like this. A teary-eyed mess. Her legs to her chest, her arms kept them close. Her head pressed to her knees. His boots hit the ground with a familiar thump as he approached.

A bag crinkled beside her, and she heard his footsteps receding. She lifted her head, and he was getting back on his bike. She looked down and saw a small brown paper bag and a coffee from Bernie's.

"What the hell are you doing?" she yelled at him. He raised his eyes to hers.

"Lex said you wanted to be alone," Drake said.

"She told you Randy fired me?" Elle said, and Drake ran back.

"Fired?" He slid down next to her on the ledge. "What the fuck are you talking about? All she said was that I'd find you here, and you didn't want to be disturbed."

"And this is you not disturbing me?" She motioned to the bag and cup.

"I figured you didn't eat," Drake said. "And Bernie said this is your favorite."

"Yes," Elle said and lifted the straw to her mouth. She could tell from the light purple coloring, lavender honey. A ham and cheese sandwich on a croissant was in the bag. Elle handed half to Drake.

He took a bite and fully chewed before he asked, "Why were you fired?"

"I didn't take any photos of the second race." She stopped and closed her eyes. "I messed everything up."

The lights in the Cove were shining, and the tears in her eyes made everything double. Lex's favorite yellow one now looked like a blob of sunlight. She wiped her eyes before Drake responded.

"They fired you because you were busy saving my life instead of doing your job?" He put his hand on his head.

"I don't regret it if that's what you're thinking," Elle said.

"How could you not?" He shook his head and looked at the view.

But she didn't. She didn't regret any of it. It sucked she got fired. Still, she wouldn't change a thing. Elle watched Drake for a moment. How he took a bite of the sandwich. Wiped his hands on his jeans. The way his jaw moved when he chewed.

"You could do a blog," Drake suggested.

She was not expecting him to suggest anything. A blog? That's what she'd thought of a while ago. "What?"

"Do what you were going to do for the magazine but online. You could make one about the team even." Drake shrugged.

"About the team?" she asked. So it really was about fame? They were using her like Kannon and Randy said. She should have never done this stupid article. She should never have gone to that first meeting. Or the first race. Let alone the second one.

"You could have different albums for different things in your life. Even do one for Sarah and the kids. One for your damn tree, even. Whatever. Lex could model for you. She'd love it. You could do all kinds of weird shit. I don't know. You're talented. So, people will want to see more. Plus, you could do some paid work for other teams or some shit. Halo wanted you to give them press, right? Why not have them hire you? For a photoshoot or whatever," he spoke quickly but softly. Like he was thinking as he was speaking.

"You'd want me to take photos of other teams?" she asked. Now she was confused.

"Whatever you need to do," Drake said. "I mean, I'd hate for anyone to use you, but if they paid you, then you'd come out better off, right?"

"You wouldn't mind if other teams got more press than you?" She didn't understand. Didn't he want to win the race?

"What? I didn't want the press to begin with, remember? What are you talking about?" Elle didn't want to cry again. Couldn't help it. He started to fidget. "What'd I say?"

"No, it's alright." She wiped her cheek, and he stared. "Sorry, I'm a mess. It's just Randy."

"Your boss?"

"Yes, he just—well, Kannon said—and then you were saying—I almost believed them, and that's stupid," Elle said. Drake handed her a napkin from the bag. She hated that she was crying in front of him. She smiled at him.

"What?" Drake chuckled.

"Nothing. Thank you."

"Sure," he whispered.

They sat there in silence until the moon was above them. She finished her coffee before speaking again.

"Race is tomorrow," Elle said. "Are you nervous?"

"You already asked me that."

"That was last time. This is this time."

"People are going to think we're a couple this time," he mumbled.

"I forgot!" she yelled and sat up straight. "Drake! You're a genius! Randy didn't know that was my photo!"

"What?"

"I didn't send it to him as myself. I sent it anonymously. So they wouldn't assume it was me in the photos. That would be weird. So I can use that to start a blog! Genius! Drake! Genius!" she yelled, and he smiled at her.

"Whatever you say," Drake said.

"How do you even start a blog? I'll figure it out, I guess. With the photos of us about to blow up, I'm sure I could get a following from that. That can be my hook. Then I'll branch out. Like you said, I can have different albums and stuff. Or different blogs altogether for different aspects of my life. I can even post some of my old work too. Like landscapes and stuff."

She stopped abruptly, and Drake turned toward her.

"I was rambling," she muttered.

Drake sighed. "You're overly self-conscious about that. I want to hear what you're thinking." He poked her temple, and she laughed. She bit her lip, and his eyes dropped to her mouth again.

"You were really going to drop this off and leave?" she asked and motioned to the sandwich bag and empty coffee cup. He nodded. "Why?"

"Lex said you wanted to be alone."

"Not good for your reputation," Elle whispered. "Assholes aren't supposed to be nice."

"Maybe I don't want to be an asshole all the time."

Elle sat with Drake another few minutes before they decided to head out. Drake got on his bike next to her car, and she noticed he didn't have his helmet with him.

"You better be fully covered tomorrow," Elle said.

He smiled at her. "Or else what?" he said and leaned toward her on his handlebars.

"Don't test me, race boy," she taunted.

Drake laughed as he shoved off the ground to slide his front wheel and face the proper way. He hit the gas and waved to her as he fled down the hill.

twenty-one

Elle woke up early and started to bake. She had to double-check Mrs. Francine hadn't depleted her stock before she began, but she was safe. Elle grabbed the album for Lex and then the small box for Drake. She shook off her nerves and drove over to Lex's. Luckily they were still getting ready for the race when she arrived.

"Yo, Elle, what are you doing here?" Vero asked when she answered the door in her pajamas.

"I have a gift for Lex." Elle handed her a bag with Lex's name on the side.

"What the hell is this?" Vero raised it and peeked inside. "Looks like a book."

"Hey! It's for Lex." She smacked her hand.

"Are those cupcakes?" she asked, trying to open the box.

"Not for you," she scolded.

Lex entered the kitchen and started the coffee pot. The logo on the back of Lex's jacket wrinkled as she lifted her arms up. The top cabinet was too high for her to reach. She pulled out a small step stool to grab a mug down. Vero chuckled, and she groaned.

"You're being mean." Lex laughed and then looked at Vero across the room. "What's that? You got me a gift?"

"Elle brought it," Vero said and handed her the bag.

Lex smiled wide as she opened it. Tears sprung in her eyes as she flipped through the album. Elle added the photos from the other night, and everyone agreed Drake would've deleted it had he seen it.

"Thanks, Elle, this is amazing. I love it." Lex went around the table to hug her.

"You're welcome, but it does come with a price." Elle smiled at her. "You have to model for me. I have some ideas." She turned to Vero. "And maybe you could be my assistant?"

"Oh, hell yeah, Vanilla." Vero punched her shoulder.

"Yes! A million times yes!" Lex jumped up and down twice before Elle calmed her down. Elle was happy to finally have some female friends, especially ones who went along with her ideas.

Elle pulled into Drake's driveway. It was empty. No cars or bikes. Was he even home? The three girls got to the door, and Lex knocked loud.

Vero sighed and groaned. "He is never on time, I swear."

"Shut up, Vero," Drake said on the other side of the door. He opened it in his usual jeans and black T-shirt. He also had a line of flour high on his cheek. Elle chuckled at him as she walked past him into the living room. Vero flopped on the sofa and put her boots on the coffee table. Lex sat in the armchair across from her.

"Is Riley here?" Lex asked, searching the room.

"Yeah, she's almost ready. I have to take her to Jane's shop before I head to the arena," Drake explained as he put his boots on by the door. Elle was going to meet Riley? She gulped. What was she like? Tall, dark, and gorgeous, most likely. Heat crept up her neck.

Drake went to the kitchen and came back with his leather jacket. When he approached Elle, he stopped. The box she was holding suddenly felt like a ton of bricks.

"Oh, these are for you." Elle held it out to his chest. He raised a brow with apprehension. He took it and opened the lid to the six frosted delicacies.

"Cupcakes?" he asked.

"For your birthday," Elle said. Drake stared at her. "You don't like chocolate?" she asked. "Everyone deserves cake on their birthday. And since somebody didn't want to tell me..." She glared at him. "You get yours late."

Drake cleared his throat and took a step from her. "You made these?"

"Yes." She chuckled. Drake didn't look away from the box in his hands. He opened his mouth and closed it. "You've got flour on your face. Did you know that?"

"Fucking Riley," he said. He wiped it off and looked up at Elle. "Thank you," he mumbled. His eyes were clear by the time he looked away from her. Sweat had formed on his forehead.

"You're welcome," she said.

"Riley! Let's go!" Vero yelled at the ceiling. Elle flinched. Drake put the box down and picked a cupcake up. He bit into it and nodded at her. She smiled.

"Best gift I've gotten since getting to the Valley," Drake said. "One hundred percent."

Footsteps came running down the hall. Elle went wide-eyed when she saw the girl enter the room. Long black waves came down around her shoulders. Blue eyes. Pale skin against her forest green overalls. Yellow rain boots on her feet. Elle guessed around eleven years old. She wanted to laugh. What an idiot. This was who she was getting worked up over? Jealous even. She wanted to scold herself.

"Whoa, Squirt, cool it." Drake stopped her mid-run and picked her up into his arms. She squealed into his neck, and he laughed. A genuine smile on his face.

"Dee, put me down!" she yelled, and he obliged.

Elle looked at Drake. "Dee," she mouthed to him, and he flipped her off behind the girl's back. Riley turned and froze when she saw Elle by the door.

"Who are you?" she asked and walked up to her.

"Riley, this is Elle," Drake said. "She's new to the group."

Riley looked up at Elle and didn't speak for a minute. Her eyes roamed from her dirty scuffed shoes to her plain dark t-shirt to her brunette hair. Elle looked away from the kid's scrutiny and noticed a wall of photos. None with Drake in them. She turned her focus back to the little girl.

"Hello," Elle said.

"You're pretty." Riley raked her hand through her hair and pulled it over her shoulder like Elle's.

"Oh, thank you." Elle smiled at her.

"No, I don't think that!" She stuck her tongue out in disgust.

"Riley," Drake gasped. Elle wanted to laugh at him. She'd heard worse at home.

Riley pointed at Drake and yelled. "That's what you told Mommy! I heard. I wasn't supposed to hear. I know. Because Daddy always tells me not to listen from the other room. But you said it super loud."

Drake closed his eyes tight. "Here we go," he whispered.

"Drake!" Lex sang.

Elle felt her face splotching. She wasn't sure if she should feel embarrassed or excited. Or mad that he told his mom that. Did that mean he talked about her? She had talked about him to Sarah. Was it the same?

"Yeah," he said. "Okay, let's go. Everybody out! Race day. Come on."

"Drake!" Lex repeated. Elle hadn't moved. She was still in shock. "Drake! You think Elle is pretty!" Lex shouted as they left out the front door.

"That's been established. Can we go?" Drake asked.

Elle laughed as she followed him around the back of the house. The truck was in the backyard. That was odd. She knew it was. Still, she didn't ask. The trailer was already attached with the bikes inside, ready to go. She climbed into the back seat next to Riley. Lex got in after her.

Elle reached over and helped Riley buckle in. Drake smirked at her from the rearview mirror.

"How old are you, Riley?" Elle asked.

"I'll be ten in two months." Riley grinned. "I want a camera. Daddy said I had to wait until I turned eleven, but I think that's bullshit."

"Hey." Drake glared.

"Right, um, bull. I think I should get one this year. That way, I can document my life turning eleven." Riley clapped her hands twice and smiled wide. Her hair flowed back and forth because she didn't sit still.

"Makes sense to me," Elle said.

"See Dee!"

"Yeah, I know. They're also expensive. I know you've been saving up, but it's a lot of money to spend on one thing."

"But I could use it for the rest of forever," she whined. "How long have you had your camera?" Riley pointed to the one in Elle's lap.

"Oh, um, about ten years now." Sarah had found this one at the thrift store for her eleventh birthday. She wasn't about to tell Riley that, though. Poor girl would be crushed to wait another year.

"You're old!" Riley said, and Elle laughed. "Super old."

"She's younger than me, Squirt," Drake said.

"How old are you, Dee?"

"Now, I'm twenty-five." He said it as if it was a death sentence. His smile vanished.

Four years wasn't so bad between—stop. Stop thinking about him. She looked out the window. Just because he said she was pretty didn't mean anything. Could never happen. Plus, they were about to win the Championship, and she'd never see him again.

A storefront came into view, and Vero yelped. She hid her head in her hands. Elle glanced up to see Aster coming out of the store in front of them. Cigarette in hand, in her usual black baggy pants, paired with a hot pink sports bra under a black sports jacket.

"She is pretty hot, Vero," Elle whispered to her, and Vero blushed. Drake laughed, and Riley jumped out of the truck.

"Hey! I like your shirt!" she shouted at Aster. She jumped at the kid in front of her before Vero hopped out of the truck.

"Riley! We don't yell at people, damn." Vero grabbed Riley and pulled her toward herself.

"Hey." Aster smiled at Vero.

"Hi. Sorry, rascal is Drake's. Can you tell?" Vero laughed. Aster smiled. Drake took Riley's hand and walked inside the store. Lex stayed in the truck, and Elle wondered if it was to give Vero alone time with Aster. Elle followed Drake inside.

"Good job, Squirt," Drake said.

Elle smiled at that. They walked inside the store, Scents for Cents. Lavender and vanilla were the strongest. Once she got to the middle of the store, it became more orange and lemon.

Drake walked them back to the counter. A short woman with gray hair smiled at them. She gasped when Elle came into view.

"Fuckin hell," Drake whispered. "Jane, this is Elle."

"I figured." Jane smiled at Drake. Then she turned to Elle. Her smile widened. "Hello, it's so nice to meet you."

"You too," Elle said and waved at her. She just had to be awkward about it. She squeezed her fist at her side. Don't raise it again. Stupid. Waving at a woman a foot from her.

Drake let Riley go, and she grabbed her bag from him. She ran to the back room around the corner.

"See you later," Drake said to his mom.

"Be careful. I love you. Please don't do anything stupid out there. And please, please, please call us when it's done," Jane said.

"Will do. Please don't cry again, Mom," he said, and she shook her head at him.

"I will do my best. And, Elle." She paused. Her hands clasped in front of her as she turned her attention to her. "Thank you."

"Excuse me?" Elle said. She desperately wanted her jacket with the silk pockets right now. Being this close to Drake and then his family on top of it. His mom thanked her?

"You saved him. And I can't thank you enough," she said softly.

"Oh," Elle said. "He would've done the same for me."

Drake laughed. Harder than she was expecting. What the hell? He covered his mouth and took a step away from them. He shook his head at her.

Maybe he wouldn't.

Drake went around the corner to find Riley. He said goodbye to her, and then she ran out to say goodbye to Elle too. Elle got down on her knees to get more on her level. She tucked her hair behind her ears, and Riley giggled at that.

"See you soon," Elle said. Riley hugged her, and Elle stood up.

Drake walked her out to his truck, and Aster waved goodbye to them. She walked across the street to the bright purple bike parked there. Vero sighed as Drake got on the road.

"I can't speak right when I'm around her. It's so dumb!" Vero put her head in her hands and groaned. Lex laughed.

"V, you're being absurd. Ask her out," Drake said.

"Right, sure. Hey, Aster, will you go out with me? HA! By the way, I'm racing in the Championship, so it's a possibility that I'll die before we even get to go out. Also, your cousin is on an opposing team. So, I hope he doesn't beat us. Hope he doesn't die. Also hope he doesn't win. HA! Oh, also, you're super hot. Please sit on my face," Vero said and hit her forehead on the dashboard. She groaned and bit her thumbnail.

Elle laughed hysterically in the back seat. Drake rolled his eyes at her. Vero leaned her head on the window as she closed her eyes and groaned loudly. Lex reached over the seat and rubbed her shoulder.

"Why don't you ask her to grab coffee with you or something more mellow? Don't add pressure for it to be an official date. It adds anxiety to the mix. You just want to spend time with her, right? So do that." Elle suggested.

"See, this is why we keep you around, Elle. You have good ideas." Lex said.

Vero turned toward the girls in the back. "Think she likes coffee?"

"Who doesn't?" Elle said. "Take it easy with her. Chill out. Don't have to rush into anything. Or rush into a dinner date. That's insanely intimidating."

"It is?" Drake asked.

"Too many expectations go along with a dinner date. Like dressing nice and eating the right amount and then the kiss at the door at the end of it, blah blah," Elle said. "I can't even imagine."

The town turned to a tree line as they headed out to the arena. A bunch of ChaosMotors bikes passed them on the way there. Some did wheelies and tried to show off beside them.

"You've never been on a date?" Lex asked.

"Hell no, I'd probably hyperventilate on the way to the car," Elle said, and they laughed.

"Drake?" Vero asked.

"What?" He put his window down and rested his arm there. The wind blew his hair around his face. The air he let in smelled of gas from all the bikes going past them on the street. One day she'd get used to the scent. If her team didn't die on the track today, of course. He turned the radio down, and Vero glared at him.

"Have you ever been on a date? Like a real one?"

"You think I took Sloane on a fucking date?" He scoffed and shook his head.

"I don't know. You didn't tell us much about that, remember?" Vero said.

Drake sighed. "She was crazy. We hooked up a couple times. And then she wanted me to be her fucking boyfriend, and I said no. Then she died. Best thing to happen to me. Got me out of seeing her again."

Elle laughed, but she wasn't sure that was the appropriate response. "Sorry," Elle whispered and covered her mouth.

"Dude, you're happy she died, so you didn't have to tell her no?" Vero asked.

"Let me repeat; she was crazy. She showed up at my house. Nobody knows where I live, Vero. Then, I almost killed her when she showed up. And she still wanted me. I don't understand girls, but I know when I find a crazy one," Drake said. "So, yeah, I'm glad she died."

"I guess I can understand that," Vero said.

They drove in silence for a moment before they pulled into the arena. Elle didn't know how to turn her brain off. The girl's name was Sloane. Elle wondered what she looked like. How she acted. What did they do together? Other than the obvious. Elle's stomach flipped.

They parked and got out of the car. Fans were screaming for Team Evolution. Posters with Elle's face on it held by teenagers near the gate. A chill went down her spine.

"Unnerving, isn't it?" Drake asked her.

"Definitely," she said.

"What was it you said? Wink if you get close to any of them?" he teased.

"You get to be on the track. I'll be in the stands with them all. How do I get away from them?"

"Feel free to join us on the track, Elle." Vero laughed.

"Not a bad idea." Elle pointed at a group of boys holding up a big sign that said, 'Matthews, when you're done with her, we'll have her.' Drake gripped his hand tight, and Elle laughed at him. "It'll be alright, Drake. Nate will protect me."

"Noodle-arm Nate?" Vero joked.

Drake helped Vero get the bikes out before Nate joined them. They all walked together toward the gate. The crowd screamed louder as they got closer. Elle looked and made sure every inch of them was covered this time. Three helmets, three pairs of gloves, three pants, three jackets, she went down a list in her head.

"Elle," Nate said beside her. She flinched.

"What?" She stopped walking.

"I was saying your name. We have to go this way." He pointed to their gate, and she nodded.

"Oh, sorry." Elle started toward him, but Drake grabbed her hand. She looked up at him and remembered. "Right, we're a couple." She slowly put her arms around him and gave him a light hug. She didn't want him to feel like she was crushing him. Instead, he squeezed her to him. His chest against hers. His chin on the top of her head. She breathed him in deeply. She mumbled into his chest, "don't die."

"Try my best," he said and released her.

Nate waved at them. Elle hugged Vero and then Lex. They were quiet as they split up. Nate led the way to a good place to sit. Race three was about to begin.

twenty-two

Ten teams remained. Which meant they would fight harder to kill each other. Only one more after today. Elle took a deep breath. She held Nate's hand through Cyra's speech. Drake, Lex, and Vero walked out onto the track. The crowd was so quiet Elle could hear the snow crunch under their boots. Flakes fell on their shoulders. Lex shivered as they mounted their bikes. They were third in line this time. Blue Falcon was last.

Elle yelped when someone jumped over the bench and landed on two feet beside her. Aster sat down in the empty spot.

"Cool if I sit with you guys?"

"Of course," Elle said. Nate introduced himself.

"Fair warning, I might cry." He smiled at her, but it didn't reach his eyes.

Aster slid a cigarette behind her ear. "Fine by me as long as you don't tell Vero if I cry too."

"Secrets are safe with us." Elle smiled at her. She had no idea.

The first gun went off. And then the second. The bikes weren't as loud with all the snow to muffle it around them. Ice patches were throughout the track. Ramps covered in them. Turns were harsher than the last race. Jumps were further. Pits filled with thin icicles pointed up toward the sky. Elle didn't want to know what that would feel like. A spear like that shoved through your body couldn't feel great.

There were small ponds on the sides covered in a thin layer of ice. She wasn't sure what was in them, but she assumed she'd find out soon. Thin dying trees lined the track with small black birds waiting for riders to pass. She remembered the firebirds. She wondered what these ones did. Couldn't be good.

The third gun popped, and Nate squeezed Elle's hand. She felt like her hand was going to fall off but didn't want him to stop.

Inhale.

Exhale.

Drake made it to first place in seconds. Around the first bend, a round black glob poked out of the pond. It rose to a standstill and tilted its head. Three purple orb eyes found him. A hole opened in the middle of the glob, and a hundred razor-sharp teeth sang as they spun around in circles. The screech it created made Drake falter. He slipped on a patch of ice but made it past the creature. The next rider stabbed it with a wooden spear and the creature ate it in seconds. The teeth churned, and wood chips came out the other side.

Lex shot a fireball and missed. The creature picked it up and spat it at the rider behind her. Their body hit the snow with a thump. Scrambling to get back on the bike, they underestimated the creature. It crawled out of the pond at lightning speed. It had no arms but six legs. They came out of the creature's chest like a spider's. It slid through the snow to get to the rider. They didn't stand a chance.

The mouth started to spin and the rider screamed as the creature started on their arm. It took less than a minute for their entire body to be gone. Only blood was left. The Guard pulled the bike off to the side when the creature slipped back into the pond.

Vero went over a jump and slid on a patch of ice. She rammed into another rider who kicked her into the sidewall of the arena. Her helmet went flying.

"Fuck," Aster whispered and leaned onto her knees. Elle grabbed her hand with her free one and squeezed.

"She'll be alright," Elle said.

Vero stepped on the gas and caught up to Lex. She signed to her, and Lex dropped back behind her. A rider in white came up behind them fast and side-swiped Lex. She hit them with a spear and they kept going. They hurled a fireball at Vero. She dodged it. She hit her brake and let the rider pass. She sped up, got on their ass, and hit them in the back with a spike. Blood oozed out of the wound. The crimson so prevalent on the pasty white suit. Vero went around them and caught up to Drake.

Drake signed to Vero with his right hand, and she nodded. He stomped on his brake, and she went ahead. Four riders passed Drake before Lex did. She signed to him, and he nodded.

"What are they doing?" Elle asked Nate.

"They must know who that rider is." Nate pointed at the one in white.

"What do you mean?" Aster asked.

"They put a target on their back. I think Drake is going to finish him off," Nate explained.

Elle sighed. She understood, but she didn't like it. "Who is it?"

"That's Seth. He's on Team Halo. Real dick if you ask me," Aster said. Elle blushed. Nate laughed. "What?"

"Nothing," Elle whispered. Remembering his hand on her arm. Vero's fist hitting him. Drake holding him against the tree.

"Drake's going to rough him up for sure." Nate laughed harder.

And he did. Seth tried to get around Drake, but he blocked him. He rammed his tire into the bike, and Seth swerved. He missed a pond, and Drake bashed his elbow into his side. He doubled over but kept going.

Seth got around Drake and went over an icy jump. Drake followed, and once they were in the air, he shot another spike into his back. However, this spike had a chain on it. Drake yanked it when they were about to land, and Seth hit the snow on the edge of the jump. He screamed as he slipped into the pit of icicles below him. Drake flipped him off as his body was impaled.

"Team Halo; fatality."

That was only the second death of the race. Elle realized this was the best of the best now. It would be a lot harder to kill these riders off. The track was getting less hard. Now, the real threat was other riders. She wondered what would happen if none of the riders hurt each other. How many riders would actually be injured by the track alone?

Gage went around his second lap and had to fight off a few creatures. Aster cheered for him as he split one in half with a sword-like weapon he had. Elle shot her fist in the air for her friend.

Josh was right behind him. He gained speed and slipped on ice. He hit the wall of the arena and the rider behind him pushed him off the bike.

Aster stood, but Elle pulled her back down.

"Get back on!" she screamed, and people behind them told her to shut up.

Josh got back on and slowly made his way back to the track. He crossed the finish line and started his third lap. He held his knee with his hand as he went over each jump.

"I think he's hurt," Elle said.

"He's got a bad knee." Aster nodded. "He might've just messed it up worse."

Vero was in first place. She entered her third lap when the birds started to whistle. One darted down and hit her in the shin like a rocket. Another smacked her head. Blood trickled down. Her helmet was in the stands somewhere. Another bird catapulted toward her.

Then another.

And another.

She punched one into a tree, and it exploded on impact. The next, she dodged. She got out of the flock and went around the next bend. Two riders on the same team were behind her. They got on either side and slammed into her.

Aster gasped and took Elle's hand with both of hers.

Vero went faster, but the birds kept following. Too many blows to count.

Then the creatures came out of the ponds.

One stood in the middle of the track and turned its teeth like a vortex. She hit it with a fireball and then a spike. It didn't move. She rammed straight into it with her bike and shoved it to the ground. The next one latched onto her leg and pulled her off her bike.

"Vero!" Elle choked on her scream.

She kicked one of its legs and then snapped the next in half like a twig. Blood pooled out of it. Thick, dark, and sticky, like sap. Vero grabbed onto another leg and yanked herself up. Punched it squarely in the eye. She stepped on a broken piece of leg. She picked it up and swung it like a bat at its head.

Ten swings, maybe twenty, before it was motionless. Vero flung the leg into the stands, and the crowd cheered for her. Another bird came flying toward her, but she jumped out of the way. Another creature grabbed her and swung her face-first into the ground, grabbing her leg in the process. The snap echoed in the arena, and Elle yelped into her hands.

"Get up!" Nate yelled.

Aster stood and ran to the fence. "Keep going!"

"You got this, Vero!" Elle screamed beside her.

Vero kicked the creature with her other leg and wobbled back to her bike as fast as she could. She mounted and only had three jumps to make it over the finish line.

Drake impaled the creature in the chest with a blade as he passed. It evaporated. Vero struggled to keep up. Drake went over the last three jumps and finished in second.

Lex came in fifth, and Vero in seventh. She hobbled over to the side, and Drake helped her sit down in the snow. Drake flung his helmet off and Vero punched the arena wall. Elle could see their breath from where she was in the stands. The cold air not helping their situation.

"Shit!" Vero shrieked.

Nate, Aster, and Elle ran down to the gate and waited for it to open. Aster bounced on her heels until the Guard opened the gate. Blue Falcon stood next to Lex. Rafael seemed to be hurting too. He leaned on the wall and held his arm close to his chest. Lex sat beside Vero on the ground. The other riders rushed out to the parking lot. The losing teams shoved each other out the gates.

Elle ran to Vero and slid in the snow in her tennis shoes.

"Don't touch me!" Vero shouted at Drake. "I need to stand."

"Let us carry you," Drake protested as he stood in front of her.

"Vero," Elle said, and Drake jumped. "Let us help."

"No," Vero said.

"Let me see," Lex said and pointed at her leg. Vero shook her head and bit her thumbnail. "That bad?"

Everyone watched from a distance as Vero got herself standing. Drake held his hands out, ready to catch her as she relied on the arena wall for support. Lex got up and stood behind her in case she fell backward.

"She doesn't want to go to the hospital," Gage said.

"Don't be stupid," Aster said.

"Not happening. Not again. I can't go back there again." Her breath was harsh. It came out in spurts. Spit flew from her mouth. Her foot poised in the air. She wouldn't put it down.

"Vero, if you don't, it'll be worse," Elle tried to reason with her.

"Stop being stubborn. We'll take you," Drake snapped at her.

Aster took another step toward her. "You won't be alone."

"Yeah, we'll all go," Lex said.

"Just what I want." Vero glared at her.

"Alright, so only Aster and Lex will go with you. How about that? Drake, Nate, and I can meet you later? Is that okay?" Elle offered. Vero froze. Her eyes wide. Mouth agape. She wasn't responding. Her face paled. Eyes red. "Vero?"

"Velorum Corruption," Vero mumbled.

Drake stiffened and grabbed Elle's hand. She gasped. He put himself in front of her. Nate stepped back, confused. Lex leaned towards him and grabbed his hand to pull him closer to her. Elle felt Drake squeeze her twice.

"What?" Aster turned around. Her eyes bulged.

"What is going on?" Cyra approached the group of them. Three Guard members on her left. "Your name, rider?" Her eyes on Vero.

"Veronica."

The arena was almost empty by now. They were the only ones left. The snow was melting by their feet. The Guard must've turned off the air.

"Team?"

"Evolution, ma'am, Superior."

"I hear your team more often now. Must be getting some press." Cyra smiled at her. Her silver gown shining back at the cold puddles. Her arms were covered with long jeweled sleeves to keep her warm.

"Yes, Superior."

"Hurt your leg, I see, tsk tsk." Cyra paused and looked at each of them. "And you are?" she asked Josh.

"Joshua, team Blue Falcon." He teetered on his leg. Keeping all his weight on the other one. He'd definitely messed it up.

"Opposing teams? Getting along?"

"No, Superior," Drake spat. His free hand turned into a fist at his side. His eyes glowered.

Gage locked eyes with Elle. He crossed his arms in front of him. Puffed his chest out. They were putting on a show. Elle wasn't sure how to handle this situation. She tucked farther behind Drake and stayed quiet.

"Excuse me?" Cyra turned her attention to Drake.

"They were trying to start a fight," Drake said through his teeth. "We'll settle it on the track."

"I see." Cyra laughed. "And you?"

Elle didn't realize she was speaking to her until Drake squeezed her hand. "Oh, Elliot Winters. ChaosMotors Mag."

"Hm." She looked down at Drake's hand in hers. "A generous match for a rider. Teams can use all the press they can get these days."

"Yes, Superior," Drake said through his teeth.

"Now, get out of my arena before I have the Guard take care of you." Cyra smiled at them. Her teeth white as the snow around them.

"Yes, Superior," Vero responded.

Cyra turned on her heel and went out the gate to a lot full of photographers. The tail of her dress just barely hit the ground as she walked. Cameras flashed, and Elle turned back to Vero.

"What the hell," Vero said and held her chest with her hand. Lex bent down and lifted her pants leg. Her ankle was purple and red. But her calf was ripped open. Bone stuck out from the back of her leg, and Elle covered her mouth and turned away.

"Let's bolt," Aster whispered. She went to Vero's right, and Nate went to her left. They helped her wobble out of the arena.

"I'm going to help Josh and Raf to the hospital. Take our bikes. You know my garage." Gage tossed Drake his bike keys, and he caught them with his left hand. He put them in his pocket. Lex followed Nate and Vero out to his car. Drake and Elle stood by the five bikes.

"Drake," Elle said. His hand was still in hers. She squeezed him. He dropped her and put distance between them.

"Drake," she started again until he shook his head. Held her words.

Elle helped him load the bikes onto his trailer. They got in the truck, and he sped off.

She tried again. "Are you okay?"

He laughed. Sweat dripped from his head. Dirt covered his jacket and neck. Snow soaked through the bottom of his jeans. He didn't speak, but he wasn't hitting anything. Not yet, anyway.

Elle leaned back in the seat and took a deep breath.

"Are you?" he asked.

She looked over at him. "Me? I was sitting the whole time. You were the one getting attacked and hit and thrown around! And I can't believe you went after that rider from Halo! You should not have done that! How'd you even know it was him?"

Drake chuckled. "Please, I could point that cocky asshole out in a crowd full of riders. Chalky bleached idiot."

Elle wanted to be angry. Couldn't. *Chalky bleached idiot.* She chuckled.

They pulled into the driveway made of bricks. He pulled up to the entrance and got out of the truck. Elle jumped down and walked up to the door. Drake felt the frame above the door but came up empty-handed.

"Well, that's not good." He looked around on the ground and then up at the door. Elle turned toward the truck. She took a few steps back, and Drake tried to turn the handle. It didn't budge. Elle looked down, and one of the bricks was raised more than the others.

"Got it," she said.

Drake raised an eyebrow at her. Elle picked up the brick and handed him the key. "How the hell did you see that?" he asked. She shrugged. He unlocked the door, and she put the key back where it was.

They walked inside, and Elle helped him put the bikes where they belonged. Elle walked around to the desk in the back of the room. A hundred pictures hung on the wall of the team. And about a hundred more of Josh and Gage making out. Elle chuckled as she looked at them. All she could think of was the photos she'd deleted of them on her camera.

"I should've paid more attention when I came here last time," Drake said. He shook his head at the wall of photos.

"What do you mean?" Elle glanced at each photo. She didn't see anything out of the ordinary. Normal photo wall.

"I thought." He stopped. "Never mind."

"What?" She laughed at him. He swayed on his feet and headed back to the truck. This guy was going to be the death of her. Infuriating.

"Do you ever say what you're thinking?" Elle asked. She followed him out, and he locked the door behind them.

Drake sighed. "I thought Gage was into you."

"What?" Elle laughed and turned toward him. "Why the hell would you think that?"

"At the party." He stopped and wiped some dirt off his jacket. He gave up and threw it in the back of the truck bed. "He kissed you and said you were gorgeous or something absurd."

"Absurd?" Elle scoffed. He really knew how to make a girl feel special.

"You know what I mean," Drake said. He rounded the back of the truck to stand beside her.

Elle crossed her arms in front of her. They were going to do this now? "No, I don't. You never say what you mean." Elle let out a loud groan.

"Can we just go see Vero, please? I don't want to have this conversation with you right now."

"You want to have it at a more convenient time?" Drake took a step toward her. "I thought you wanted him."

"Gage?" She put her hand on her forehead. "First, he's gay. Second, are you insane? Every comment out of your mouth is about how hot you are! You're always so cocky! Yet you can't tell when someone agrees you're the only one in the room?" Elle yelled at him. She was over his stupidity and male ego bullshit. He wanted to do this now?

"Elle."

"Shut up. Get in the truck. Let's go." Elle opened the passenger door, but he slammed it from behind her. "Drake, seriously," she said. Elle turned back toward him. He was even closer. He gently pushed her against the truck and leaned toward her.

"I never say what I mean because half the time, I can't figure it out. I can't figure *you* out. I don't know if I like the fact that you have no problem challenging me. Or yelling at me. Or getting on my last nerve." He rocked back on his heels and locked his eyes on hers. "But I do know that I want to feel you." He brushed his thumb down the length of her jaw. "Kiss you." He moved his fingers to her lips. "I want to know what my name sounds like coming out of that fucking mouth of yours," he whispered.

Elle sucked in a breath as he pressed his lips to hers.

His arms were around her. Her hands on his chest. His tongue flicked her bottom lip, and she wanted more. She gripped his shirt and pulled him closer. Elle felt herself melting into him and didn't want it to stop. He ran his hand down her side and dug his fingers into her.

His phone rang, and she jumped. Her back pressed to the truck, and a cold chill ran down her spine. Drake pulled the phone out of his pocket and answered on speaker.

"Lex," he said.

Elle put her forehead on his chest. She took three deep breaths. Drake had kissed her. On the mouth. She put her fingers to her lips. She'd been kissed before. Never like that. Like she was the only person in the world, forget about just a room. She could feel his lips on hers still. Rough. She leaned back against the truck to look at him.

Do it again, she pleaded in silence.

"You guys can come now. Josh can't race. Vero can't race. What the hell are we going to do?" Lex was hyperventilating. "Where are you?"

"Gage's garage. Dropped off their bikes. We'll drop ours next and then head to you." Drake turned to check the garage door before he opened the truck door for Elle.

"You're not even at ours yet? What are you doing?"

"Making out," Drake said. Elle smacked his arm.

"Very funny. Hurry up," Lex said.

Drake slid his phone back into his pocket. He smirked at her.

"Get in the truck." Elle smiled at him. He went around the other side and hopped in behind the wheel.

twenty-three

Drake found out which room Vero was in. They got in the elevator at the hospital. The ride up was silent. She wasn't sure where they stood now.

They made it to the sixth floor and saw Lex first. She sat at the end of Vero's bed and cried into the mattress. Aster held Vero's hand from beside her. Her yellow hoodie stood out in the bland room. Nate was half asleep on the sofa by the window.

"Hey," Elle said.

Vero looked up at her. A dopey smile on her face. "They gave me drugs."

"Oh yeah?" Drake snorted.

"Yep!"

"Come." Aster pulled Elle to the hallway and waved Drake along. Nate joined them and sighed when they got out to the hall. "The doctor came in. They have to amputate from the knee down."

Elle's throat closed up.

Amputate.

Vero would lose her leg.

No amount of Sludge would fix bone. She couldn't fix this. Amputate? Inhale. Her eyes clamped shut. Exhale. She might never ride again.

Muffled screams echoed in her memory. Bubbles began to pop.

No.

Not again. No.

She opened her eyes. Everything was blurry due to the waterworks about to start.

"Amputate?" Drake repeated. "They can't save what's there?"

Aster shook her head at Drake. Elle looked to Nate. His glasses slid down his nose. His shirt lay untucked, and his hair a mess.

"There's too much damage. It could get infected, and they'd have to cut higher." Aster bit her lip. Tears brimmed her eyes, and Elle put her hand on her shoulder.

"Aster, it's okay," Elle whispered. "She's going to need support through this. And I know you'll be there."

Nate clasped his hands together in front of him before he ran them through his hair.

"Unless I'm next." Aster scoffed. "Rafael can't race. He messed up his leg and his arm. Means I'm in the fourth. And Josh isn't in great shape either."

"You're racing in the Championship?" Drake asked. She nodded once.

Elle wiped her tears. Tried not to unfold in front of her as she said the words, "I'm sure you'll do great."

"Thanks." Aster gave a small smile before they joined Vero again.

Drake stood next to Lex, and they locked eyes for a minute. Silent understanding passed through them. Nate rubbed Elle's shoulder as she cried on the side of the bed.

Elle put her hand on Vero's. "How are you feeling?"

"Great. I know about the leg. It's a goner. Don't know why everyone is crying about it. Means I get a super cool metal one. I'll be like one of the creatures on the track. Maybe next time one of them grabs me, I'll rip my own leg off and beat them with that!" Vero laughed.

"Sounds like a good plan." Elle started to blubber and cleared her throat to start again. "Do you know when the surgery is?"

"Tonight! Tonight's the night!" Vero shouted.

"Alright," she whispered. Wasn't sure she could accept it.

Nate filled a cup of water and handed it to Vero. The chair scratched on the floor as he pulled it closer to them. Drake took a step back.

A doctor came into the room. She gave Vero a shot so she wouldn't be as loopy. Her pain would return gradually, but Vero would get to talk to them like normal before they took her to surgery. Lex spoke with the doctor in the hallway before she left.

"You have an hour," the doctor said.

Vero nodded at her. They all knew her fate.

Nate pulled Lex out to the vending machines, and Aster followed.

Drake stared at the white tile floor. His nostrils flared as he breathed in and out hard. His fists clenched around his abdomen.

"Can I have a minute with Drake?" Vero asked Elle.

"Of course, I'll be out here." She motioned to the hall and noticed Aster sitting in a chair by herself.

Elle sat next to her. She couldn't imagine what Vero was about to endure. Years of training and racing all for it to end like this.

"Think she'll be okay?" Aster asked as she put her hands in her pockets. The yellow jacket had seen better days. Elle could see her fingers poking through a hole at the center.

"Definitely," Elle said. She could see Drake in the room from her seat. He stood tall with his shoulders broad and back straight.

Aster sighed. Rubbed her head with her hand. "What if she doesn't make it?"

Vero was the strongest woman she knew. No way was this her end. "She will. She has to." Elle caught herself saying that a lot these days. But it didn't make it less true. She refused to believe they wouldn't survive. They had to. For each other. For her. Crying became the only thing she felt she could control. She lifted the dam.

"She is tough," Aster whispered. "She'll be okay." Aster nodded at her, and Elle wiped her face. Dr. Gordon's voice echoed in her ears to tell her to do her breathing exercises. So that's what she did.

Vero laughed, and Elle looked up again as Drake sat down on the bed. His head drooped between his shoulders, and his whole body started to shake. Vero put her hand on his, but he rose up. He shook his head. Her hand dropped to the sheets.

Machines beeped, and people spoke around them in hushed tones. Aster's leg bounced up and down. A nurse walked by, and she pulled her feet under the chair. Her shoe squeaked on the tile. Aster brought her hand to her neck and stroked her scar absently. Elle wondered if people had asked her about it all the time.

"What do you think she's saying to him?" Aster asked.

Elle brushed her hair with her fingertips before deciding to put it on top of her head. "Something he doesn't want to hear. Like how much she loves him."

Aster laughed. "I'm thinking she's telling him what to do if she dies. Outside of the track, the beneficiary sheets don't matter. Goes by blood."

"Aster," Elle started.

"I've seen enough death. Doesn't make it easier. We all die. It's that in the Championship, it's a—"

"Side effect. Yes," Elle finished the saying they all knew.

Aster nodded. "Exactly. So, make the days count. These minutes we get here might be our last. You gonna wait around or do something?"

"What do you mean?"

"I mean life, Elle. Is there anything you want to do before you die? Think about it. Make a list. Do it all."

Elle realized it would be a short list. All she wanted was time. "Do you have a list?"

"Yeah. Just one thing right now." Aster smiled. She crossed her arms in front of her. "Kiss Vero. At least once. Once is all I need."

"You think that, but it's not true," Elle sighed. Drake sat down again. She assumed Vero had a lot to say. The hour would be up before they knew it. "One kiss makes you think a second one is never going to happen. Makes you crave it."

"Damn." Aster laughed. "You're worse than me." Aster winked at her before she got up. She walked down the hall for some air. Elle put her elbow on the armrest. She closed her eyes and drifted with her cheek on her fist.

"Elle, Vero's going now." Drake rubbed her arm. His eyes were red and puffy. But she probably looked worse than him. Everyone packed in the room; Josh, Aster, and Gage sat with Rafael in the corner. Rafael was in a wheelchair. A cast on his arm and leg. Elle smiled at them all. Tears welled in her eyes as a nurse prepped Vero for transport. Drake stood at the door. Trying to keep his distance from the crowding room.

Josh gave her an awkward one-armed hug, and Gage wheeled Rafael out of there to give them room. Vero waved at the boys as they rounded the corner.

Nate gave Vero a small hug and then stood in the hallway. Lex stayed at Vero's side. Tears streamed down freely.

"Dude, come here." Vero waved Elle over. She gave her a hug, and Vero put her mouth to her ear. "Don't let him push you away, you hear me? He needs you."

"He needs you, too," Elle whispered.

"Like a hole in the head." Vero laughed. "Take care of Lex. Yourself. Everyone."

"Vero, you will be able to when you wake up in the morning," Elle said and wiped her tears. "You'll be able to fight crime with that metal leg. Promise."

"I'll draw comics of myself beating the shit out of people with my leg. I'll be a millionaire." She winced and grabbed her thigh. Elle brushed Vero's hair to the side. She wanted to braid it in the morning for her.

"Definitely," Elle said.

She stood and let everyone else get a turn. They each got a hug before filing out to the hallway. Drake held his breath and put his arms around Vero. She choked on a sob when he let go and stood in the doorway for a moment before stepping out. Aster waited until everyone left to sit on the bed again. She hugged her tight.

Elle heard Vero groan as Aster started to stand. "You're really not going to kiss me?"

Elle laughed as she stood next to Drake in the hall. He swayed on his feet and crossed his arms in front of him. The doctor came and wheeled Vero to the elevator. Everyone waved and wished her well. Lex cried into Drake's chest as she passed by. Elle could tell he wasn't a fan and pulled Lex toward herself instead. Aster rubbed Lex's back as they watched their friend go.

"How was it?" Elle asked Aster. Drake looked at her with a raised brow.

"You were right," Aster said. "I hate that you were right."

"Right about what?" Drake asked.

"None of your beeswax, race boy," Elle said.

Aster gave a lazy salute and headed outside for a breather. Probably a cigarette. Elle could hear her sniffle as she walked away.

Elle felt the rug being pulled from beneath her. Her eyes burned from crying so much. Sweat beaded on her forehead. Her palms clammed up.

"You should go see the boys. Raf is in Room 693," Lex suggested. Lex sat down in the hall. Nate handed her a tissue box.

Elle felt herself nod. Collected herself. Took a deep breath and headed down the hall. Drake tagged along.

Josh stood outside the room. He had his right arm in a temporary sling. Rafael sat up in bed. His beard more silver than blue today. His eyes and cheeks wet. Gage got up and waved them in. The group parted. Josh went to find food after greeting the pair.

"How are you doing?" Elle asked Rafael. They didn't know him that well, but she could tell he was in a lot of pain. His leg was in a thick white cast, and his arm was in a gray sling, also wrapped but in a thinner casing. Cuts and bruises covered the arm she could see. Drake and Elle stayed by the foot of the bed. Gage hugged her and raised his fist to Drake. He tapped it.

"They say I'll be fine in a month or so, but I can't race. Now Aster has to join because of me. I can't believe this. And Vero's hurt... everything went to shit this year," Rafael whined. He looked pale. Dark circles under his eyes.

"Yeah," Drake said. He looked out the window. The moon started its ascent. The sky began to darken.

"It was wild that Cyra came up to us. Don't you think so?" Gage asked.

"Definitely," Elle said. Rafael bit his lip and squeezed the sheet in his hand. "What's wrong with your leg exactly?"

"I have cuts all over my right leg, but my left is fractured. I'm fucked." He pulled out his right leg, and Elle could see the marks from the creatures and birds. The injuries that pained him.

Elle looked up at Drake. He nodded at her. He stood in the doorway to block the view. Elle pulled out her tin and quickly put some Sludge on his leg.

"Whoa, where'd you get that?" Gage said.

Rafael had tears in his eyes as he concealed his leg again with the light sheet.

"Don't worry about it," Elle whispered. She shoved it back in her pocket. He looked better already. Even around the eyes. Gage stood and brushed his friend's hair to the side and smiled down at him.

Then a Guard member walked in.

Elle grabbed Drake's hand. He pulled her behind him. Her heart raced. Pulse quickened. He squeezed her hand. Like they were back in the arena.

"Surveillance," the Guard said. His voice crackled from the helmet between them. He pointed at the corner of the room. A camera the size of a cherry flashed at Elle.

Her spine went rigid. Air froze in her lungs.

"Fuck." Elle let go of Drake's hand. She knew the consequences. Knew her time would come to an end.

"No," Drake exhaled.

"Do not do anything stupid," Elle warned. She reached into her pocket. The tin of Sludge was cool as she gave it to the Guard.

"Where did you get this?" he commanded.

"Found it," she lied. The words came out smoothly. Just like she practiced. All those years knowing the risks. Knowing she could get caught.

"Where?" His voice through the helmet was stern.

"Corner of fourth and twenty-second. It was on a bench. I picked it up," Elle said.

"You're coming with me," the Guard said. Elle nodded. He put cuffs on her, and Drake grabbed her shoulder.

"Don't," Elle scolded him. "Do not."

"Elle." Drake shook. His eyes popped out of his skull. His knuckles were white.

"Do not follow," Elle whispered. "It's alright."

"We'll let Cyra decide what's next," the Guard said. Drake stiffened, and Gage put his hand on Drake's arm. He took a step away. The dread in the room was palpable.

Elle let the Guard take her down the hall. They passed Lex and Nate sitting in the chairs Aster had been in a short moment ago. Elle locked eyes with Lex. She silently wished Lex wouldn't react. It was useless.

"Elle?" Lex exclaimed, flying out of the chair. It fell on its side as Nate pulled her back. "Elle!"

Nate held her around the waist from behind, trying to keep her from interfering.

"Drake! Drake, what's going on?" she cried. Elle couldn't hear Drake's response. The Guard had brought her to the elevator so fast.

Elle could hear her friends' screams back and forth. They waited for the doors to open. She got on and turned to face them. Nate still held onto Lex. Aster and Josh were running down the hall toward them. Drake had his hands on his head. Tears streaked his cheeks. Elle smirked at him. They had a good run.

She knew what was next. Any mate caught with Sludge would receive a death sentence. It would be better to not die in the small room while your friends watched. They had enough to deal with. They needed to find a third rider.

Drake had kissed her. One kiss. Maybe she'd be able to replay it in her mind wherever she ended up. She thought of Lex. Her happiness wouldn't fade. She'd be there to lift everyone up, like she always does.

And Nate would be there for her. Vero would live forever for sure. They'd win the Championship and bring Aster and Nate with them to the Cove. No doubt. At the very least she hoped Aster got a second kiss. Elle would never. At least someone deserved theirs.

twenty-four

The Guard pushed her into a black van. Identical to the one they forced her into when she was six years old. The same stale smell. The same leather seats in the back. She was teleported back in time. Crying as she watched the Guard kill the boy who saved her. Shot him right in the head.

She refused to cry this time.

Refused.

Something shiny reflected off the ground, and she put her shoe on top of it. Dragged it over to her and picked it up. A hairpin. She wasn't sure if it would help, but anything was better than nothing. As she put it in her pocket, something cool touched her fingertip. It was the small purple rock Samuel had given her that day she went to see Sarah. She must've washed the pair of pants with the rock still inside. She didn't have her silk. But this would suffice.

Poor Sarah. She'd never know what happened unless Nate went to explain. He'd be a blubbering mess. Drake or Lex could do it, too, she supposed. She could not imagine Drake talking to her mom. Sarah would give him a piece of her mind for allowing Elle to do such a stupid thing. Elle almost laughed, thinking of the scenario. She wanted to be in that room with them. Wanted to watch Sarah laugh at his one-liners. Spend a morning with him flipping pancakes for the kids.

They parked outside the manor, and the Guard stopped at the door. A small fingerprint scanner was beside her. Elle looked over her shoulder at the pine trees nearby. The scent hit her hard and made her think of the night she left Drake standing by the fire. The Guard took his glove off and pressed his thumb to the scanner. She was wrong. It sliced him. Took his blood.

She'd heard of the massive amounts of security at the manor but hadn't thought about using DNA to keep people out.

He pressed his thumb to the small machine underneath the scanner. When he pulled his glove back on, the cut was gone. Elastaderm? Could be.

The Guard knocked four times fast and twice after. Another Guard opened the door. They were silent. Only the creaks of the door sounded. Their footsteps echoed in the foyer.

They entered a small room off of the main hallway. Cream tile flooring, dark green curtains covered the floor-to-ceiling windows, and a large oak desk sat in the middle of the room. She knew where she was. The room Cyra killed the Guard. She could still see his dead body in the middle of the floor. Her eyes found the secret door in seconds. Cyra sat on the edge of the desk. Her ivory gown flowed past her heels.

"What?" Cyra snapped at the Guard.

"Ma'am, she used Elastaderm on an injured rider. The container was unrecognizable." The Guard handed the tin to Cyra, and she examined it.

Elle knew her fate.

And it was in the executioner's hands.

"Where did you get this?" Cyra asked. She didn't look up at Elle. Her eyes stayed on the small tin. She turned it over and over in her hands as she examined it.

Elle repeated the lie.

"I saw you earlier," Cyra said. Elle kept her voice steady. Kept her head held high. She wouldn't die on her knees.

Elle nodded. "Yes, ma'am."

"You don't want to beg for your life?"

Her time was up. She didn't feel the need.

"Do you know why you will be punished? Killed?" Cyra smiled at her.

"The Sludge, Superior."

"How naïve of you to assume you'd never get caught. We have you on camera at the second race." Cyra paused.

Oh shit.

"You didn't think you had gotten away with it the first time, did you?" A laugh slipped between the Superior's lips. "You know, I love playing games, but it was fun watching you make a fool of yourself. Every single year there is one. One that thinks the rules are above them. Every ye—"

"Hey!" Drake yelled from the doorway. Dripping in sweat. His jacket was on again, caked in mud. He panted as he took a step into the room. Elle jerked at his sudden appearance.

Cyra chuckled. "Well, well, a knight in leather?"

Drake punched the closest Guard member, and his helmet shattered. Blood spurted from the bridge of his nose. He screamed, and Drake pulled the gun from his belt. He shot him in the throat, and Elle shrieked and ducked down into a ball. Her chains rattled at the movement. Drake shot three of them and got behind Cyra. Out of bullets, he pulled out his knife and put it to her neck. His arm rested on her shoulder.

Elle stood back up with her hands raised. "What are you doing!"

"Oh, how exciting!" Cyra laughed. She held her hands up to the other Guard members, that rushed into the room to stop them.

"Here's what's going to happen." Drake put his mouth to Cyra's ear. His words came out like venom. "You're going to let her go. And if I win the Championship, she gets to live. And if I lose the Championship, you can kill me." Drake held the knife to her carotid, and a trickle of blood traveled down her dress.

"What! No!" Elle cried.

"How fun!" Cyra grinned. "And why would I agree to that?"

"You've always liked games. Lollipops and sunshine, right?" Drake gritted his teeth. His eyes darkened. Jaw clenched.

Cyra's eyes were wide. "Lollipops and sunshine? Where'd you hear that boy?" Her words came out soft. That phrase meant something to her.

"From the horse's mouth," he said and pushed harder into her throat. She coughed. "So, fun and games? Agree to my terms."

"How'd you get in here?" she asked. Elle looked around the room. That was a good question. She would've noticed him come through the secret hall. The Guard were everywhere. Drake locked eyes with Elle. Blood dripped from his pointer finger.

She swallowed her gasp.

No.

"Lincoln," Cyra said to a Guard member. "Who was guarding the door?"

"Hayworth." The Guard responded immediately.

"Kill him," Cyra grunted. Lincoln grabbed the gun from his belt and shot a Guard in the entry. Elle yelped from the floor. Drake didn't flinch. Cyra tried to face him, but he tightened his grasp. "Only someone with my blood can get in. Other than the Guard. So, how did you get it? Steal it from my doctor?"

"What's the matter, Mammie? Can't see the resemblance?" he snapped at her.

She went rigid. Drake slowly came around to face her. The knife still at her jugular. Cyra tilted her head and looked him up and down. Her eyes stopped on his face.

"Well. Things have certainly become interesting." She smiled.

"If I win, I'll tell you everything," he said. "How I hid all these years. I'll tell you if you let her go. She lives. Those are my terms." He kept his eyes and blade on Cyra.

"Why?" Cyra said. The silence hung between them. He stood his ground. "You've been hiding all these years to come out now? What makes her so special?"

"Does it matter?" Drake shouted. "She lives. Those are the terms."

"Your name?" Cyra looked to Elle.

"Elliot Winters." Her voice soft in the thick room.

"Winters," Cyra said. As if she was trying to remember. She turned back to Drake. A grin on her face. "Interesting last name."

"Not really," Elle mumbled. Confusion played on the tip of her tongue.

"Significant, wouldn't you say so, Drake?" Cyra said. "You were in the paper a long time ago, yes? A crash of some sort?"

Elle stood and took a step toward them. The air left her lungs. Her eyes began to sting. "What did you just say?" Elle asked. She looked at each of them. Cyra laughed. Drake twisted the dagger, and a little more blood came down her shoulder.

"Aw, you didn't tell her? How romantic!" Cyra's words echoed in the tall ceiling. "Oh, what a treat! Lies upon lies!"

"What's she talking about?" Elle said. Drake didn't look up at her. But his jaw tightened. His arm tensed.

"Fuckin' hell," he mumbled.

"This is why you think you need to save her? Because you killed her family?" Cyra turned to Elle. "When they died, did you think it was an accident?" A maniacal laugh erupted from her. "Idiot girl. It was all planned! Except for your car to be a part of it. I was trying to kill *him*!" Cyra tried to slap the blade out of his hand, but Drake stood strong. He didn't budge. He pushed harder into her. She laughed as she sat down on her desk. He repositioned himself to look at Elle. His eyes pleaded with hers. He was always hard to read. But not now. Remorse and regret waved off of him and crashed into her.

"How?" Elle whispered. "It doesn't make sense. They killed you. I saw them murder you."

Drake shook his head at her. "I was in the back seat when our car hit your van. Both went into the lake. My parents died on impact. But I sank. When I got the chain unhooked from the seat and surfaced, I realized I was alone. I went down to check the van. I broke the window with the chain. You were the only one breathing."

"But—but they killed you. I watched them kill you." Elle started to cry. She hated that this was all happening. He was the boy? Impossible. "The Guard killed you."

"They tried. They shot a round beside my head. I grabbed the other Guard's gun and killed him before killing the other. You were so young, Elle. Your mind made you see what it wanted."

Cyra hummed with joy. "Lies upon lies! You see, you don't want to be on his team."

"You lied," Elle whispered. "You knew this whole time!"

Cyra liked games. She lived on drama. Her smile was widening.

Elle pieced it together. "When Randy sent that message, you knew once you saw my name was Elliot."

Drake nodded.

"Lies upon lies!" Cyra laughed. "No trust in this place!"

"Should've known," Elle whimpered. "Everything is always a secret with you!" She shook her head. She could see the lights go on behind Cyra's eyes.

"I've got a fun idea!" Cyra yelled.

"No," Drake snapped at her. "Fun's over. Agree to my terms. I win the Championship, she lives. If I lose, you can kill me. It will be a redo of what you failed at fifteen years ago."

"If you win, she will live. If you lose, your neck is mine. But let's make it even more... fun. Shall we?" Cyra giggled.

"No." Drake shook his head.

"She must race too." Cyra pointed at Elle.

"No," Drake said. "Absolutely not."

"Alright." Elle took a step toward her. The chains around her wrists clanged as they swayed. "Yes."

"No!" Drake turned to her. His chest heaved up and down.

"Agree to the terms," Elle snapped at Cyra. "Agree."

"I agree that if both of you survive the race, you'll be free from my grasp. You don't even have to win," Cyra said. "Let's make it more fair. Though, if one of you dies, you both will have the same fate."

"Agreed," Elle said.

"Agreed," Drake snarled.

Cyra smiled. "Agreed. Oh, how fun! Now, off you go!" Cyra waved them off but then held her hand up. "One more thing, Drake?" They turned to her. She crossed her arms over her body. "Don't bother trying that door again."

twenty-five

Drake opened the passenger door of the truck and helped her get inside. He sat behind the wheel and got them out of there. Elle dug in her pocket to get the pin and put it between her teeth. It took her three tries to get it lined up. Drake flinched when the chains clunked to the floor by her feet.

She rubbed her wrists. "Sorry, I didn't want to wait for you to get them off."

"How the hell?" He shook his head. "Never mind."

"Drake, I told you not to. I told you not to!" she yelled, but all he did was shrug. The window was down, and his arm lay on it. The roads were dark. The lights on the street were dim. And he was calm. How was he so calm? What the hell was wrong with him? "What's wrong with you? She could have killed you!"

He raised his voice at her. "Me? She was going to kill you!"

"I know! That's why I told you not to."

"And I didn't listen!" he yelled. "Get over it. Now, we have a bigger problem."

"That you lied? Big shock." She rolled her eyes. "What a way to find out that the kid who saved your life and died for you didn't. In fact, he's been a foot from you for weeks. He figured it out. But didn't want to tell you."

"Elle, you don't understand. I couldn't tell you. Then you'd know who my grandmother was. Then you'd be in worse danger. And everything else would've fallen apart with it. You would run away."

"Run away? Why would I run away?"

"Because I killed your family!" he yelled. "Were you not paying attention? I fucking killed your entire family. Every single one of them. Their lives are on me." Drake stopped at a stop sign. He put the truck in park. Elle took a deep breath. He was delusional.

"Are you insane?" she said. She closed her eyes. It came out smooth, but on the inside, she was screaming. She opened her eyes to glare at him. "Their blood is not on your hands. You didn't kill them. Cyra did. I wanted her to think I was upset with you. I wanted her to think we weren't going to beat her at her own game." She paused, and he stared at her with wide eyes. "I have ideas. I have to look the rules up. It'll be alright. We'll get through it. And we will live. We have to. There's no other option. If you die, I die, and if I die, you die, so therefore, we must both survive. Simple."

"Elle."

"Shush. You're forgiven. Don't make me regret it. You're an ass for not telling me, but I am letting it slide on account that you saved my life. Well, you delayed my death for four days at least. Maybe," Elle said.

"Elle, you can't race. It's not that easy." Drake ran his hand through his hair. "It's crazy out there. You've never even been on a bike."

"I've been on other bikes. You can teach me."

"In four days?"

"Yes." Elle nodded. "Yes, in four days. That's all we get."

Drake was silent on the way to the hospital. He parked the truck and climbed out. Elle put the chains on the back seat. The moon was high in the sky as she climbed out.

Drake was usually quiet, but this time her mind raced. Circling what he could be thinking. What he thought of her. Probably thought how pathetic she was for even agreeing to Cyra's insane plan. She couldn't blame him for thinking that, though. She was a nobody. Untrained. Untalented. Not even coordinated half the time. How was she going to do this?

Her breath started to come out shaky. This was a terrible time to freak out. But she had agreed to be in the Championship. ChaosMotors Championships were for the best of the best. She had to, though. For Drake. For Vero. Lex. She'd die trying to save them all. She knew that for certain.

"Elle," Drake said. She jumped. Had he been trying to get her attention? She stood in front of the truck.

"Sorry, what did you say?" Elle took a deep breath, and Drake wiped his hand across her cheek. She didn't remember starting to cry. Her mind couldn't focus on one terrible part or the next. Vero's leg. Drake had an even bigger target on his back than she did. Lex would be next in line to get attacked. She couldn't take a breath. Her exercises were failing her. She couldn't remember the first step.

Everything started to spin.

"Elle!" she heard Drake yell, and suddenly she was sitting on the ground. His hands on her cheeks. "There you are," he whispered. "Breathe. It's alright. You're fine," he said over and over. She finally inhaled, and he nodded. "Good. In. Out."

Her eyes burned. Her head throbbed. Arms began to still from shaking.

Drake put his forehead to hers and closed his eyes. "Listen, I will train you. You'll survive."

"What about you? What about Vero? Lex?"

"Somebody once told me to trust them more. You should give them more credit," he said. His mouth twitched with a smirk.

Elle finally took a normal breath. She locked eyes with Drake and felt her lips tingle. He had saved her life. And then coached her out of a panic attack. All she had to do was lean in.

Tires on gravel came up fast. Drake jumped up. Eyes wild.

"What is that?" Elle asked.

"Those are not Chaos bikes. She sent her dogs." Drake pulled her up.

A smoke bomb barreled at them. Drake rolled her to the side. Elle coughed as she steadied herself. A Guard tried to side-swipe them. Drake pushed him off the bike. He flung off and smacked the dirt.

"Come on!" Drake yelled. Elle clambered into the truck. She could barely see out of the window. Drake dodged another blow, and the next one hit his head. Elle screamed. He got up fast and jumped behind the wheel.

"What the fuck is going on!" Drake screamed. Blood ran down his face. They struck him in the temple. Elle didn't have any Sludge with her. It was in her car at Drake's. She looked to see if he had a towel or napkin in the backseat. A Guard came up to the tailgate and shot a spear. Drake gasped as she grabbed the wheel and jerked it towards her.

The spear whizzed between them, bursting through both panes of glass. A hole the size of an orange was in the back and the windshield started to splinter. The sound was like ice cracking on a pond.

"On your left!" Elle pointed to the bike, and Drake grunted. He stomped on the gas pedal. His eyes on the Guard, he reached over and grabbed the seatbelt across her chest and tightened it.

Drake rammed the truck into the side of the bike. He locked his jaw. Gripped the wheel with both hands. Then hit him again. Blood splattered the driver's side window, and Elle wanted to vomit.

"Glove compartment," Drake shouted at her. The wind whistled through the holes in the glass. She opened it up. Empty. He slid his hand inside and pressed a small hidden button on the side closest to him. A section popped out, and Elle reached in to grab the revolver. It was a Guard weapon. Old. Six shots left.

"Where the hell—" She stopped. Better to not ask. Did he kill a Guard to get this? She didn't want to know. Not right now.

"Do you know how to use it?" he shouted over the wind.

She gripped it in her right hand. Nodded. Pursed her lips. She knew how. But could she?

Another Guard came up on the right, and Drake hadn't seen. She put the window down and Drake yelled. Couldn't hear the words. She slammed her fist into the Guard's helmet. Pain shot up her arm to her shoulder. He pulled off to go around a parked car.

Elle reached into the back and grabbed the chain. He collided with the truck, and she shrieked. The metal screeched as it scratched down the side. Drake sped up and took another turn. Elle waited until the Guard was closer before she whacked him with the chain. She went to hit him again, and he grabbed onto it. He busted up her palms by pulling it. She let go, and he threw it into the street.

"Shoot him!" Drake growled.

The Guard reached for his belt. Elle felt the bile rising inside her. She put the barrel on his helmet and closed her eyes as she pulled the trigger. His body slammed into the pavement. Blood pooled out of him. She put the window up. Don't cry. Don't.

She killed someone.

Somebody she didn't even know. Killed them. They deserved it. But did they? They were just following orders.

No.

They were going to kill them. Kill her. Kill Drake.

She'd never let them. Not without a fight.

She reloaded.

"We can't go anywhere until they stop following," Drake mumbled to himself.

"The lookout," Elle suggested. Drake nodded and told her to hang on. He whipped the wheel to the right and took a dirt path out of town. Three Guards trailed behind them.

Elle sighed. She turned around and aimed the gun out of the broken glass. She shot and missed. Reload. Shot again and hit his shoulder. Reload.

The truck bounced with every slight bump. She couldn't get a good shot like this. She held her breath and closed one eye.

"Slow." Drake put his hand on her leg to steady her. He was trying to help, but all his touch did was send a heat wave through her.

She had to refocus all over again. Her finger steady on the trigger. Released a breath. Squeeze.

Headshot.

He flew off the bike and hit the Guard behind him.

"Team Superior, fatality," Drake said.

Elle laughed as she wiped the blood off his face. At least it was red this time. More trickled down at a slower pace. "What's your plan?"

"Try and make him go over the edge."

"Preferably alone, right?" Elle asked as he barreled up the hill.

"Preferably," Drake said.

The Guard came up on Drake's side. His tire on the very edge of the cliff. "Almost," Drake whispered. He went faster. Turned sharp.

Elle wished for the best. The worst? She wasn't sure how to look at this.

The Guard turned with them. Hitting his brake, he didn't take the bait. Drake stopped abruptly and kicked his door wide. The rider collided with the frame and fell to the depths. The truck shook from the impact. Elle held onto the door handle on her side. The riders' mangled remnants forced a cloud of dust to rise.

Drake put the truck in park. His phone rang. The ID read unknown.

He slammed his fist on the wheel. Elle recoiled. Drake took a breath and pressed the green button. Didn't speak. He put it on speaker.

"Just a little fun," Cyra said on the other end. Elle could practically see the shit-eating grin on her face.

Drake hung up and slammed his fist again. "Fuck!"

Elle unclicked her seatbelt, raised the center console, and scooted over to him. She ran her hand up his arm and back down to intertwine their fingers together. Her palms were rough from the chain, but she didn't mind the sting. His hand shook in hers. She brought his hand to her mouth and kissed it.

"It's alright. We can hide," Elle whispered. "I have some ideas, remember?" Elle paused. His hand stopped shaking. "The beast rests again." She chuckled. Droplets of blood formed on his knuckles. He closed his eyes, and she realized she had moved too fast. She tensed and released him.

"Oh, sorry." He didn't like to be touched and that's all she ever seemed to do. She needed to learn to keep her hands to herself. "Sorry," she said. She started to move back, and he glared at her.

"What are you doing?"

Red ran down the side of his face. His hand. Busted glass on either side of them. Wind blew between them. Cyra was after them. She loved playing her games. Was this a game to him? Was he like her?

No.

He wasn't anything like her. He had saved her. Risked his life for her. Didn't like when anyone touched him though never seemed to push her away. Maybe he didn't mind her touch.

Elle slowly moved back. Raised her hand to cup his face and pressed her lips to his.

This was nothing like their first kiss.

Soft. Gentle.

He slid his hand to the back of her neck and pulled her closer.

twenty-six

They parked the truck at the garage, and Drake got on his bike. He helped Elle get on behind him, and she wrapped her arms around his torso. She pressed her cheek to his back and closed her eyes as the wind whipped.

Drake hid the bike near the back exit of the hospital. They kept their heads down as they passed each camera. This time they took the stairs up the six floors. They entered Rafael's room, and Drake put his finger to his lips to tell them not to react. Gage stood and took Josh's jacket off the hook behind the door. He handed it to Drake. He hesitated before he took it. Their logo on his back would throw off any Guard member for sure.

Aster shrugged out of her yellow zip-up. Elle groaned as she put her arms through it. Drake pulled the hood up for her. Her arms swam in it. At least it was the right length.

Lex stood from the corner and wrapped her arms around Elle. She sobbed into her, and Elle tried not to melt down with her.

"I'm okay," Elle whispered.

"You almost died because of me," Rafael said.

"No, no, no." Elle went over to him. She sat down beside him. "No. It was my choice. I've been using it for years. I knew the consequences. I would never want any of you to think that." Elle looked at each of them.

Drake stood with his arms crossed by the door. Keeping his distance from the crowd.

Nate put his arms around her next and gripped her tight. Elle pulled away from him and smiled at his red eyes. Lex joined Aster and Josh on the small sofa under the window. She looked at her group of friends.

Her family.

Only missing one link. But they were here for Elle. Glad she didn't die. Glad she was part of their group. She'd never felt like this before.

"We don't have a lot of time. They're after us." Drake sighed. "Cyra likes to play games. And now we're in one. Elle has to race."

"Whoa, what?" Nate stopped him. His eyes on Elle. His hands shook, and she silently told him to calm down. He didn't get the message.

"If one of us dies, Cyra will kill the other. We have four days to train. The fourth race is always the hardest. In terms of the track anyway," he spoke quickly. Trying to shove all the information in.

"You've driven a bike before?" Nate asked Elle.

"Motocross bikes," Elle said. She thought back to her early teens riding around with her brothers.

"Cyra sent the Guard after us. The truck is dead." Drake turned to Lex. "I need you to go to my house. Now. Move Elle's car somewhere safe. So they can't find it."

Elle handed her the key from her pocket.

"I'll go with you. I need to get out of here." Aster followed her. Elle figured it might help Drake calm down. Too many people in one room.

Drake turned to Gage. "We'll stay at Elle's tonight. And we'll find somewhere to train tomorrow."

"Use our garage," Gage offered. "Alliance?" he asked Drake.

He stared at Gage. He looked at Josh. "Why would you do that? You still want to win the Championship. We're a team in your way," Drake said.

"There are more important things than winning." Josh smiled. Gage winked at Elle. "We can help protect her from Cyra."

Elle had tears in her eyes again. They were willing to do so much for her. "Don't put your life on the line for me."

Gage huffed. "You're one of us. Can't back out now."

"Deal." Drake held out his hand to Gage. Gage took it and laughed at him. He knew Drake didn't like being touched.

"If you fuck up…" His eyes became slits. His mouth tight.

"You'll kill me, I know, Drake. I've known you my entire life, remember?" Gage chuckled, and Drake nodded once at him.

"Drake," Elle said. "You will not!"

"I'd do the same thing for Josh." Gage shrugged.

Elle turned pink. Drake didn't react. Nate grabbed everyone's attention next.

"What about Vero? What should we tell her?" Nate asked.

"The truth," Drake said.

Elle grinned at him. He was free of his secrets. Most of them, anyway. She had so many questions. Would he actually answer them if she asked?

"How did you get her out?" Nate asked. "Did you get into the manor?"

"Yeah," Drake started. "I walked through the front door."

The replay started in Elle's head. The pine smell from the walk from the van to the manor door. How Drake barged in and saved her. Cyra's expression when he held the blade to her throat. The sound of the chains rattling around her wrists. She almost died tonight. Drake saved her. Again. This time she didn't mind so much. He didn't die. Not yet, anyway.

"What do you mean? I thought you could only open it with Cyra's blood?" Josh asked.

"You had some of her blood? Ew, Drake." Gage shook his head with his tongue out.

"No, I used my own blood," Drake admitted.

Drake filled them in as fast as he could, leaving out the part where he saved Elle in that very same crash. Too much drama for one night. Elle appreciated him not transferring the spotlight to her. On the same note, she was glad to have some space with it. It was still impossible for her to see him as the boy from her past.

A Guard walked by the room, and Drake grabbed Elle's hand. She pulled on her hood more, and Gage eyed their hands. Elle blushed. Did he want to keep them a secret?

Drake whispered to them. "We have to go."

"Tell Vero I love her," Elle said to Nate. He pulled her in for a quick one-armed hug.

"You'll be alright, kid."

"Good luck. See you on the track," Gage whispered.

Drake got them out of there without getting detected, and they ran to his bike. She squeezed her eyes shut as he rounded corners and sped up the hill to her apartment building.

He hid his bike behind a dumpster, and they made it inside her building. They ran into the elevator, and Elle hit the close door button as soon as she could. She was ready for this to be over.

Drake locked the door once they were inside and then pulled her coffee table over to the door and propped it up to jam it. Elle checked the locks on the window above her kitchen sink before pulling the curtains. The moon shined through the fabric so she could still see in the room. She reached for a light, but Drake stopped her.

"No, they'll see."

"Good thinking. Now what?" she asked.

"Now you can relax."

"Relax? Are you insane?"

Drake laughed. "I figured you might say that. Can I shower here?"

"Yes." She went to her closet and opened the bottom drawer. She handed him a pair of black pants one of her older brothers had left and grabbed his T-shirt from under her pillow. "Don't say a word."

"Wasn't going to." Drake chuckled.

She pulled the yellow jacket off and changed into a different pair of pants and a clean shirt while he cleaned up. She slipped the purple rock from Samuel back into her pocket. Then she opened her safe and grabbed a tin of Sludge so he could fix himself when he was ready.

Drake came out and put his dirty clothes on the floor by her bed. Elle sat under her window and grabbed her laptop.

He sat down beside her as she watched video after video of Cyra's Championship speeches. She pulled up the rules and read them three times before going back to the videos.

"What are you doing exactly?" Drake asked.

"Shush." Elle waved him off, and he chuckled at her. He leaned his head back on the windowsill and closed his eyes.

Another hour of videos went by before she realized he was asleep. She closed the lid and rubbed her eyes. Drake sat up and looked around the room.

They stood up, and both got into her bed. Elle couldn't help the butterflies crowding her stomach. Even though he had so many secrets. Cyra and her Guard were after them and Vero's leg. She was still a girl falling for a boy who was about to sleep beside her.

She rolled to face him and took a deep breath. He didn't smell like he normally did. She should've taken him up on his soap deal.

"Go to sleep," Drake whispered.

"I can't. I have too many questions," Elle said.

"Like what?"

"When did you tell Vero and Lex about Cyra? Where did you really go that night when you said you went to a friend's house? How many times did you almost tell me you were the boy? How long ago did—"

Drake chuckled. "One at a time."

"Sorry."

"I went to work that night. Not a friend's house."

"Work?" Elle remembered him saying he had a job before. Why wouldn't he tell her that?

"Yeah, I work at a ChaosMotors bike shop. I repair old ones. Usually, I work overnight, sometimes during the day when I can get away. Depends."

"Why is that a secret?"

"Riders can buy their bikes there. But mostly, the Guard. Risky business. Honestly, I shouldn't even be telling you." He let out an exhale through his teeth.

"But we might die in the next few days, so might as well tell me everything, right?" she whispered, and he smiled at her in the dark. The sun was beginning to rise, but her apartment was still covered in shadows.

"Something like that, yeah."

She tried to think of any secrets she kept to tell him. She couldn't think of any worth mentioning, though. "I think I should teach you how to make Sludge," Elle said.

His eyes opened wide. "Really?"

"Yes." She laughed. "Then again, maybe not."

"Wasted effort. What if I die?" he sighed.

"Maybe I should teach Nate. He is my best friend," Elle said.

"You should ask."

They were quiet for a few minutes. Elle looked out the crack in the curtain to the full moon. The light brightened a spot on her ceiling.

"What about rooms with only a bed, a locked window, and a barred door?" Elle asked.

Drake shut his eyes and took a deep breath. "Depends." He paused. "What are we doing in bed?"

Elle smacked his chest, and he laughed in the dark. "Go to sleep." She huffed and rolled over. Her back toward him, she faced the wall. Would the Guard try to find them here? Would Cyra? Would she leave them alone now?

"What about this?" He slid his hand up her thigh to her hip and around to her stomach. His palm covered her entirely. She tensed under him until she felt his breath on the back of her head. He had scooted a lot closer. She pressed her back to his chest and placed her hand on top of his.

"I would have pegged you as the little spoon," Elle whispered. Drake pressed his forehead into her shoulder as he shook with laughter.

Elle sat up fast with a gasp. The sun blinded her, she raised her hand to her eyes. Drake turned to face her from the edge of the bed.

"Morning," he said.

Elle looked down at herself. She'd slept for hours and didn't have a nightmare? She wasn't covered in sweat. Exhaustion won that round, she guessed.

"Hey," Elle said. Drake went to the fridge, and Elle rubbed her eyes. She took a deep breath and put her fingers on the bridge of her nose. When she opened her eyes, Drake stood beside her, holding a bowl. She jumped. He kept his eyes on hers.

"What is this?" Elle asked.

"Food." Drake shoved it at her. She took it and sat up straight. Cold oatmeal with a cut-up banana and some honey drizzled on top. She eyed him. This was well put together. "Eat. I make it for Riley, so it has to be sweet, or she won't eat it. You like it?"

She nodded with a smile after the first bite. "Definitely. But you didn't have to do this. Why didn't you wake me up?"

"I called Howard earlier. Told him what was going on. Plus, you need your rest. The next few days are going to be rough," Drake reminded her.

She whispered her thanks as she finished the bowl. When she looked back up at Drake, he was staring. His eyes were so light she wasn't sure she was awake.

This was the longest they'd spent together alone. Was he regretting sleeping there? Did he want to leave? Her hair was probably a rat's nest. She put the bowl down in front of her and bit her lip. He reached out and pulled her lip from her teeth with his thumb.

"Stop stressing," Drake whispered.

Elle chuckled. His hand dropped on the bed between them.

She got up and looked in the mirror. Her guess was correct, rat's nest. She groaned as she brushed it and fixed it on top of her head in a ponytail. She put her brush in her secondary backpack. Grabbed a few outfits and shoved them in too.

Elle put her camera in her bigger safe under her floorboards. She needed to make sure that if she lived, it would still be here for her. She didn't care about anything else in this place other than that. When she opened the lid, the chip Nate had given her sat in the corner. A big reminder of the images on that card. How could she use this now? She'd think of something later. If she lived.

Drake grabbed two bottles of water. He put the table back where it belonged as she put the bottles in her bag. Elle did one last sweep of her apartment. It might be the last time she saw it. She glanced at her jacket hanging on the hooks.

"I ruined your jacket, didn't I?" Drake asked. "I wasn't thinking."

"Neither was I. They could've killed me for trying to save him." She brushed the sleeve with her fingertips. "It was my favorite jacket. It's the exact one my mom would always wear. Sarah got it for me when I turned seventeen. Finally able to fit in it." Elle chuckled as they got on the elevator. "If I'm being honest, I just like the silk pockets. Reminds me of her. I used to always put my hands in her pockets when she sat beside me. Kids are strange."

"I used to leave sticky notes for my mom in her pockets. So she'd find them later in the day. Most were smiley faces, but some were drawings. She loved them. Hung most of them on the fridge." Drake shrugged.

"That's adorable," Elle said. Her mind started to spin. She'd been so focused on her own past she never thought of his. He lost his parents too. His family. They drowned like hers did. He saw what she had seen. "Do you miss them?"

"Every day," he said under his breath. "My mom owned a bagel shop. My dad helped her in the mornings before he went to the office. He worked as an accountant or something boring. But they were happy. I remember them dancing in the kitchen." He gave a small smile. "She'd sing to me as I fell asleep. He'd play catch with me in the yard. Normal kid stuff in the Cove."

"That sounds amazing." Elle smiled. Drake peered over at her. She was getting better at reading him. He seemed relieved. Happy even.

First stop was Evolution's garage so Drake could fix Vero's bike. Well, enough for Elle to ride for the day. He taught her what every button did and which ones not to mess with. How many shots she had and how many weapons were legal, and which ones weren't.

"Why would you put an illegal weapon on the bike?"

"It's only illegal to use them. Not have them." He winked at her. "Emergency situations. Or in case you weren't on the track when something happened."

That made sense now that they'd lived through an attack from the Guard.

Drake pulled their bikes out to the dying grass. Brown was more popular than green. Elle swung her leg over the red bike. The seat was a good height, so they didn't have to adjust it. Drake shoved a helmet into her hands. She rolled her eyes but put it on. He pointed more things out to her, and she pressed on the gas too hard. She jerked forward and laughed when he gasped. He shook his head at her.

"Lightly press, Elle."

"Got it." She smiled, but he couldn't see her.

She pressed on it again and rode around the grass for a couple of minutes. Drake nodded and ran inside to grab his bike. He put her backpack on her back and grabbed tools, and put them in a bag he had in the office. He led them to Gage's, and Elle felt that familiar tightness in her stomach.

She needed to see Sarah soon. What if the Guard went to Little Hearts? They wouldn't. She tried to ease her brain. She tried.

Drake got the key from under the brick and unlocked it fast. They got inside, and Elle took her helmet off. Drake handed her a bottle of water. She sipped it as she went around the garage. The photos above Rafael's area were all in black and white. Years had passed in the instant camera photos. His hair was at different lengths. His clothes were baggy in some and tight in others. The two styles clashed. It didn't make sense until she noticed the different eye shape. She smiled.

"Rafael is a twin."

"What?" Drake said, walking over to her. She pointed at the photos. He looked at them all. It was rare to see twins these days. Especially inside the walls.

"What is this?" Elle asked, picking up a tool she'd never seen. It had the head of a hammer but on the other side a torque wrench. Awkward to hold.

Drake ignored her. "How do you do that?"

"See the obvious?" she joked as she put the tool back down on the table. "I don't know. I've always been good at it. Very observant as a child, I guess."

"It's your superpower." Drake chuckled, but his smile disappeared just as fast as it came. "Vero said she's writing a comic about herself and her leg."

Elle smiled. "And what's yours?"

"My good looks." He winked at her. He leaned closer to the wall of photos to get a better look. She could see him trying to piece together what she had.

"Right, of course. Kill anyone with a smile. Too bad you never let it show," she jabbed.

He shrugged. "It's hard being happy in a prison sometimes." Drake stood straight again and turned towards her fully.

"You need a new perspective." Elle put the tool down and picked another one up. She turned it in her hand until it was upside down. "If Cyra and the Guard weren't here, it wouldn't be so bad. Surrounded by friends and your favorite thing; grease."

"It's not my favorite thing," Drake said.

"What is?" she asked as she picked up another tool from the table to inspect.

"Today?" He pondered for a minute before he responded, "Chocolate cupcakes."

Drake helped her build the courage to go over a jump on Gage's track. It was harder than Elle thought. First, she didn't hit it hard enough, then she hit it too hard. She landed weirdly a couple of times before she got the hang of it. Once, she rolled out of a jump, and Drake sprinted to her. She was laughing so hard that Drake pulled her helmet off, thinking she was crying.

He was not happy about that.

Elle got back on the bike and went around and around until Lex showed up.

They ate in a small patch of green grass as she filled them in on Vero. She would be okay. Determined to ride next year. Lex said she was stubborn, but Elle felt the word was strong.

Lex told them Nate was with Vero, and Elle felt a flutter in her gut at that statement. He was always so caring. Would Lex see that in him?

"We need to get Elle a beneficiary form." Drake sighed.

"You ever going to add a fourth Drake?" Lex chuckled.

Drake locked his jaw. Elle eyed him.

"Did you have Elle sign?" Lex shrieked with joy.

"I didn't sign anything." Elle laughed.

Drake looked down at his hands in his lap. "So, I guess I should tell you."

Lex gasped and covered her mouth. Drake scratched the back of his head. His nose scrunched as he hesitated. Elle stayed silent. Waiting.

"I had Sarah sign it."

"Excuse me?" Elle chuckled.

Lex looked at Drake. Then turned to Elle. He was kidding. This was a joke. The smile left her face. He wasn't kidding.

Huh?

"I knew you wouldn't sign it. So I went and saw her. I made her promise not to tell you unless I died. You get a portion if I die. And if we both die, I guess she can keep it. That's fine with me," Drake said.

"Drake, what are you talking about?" Elle put her head in her hands. "When did you see her?"

"Before the third race."

"Drake!" Lex yelled.

"The day we did the photoshoot," Elle whispered to herself. She saw him on his bike heading out of town. She never thought he'd be going to Little Hearts. Why would she? She glared at him.

"You saw me?" he said.

"I'm over your damn secrets. What the hell!" she yelled.

"You're only mad because this one involves something that would benefit you," Drake said. "You can't stand that I did something behind your back for you."

"That doesn't even make sense!" She stood up and wiped her hands on her pants. "You're infuriating. You're so comfortable with lying!"

"I had to lie! Don't you get that? It's not easy to lie to everyone your entire life. It's not easy to try not to leave a footprint." Drake got an inch from her face. She didn't move away. He wasn't going to intimidate her. "Having codes in case Cyra found me and tried to kill my family again. Kill Riley. Kill Jane or Howard. Lex, Vero. You!" He paused and took a step back from her. He got quiet. His hands were fists again. Always looking to hit something. "Aren't you the one who pointed that out to me recently? That I should care about my family? Don't you realize that's all I do?"

Anger boiled inside her. She turned on her heel and started for the bike.

"Oh, now you run away!" Drake yelled at her.

"Sorry, I can't hear you over your own hypocritical bullshit!" Elle shouted over her shoulder. She got back on the motorcycle, shoved her helmet on, and rode the track three times. She had to be better than this. Had to.

Drake kept everything from everybody. Including her. She was just his newest secret.

He went to see Sarah. Sarah had kept it a secret too. Why had she agreed to that? I've seen him. Tall, dark, handsome, mysterious. That's what Sarah had said on the phone. Elle assumed she meant Sarah had seen him on the magazine covers. She was wrong. Sarah had seen him in person. At Little Hearts. They just didn't tell her. They lied. Again he lied.

She felt like throwing up. Was this how it was going to be with him? A constant stream of lies. Was she actually mad because he had Sarah sign the form? Or was she angrier that they were going to die right when things were getting good?

Elle couldn't believe her own fate. The irony of their lives. He saved her so she could save him. Not so he could save her again and again and again. No.

She knew how this would go. She would die at the race. He would live. She had to get his family to sign her form. And Sarah, of course. Now she could add Vero since she wasn't racing.

Elle's legs felt like rubber. Her arms like lead. Lex waved her over to where she was standing by the side. Drake walked toward the garage. Elle pulled up next to Lex and took her helmet off.

"He's going inside to fix his bike. You want to talk now?" Lex asked. Elle shook her head. And the tears began immediately. Lex put her arms around her. "It's okay."

"Why is he the worst?"

"The best ones usually are," Lex said.

"He can't die, Lex. He can't die." Elle sobbed.

"Neither can you." Lex pulled her tighter, and Elle started to feel light again. She let out enough. She reeled herself back in. "Should I go get a bike?" Lex asked. Elle nodded.

She was grateful for Lex. Having her, there eased some of her anxieties of racing. She even let her cry on her when she needed to. With these next few days, Elle had a feeling she was going to need to.

Lex ran inside and borrowed Rafael's cobalt bike. It was the smallest of the four. Elle smiled at her as she came to join her on the track. Lex gave her some pointers and started to ride beside her. Then she would get closer and closer. Elle had to get comfortable with riders being next to her. Without swerving off the track.

The sun started to go down, and Lex called it.

"Come see Vero later?" she said. Elle nodded. She sat down to take a break as Lex left. Tools clinked together inside the garage and echoed out to the field she was in. She laid back and shut her eyes.

When she opened them again, Drake was in a pit of fire in the arena. His skin melted off his face, and his mouth started to disintegrate. Teeth fell out of his gums as his eyes rolled to the back of his head.

She sat up fast, breathing hard. The sun was still out but just barely. Something moved beside her, and she screamed. Drake held his hands up.

"Sorry, I had to wake you," he said.

Wake her? Shit. She put her knees to her chest and her forehead down. Sweat dripped down her spine. He plopped down next to her. His hand slowly rubbed her lower back.

"Fuck, you scared me," Drake whispered.

Elle didn't respond. She peered at him from between her arms. He brushed some hair out of her eyes.

Drake took a breath before he opened his mouth again. "You ever done something so stupid it changed the course of your entire life?" He chuckled. He spoke low and soft. Slow. With intention. "I've gone every day of my life with a plan. Don't fuck up. Don't let anyone know. Cyra will kill everyone you know." Drake looked back at the garage. "And then you were gone. The girl who, at first, I didn't want to even be in the same room with." He let out a laugh. "The girl who saved my life. The girl who doesn't realize she's the smartest in the room." The wind kicked up and his midnight hair brushed over his forehead. "So nothing else mattered. You were gone. I knew the risk. And I knew what I was going to do. I told Lex I was most likely going to die. Tragic." He laughed again. "You know what she said?"

"What?" Elle murmured. This was the most he'd ever spoken to her. So honest. Open.

"You better fucking save her, or I'll kill you myself."

"She cursed?" Elle asked. That was more shocking than Drake coming to save her.

"Yeah," Drake said. They laughed. "I couldn't believe we had kissed, and she was going to kill you. Couldn't let it happen." Drake shook his head.

"It was a good kiss, though," Elle said.

"Good?" Drake scoffed. Elle knew how to get under his skin and she was getting better at it.

"It was alright."

"Now you're being an ass."

"Yes." Elle laughed. "Thought I'd never get a second. Now that would have been tragic." She unraveled her arms from her body. She redid her hair before she let out a heavy sigh. "I'm sorry I freaked out earlier. I don't like secrets."

"You shouldn't be the one apologizing," he said. "I should've told you sooner. Well, I should've asked you to sign my form."

"No, you were right. I wouldn't have done it. But I am mad I didn't see the look on Sarah's face when you were at the door. Wait till she hears you're teaching me how to ride."

"You don't need a teacher for that." He winked. "Just a partner."

What a cocky asshole.

"I should find one," Elle snapped at him.

His eyes darkened. "A better one than me?"

"One with a better mouth."

The grass stuck on her pants and she began to pick them off one by one. The sun no longer shining on them made the air cooler on her skin. He was sitting so close now she looked at his mouth. Would his lips feel colder on hers or warm like the first time?

Drake smiled at her. "I haven't even begun to show you what I—"

Elle kissed him.

She learned fast. The best way to get him to shut up was to keep his mouth busy. She preferred it on hers anyway.

twenty-seven

Elle hid her bag in the corner and cleaned up the garage a bit before locking the door. Drake led her to his bike.

"Lex got the form for you." He held up the sheet that she'd taped to his bike.

"When did she come back?" Elle turned pink. Hopefully, she hadn't seen them in the field. Drake shrugged. Maybe he didn't care about keeping them a secret after all. "So, then where are we going?"

"Sarah's," Drake said. He eyed her as if she should have known. "I figured you'd want to explain things to her. And have her sign."

"Oh," Elle said.

"You wanted to go alone?" he asked, surprised.

She shook her head violently. "Hell no." She paused. "Is it safe?"

"I don't think they'd go there. Too risky for her reputation," Drake said.

She believed him. He helped her get on behind him and she pulled on her helmet. He took off in a cloud of dust.

Elle remembered as they were pulling into the driveway that Drake had already met Sarah. A strange feeling began to bubble inside her. No awkward first meetings or stumbles over her words. She grinned as she put the helmet on the bike seat.

"Elle!" Samuel came running out of the house. Elle grunted as he slammed into her legs. Drake chuckled.

"Whoa." Elle sighed and another kid came bolting out of the house. And another. One of the teenagers, Kayleigh, came down the steps with a boy in her arms. Zach was the youngest in the house now. A two year old with a loud laugh and an even louder cry.

"Kayleigh, this is Drake," Elle introduced.

"Better be good with kids," she snapped. Zach started to squirm and Drake held his hands up to her.

"May I?" he said. Zach turned to him and Drake smiled. "Hi."

Zach rubbed his eyes and leaned toward him. Drake took him in his arms and nuzzled his head into his shoulder. He began to sway and Zach closed his eyes. Almost asleep already.

"You can stay," Kayleigh said.

Elle snorted. It was funny, but she didn't mind that her family accepted Drake as he was. Even if she didn't know where they stood. Or what would happen with them. She liked knowing her siblings approved. She rubbed Zach's back and Drake put his head on top of the boy's curls.

"Elle! Come see our rock wall! Come on!" Pedro pulled on her hand and she sighed.

"Alright, but I have to see Ma in a minute."

"Okay, okay, come on! The boy can come too!" he said and Drake chuckled at that. He followed her to the back of the house. Sarah waved from the porch and then froze when she saw Drake. He waved at her. She smiled wide.

"Well, I'll be damned," she said. Elle waved back at her before she followed Pedro into the woods. A few of the older boys were dueling with sticks by a large wall of rocks they piled together. It must have been four feet tall and about six feet wide.

"You made this yourself?" She smiled at them.

"Damn," Drake said. He seemed impressed too.

"Look! We saved you this one!" Skylar pointed at a painted purple rock. She laughed at it. It had her name on the top with a backward E. Drake stayed back until Pedro pushed him from behind to get closer.

"Here, you can do this one!" He handed him a dark brown one. Zach asleep in his right arm, Drake held the rock with his left. Elle slapped the rock with some of the putty they were using and watched him place it on top of the wall. Elle did the same, putting hers right next to his. The other boys came to add more. Zach started to stir in his arms. Drake rubbed his back and he stopped. Elle stared at him.

"Drake, one-hundred-time racer, hitman… and baby rocker?"

"Shut up," he whispered and glared at her. She laughed.

The kids let them walk back to the porch. Kayleigh came and took Zach to put him down for his nap. He cried when Drake gave him up. Kayleigh groaned.

"I can put him to bed," he offered and she beamed at him. She handed the boy back and Drake followed her inside. Elle walked Pedro to the kitchen but stopped on the porch where Sarah sat. She waited for him to go inside before she spoke.

Elle sneered. "You lying son of a bitch."

Sarah laughed and covered her mouth. "So he finally told you huh?"

"Why wouldn't *you* tell me?"

"He told me not to. For good reason. You would've never let him do that."

"You're right. I can't believe you," Elle sighed.

"You can though. It's alright honey. You should've seen how nervous he was. Boys." She giggled. "I can tell he cares. He just doesn't know what to do about it."

Elle was quiet. She wasn't sure what to say. But now she had to confess what was going on. She bowed her head. "I have to tell you something."

"What is it? Are you okay?" She stood up and rubbed Elle's shoulder.

"I'm in the fourth race," she whispered.

Sarah laughed and stopped when she looked into Elle's eyes. Her expression grew dark. "You're joking."

Elle shook her head. She started to ramble to get the words out. "It's complicated. But Cyra—sh-she caught me using Sludge. And the Guard brought me to the manor. And Cyra was going to kill me. And Drake saved me. And then she made a deal with us. If we race and live, she'll leave us alone, but if one of us dies, we both die. But we don't have to win the race. So that's good. I can skate by. It's kinda a longer story. We can't stay long. I'm worried they'll find us here."

"Honey." She stopped her and Elle took a breath. "Drake saved you?"

Elle nodded. She bit her lip. "Yes."

"And you're being forced to do this?"

She couldn't let him die. "Yes. I mean, if Evolution asked me to race, I probably would have. I mean, Vero got hurt in the last one. She had to get her leg amputated." Elle started to cry. She didn't want to but, talking about it made it real. She hadn't even seen Vero yet.

"Oh, my heavens!" Sarah covered her mouth.

A group of kids ran past them into the house. Elle waved at Christopher who walked into the kitchen holding grocery bags. Drake appeared and started to help him unload the bags. They were talking in the kitchen as kids were trying to help too.

Sarah pulled her attention back to her. "Hold on. Back up, how did Drake save you exactly?"

"He ran into the manor and killed some of the Guard and held Cyra with a knife until she made a deal. He said, if he won the championship, I would live. If he lost, he'd die. She changed it on us." Elle dropped her eyes. Tears flowed freely. Sarah raised her chin to look at her face. "There's more too. He's the boy. The boy from the crash. Ma, he didn't die."

Sarah stared at her with wild eyes. "What do you mean?"

"He's the one who saved me that day when I was a kid," Elle whispered.

Her words sunk in and Sarah's eyes were wet too.

Drake came outside and froze on the porch. His boots loud on the wood.

Sarah dropped her hand and Drake pointed over his shoulder.

"You want me to leave you two?"

"Get over here," Sarah snapped at him. Elle had never heard her use that tone before.

Drake strolled over to her. She raised her pointer finger at his face. He didn't change his demeanor. Sarah dropped her finger to poke his chest and his eyes followed her finger.

"You." She paused and he looked back up at her face. Elle wasn't sure what to do. What was happening? Should she stop it? Then Sarah dropped her hand and put her arms around him. Elle was about to step in when Drake shook his head at her. He put his arm around Sarah and let her squeeze him.

"Thank you. Oh thank you," she cried and finally took a step back from him. "You watch out for her."

"Yes ma'am."

"Sarah," she said. "Call me Sarah."

Elle put her hand over her face. Wiped her tears first before hiding from her embarrassment.

"Ma," Elle started but stopped. Drake took a step back and she could see his hands turning into fists. "We have to go."

"Call me when you can."

"Your form," Drake said.

"Oh! Right!" Elle reached into her back pocket and unfolded the piece of paper. She ran inside and grabbed a pen and Sarah signed it in a flash. She kissed Elle on the forehead and pat Drake on the back.

"I love you," Elle said.

"Love you too honey. Now go kick some ass." Sarah winked at them and they ran to his bike by the driveway. Elle got on behind him again and they sped off.

She could feel him begin to shake. Elle tapped his shoulder and pointed to a side road so he could pull over. Trees lined the dirt path. He pulled off and parked behind the first row. Out of sight. Like she'd done that day with Lex. She climbed off and he stared at her.

"What's wrong?" he asked.

Elle chuckled. She pointed at him. "You! You're practically convulsing. Can you please get off the damn bike! Walk around. Get some air." She waved her arm and he sighed. He started heading further into the woods. His stomps got softer as he got further from her. She heard a car pass and jumped. They couldn't be alone. She turned but didn't see him.

He went too far. She started to head in the same direction and caught up to him. He was walking fast. The branches hit his arms as he went by. Elle didn't have sleeves so each one swiped a layer of skin with it. She winced at the last one and Drake turned on his heel. Elle ran right into him. He steadied her. His breath came out hard. His chest rose with every inhale.

"What are you doing?" he said, looking at her bare arms.

"I didn't want you to be alone."

A snap sounded in the distance. Drake tilted his head. A deer came into view and Elle let out a sigh of relief. Drake chuckled at her.

"Fuck off," Elle said and started to walk back to the bike. He grabbed her hand and pulled her back to him. She hit his chest with her palm. "You're such an ass. All the time."

"Yeah," he said. His eyes found the trees for a moment before coming back to her.

She sighed. "I'm sorry she hugged you."

"I'm not. She needed it. I'd rather she thank me for saving your life than cry on me for letting you die," he said.

Elle crossed her arms in front of her. "If I had died, it would not have been your fault." She paused. "Either time."

Another twig snapped. This time Drake moved fast. He covered Elle's mouth with his hand and lifted her. He pulled her behind a tree. Putting his chest to hers. Her back to the bark. Drake's body covered hers entirely. He uncovered her mouth and put his finger to his lips. A group walked by them. Chatting back and forth. Laughing. She knew immediately.

Halo.

She heard Kannon's high-pitched snort. She glared under Drake's arm at the group as they walked by.

He looked down at her. She nodded at him. Drake pulled her toward the group and they stepped quietly. Kept their distance.

Once the trees started to thin, Drake jerked her behind another and ducked down. They went one by one to the next trunk and the next until they were closer to the clearing. Halo had a fire going. Throwing small bottles back and forth of alcohol the shade of lavender.

"Violet Bourbon," Drake mumbled. "Illegal in the Valley."

"How do they have it?"

"Easy to make."

Three Guard came up to the fire and Drake tugged her behind the tree again. Elle's breath left her body. Fear struck her like lightning. But nothing happened. They looked around the tree and the Guard were sitting with them. Helmets off. Drinking from the bottles.

"Thanks for the tip." One of the Guard slapped Kannon on the back.

"Sure thing. She had it coming. Stupid bitch. She chose the wrong team. I told her that." He snickered. "Cyra will find her tomorrow. I bet she's hiding in her little apartment. Those idiots won't help her. That's for sure. They'd be stupid to."

"It true Matthew's is fucking her?"

Drake stiffened.

"He killed Seth. For sure he's fucking her." Kannon laughed as he took another swig. "Poor guy."

"Yeah, going from that sexy blonde chick a few years ago to that bitch. Can't even believe he'd choose someone like her." One of the guys from Halo said throwing a stick into the fire.

"I don't know man. She was nuts when I met her," Kannon said. "Maybe that's why he likes her."

"Oh, so that's why. She's crazy!" One of the Guard snickered and stuck his tongue out. His long blond hair sticking to his neck. "Sex must be wild!"

Elle figured he must be the youngest. His immaturity radiated off of him.

Drake's jaw locked. His knuckles white in the dark forest. Elle put her hand on his, and he flinched. Taking his mind off the group of men. Elle nodded toward the bike, and he let her lead him away. They were silent until they got to the hospital.

She hopped off the bike and helped him hide it again.

"I'm so sorry," Elle said.

"For what?" Drake snapped at her.

"They're all spreading rumors about you."

"Shut up, Elle." He shook his head at her. "What are you talking about? You're sorry? They were basically calling you a Race Slut. I should be apologizing to you. These fucks think any girl in the Valley wants them because they're good on a bike."

Elle nodded. She didn't have a good response, so she bit her tongue. They walked inside and found Lex and Nate standing in the hallway. Aster walked out of Vero's room. When she turned to Drake and Elle, she smiled.

"Hey!" Aster yelled. Elle ran and hugged her.

Drake peered into the room and Vero sat up straight. He walked swiftly to her and she put her arm around him before he took a step back. Elle jumped on her bed to give her a big hug. She cried on Vero's shoulder and squeezed her.

"I hear you two have been through the wringer."

"Us?" Elle said, lifting the sheet to see her metal leg. It shined in the fluorescent light. Vero chuckled.

"Yeah, yeah, whatever. Not exciting. So, you ready to race or what dude?"

twenty-eight

Drake and Elle parked inside Gage's garage. Inside they found a stack of blankets and pillows Josh had left for them. Elle reminded herself to thank him when she saw him. She couldn't wait to sleep. Drake put a blanket down behind Vero's bike. So if anyone walked in, they would be hard to see.

Elle grabbed the pillows and put them down next to each other. She pulled her shoes off and laid down. Drake did the same and put his arm over his head.

"Think they'll find us here?" Elle asked. The lights were off and the windows were on the other side of the garage. It was hard to make him out. Elle turned on her side to face him.

"I doubt they'd look here."

"Even though we were in Rafael's room at the hospital? You don't think they'd make that connection?" Elle asked. Drake shook his head.

"They're not smart like you, Elle." He turned to face her. Brushed her cheek with the back of his hand. Elle closed her eyes and felt a blanket cover her. "Go to sleep."

"What about large rooms filled with a lot of stuff?" she asked.

"Better than tiny rooms with a lot of stuff for sure."

She was about to ask another when he interrupted her. "Why did you choose our team?"

"What do you mean?" Elle opened her eyes when she laughed. "I didn't. Lex came up to me. She didn't tell you that?"

"No." He shook his head. "So you really didn't know us before that day?"

"No. You thought I planned this? Wanted to get close to you? Uncover some insane story with Cyra and the boy who saved me?"

"I wasn't sure what to think that first day. I wasn't sure I could trust you," he said.

"Did you think I was a Race Sl—"

"Don't you dare finish that sentence," he snapped. She froze. His tone harsher than she expected. "You're nothing like that. And those riders tonight don't know you at all. You should've let me kill them. Would save us some trouble on the track." He huffed and she didn't speak.

It reminded her of the Guard she killed. She closed her eyes again.

Elle knew she had to or he would have killed Drake. It didn't make it easier for her to replay it in her mind. She tensed and Drake put his arm around her. Pulled her to him. He lay his head above hers.

"How do you kill people so easily?" she asked him.

He shrugged. "Kill or be killed. It gets easier the more you do it. The first one was the worst. Nightmares for weeks. Sometimes I still get them," he said. "Since I was fifteen, I've been trying to win to get Riley out of here."

"That's why you joined so young." Elle realized.

"I don't want her to live here. Watching people die on the streets for nothing. People killing each other for sport." He shook his head.

"So why haven't you killed her?" Elle spoke softly.

"Cyra you mean?" he asked. Elle nodded. "I would be Superior."

Oh. She hadn't thought of that. Inside it went by blood. If she died, and he's inside the Valley, he's required to take her place.

Elle woke up and Drake was gone. A note was on top of her phone.

Be back soon. Nate's being guard dog outside.

She got up and grabbed a bottle of water. Searched the fridge and found a snack to munch on. Blue Falcon's garage was night and day compared to Evolution's. Everything had a place and it was neat and tidy. Even the tools hung on peg boards around the room. Only one table was in the center of the room that seemed slightly messy.

Elle fixed her hair in the bathroom. The tile floor was light blue and a small window was covered with a dark blue curtain. She rubbed the dark circles under her eyes and splashed some water on her face.

Elle came back out when she heard a car coming up the drive. The Guard had found her. She tensed and grabbed a wrench from the nearest table. Any weapon will do. Nate was outside though. Did he have a weapon? Anything to protect himself with? The doorknob jiggled before it unlocked. She relaxed. The Guard wouldn't have a key.

Drake walked in and furrowed his brow when he saw the empty spot where they had been laying.

"Hey," Elle said. He jumped and she smiled at him. "Where did you go?"

"Come on." Drake waved her toward the door.

She looked outside to see Lex hanging out the front of Nate's car. "What are you guys doing?"

"I just went for the ride. Drake got you something." Lex smiled.

Nate joined them by the car and Elle hugged him.

Elle turned to Drake. "Got me something?"

"It's not that big of a deal." He handed Elle her keys and she patted her pocket. Only Samuel's rock remained.

"What the hell," she said. "You took my keys?"

"Had to grab something from your place." He opened the trunk and grabbed his jacket and handed it to her. The thick black leather felt smooth on her fingers. She put it under her arm and expected him to hand her a bag. She looked at Lex and she giggled. Drake closed the trunk.

"What?" Elle said. She turned back to Drake. He crossed his arms in front of him and looked at her. His jacket hugged his arms and she gasped. He was wearing his jacket. She held up the one in her arms. "What!"

E.W. on the collar. Fresh leather smell. The burning tree on the back with Evolution in bold letters over the top. Her very own jacket. She stared at it in awe.

"Put it on!" Lex grinned.

She put her arms through the sleeves and instantly felt the fabric glue to her skin. It had pockets in the front. She slid her hands inside and felt the familiar silk. From her ruined jacket.

Her eyes locked on his. He smirked at her.

She wanted to kiss him.

Bad.

But Lex and Nate were a foot away. They were still a secret. She focused back on the jacket instead. Her eyes filled. Her stomach flipped. He'd done this for her. Elle bit her lip and shut her eyes. Nate slapped her back and she laughed.

"Thank you," Elle choked. Drake gave a half smile.

Lex and Nate hung around the track for a while and watched Drake teach Elle more maneuvers. She quickly learned how experienced he was. The most difficult moves for Elle he did without fear or flaw. Gage's track was more advanced than dirt and a couple of jumps like Evolution's. Drake eased her into the track and she didn't complain when sweat dripped into her eye or dirt covered her entire body. However, once a beetle flew into her mouth, she stopped to spit up a little in the bushes.

"Whoa! Elle, you okay?" Lex ran over and handed her a bottle of water.

"Bug." Elle coughed and Drake laughed.

"You need a break," Lex said.

"I agree." Drake put his hand on her shoulder and she shook her head.

"No way, we only have two days left. I need to be better. Faster. I just need to close my helmet better."

"You also need to rest," Lex said.

"I refuse to be the weakest link."

"You're not," Drake sighed. "Vero is."

They all laughed. Elle eased up. She stared at the ground and put her hands on her new jacket. She nodded. Okay. She could use a sip of water. They all sat in the field with sandwiches and Nate ran inside to grab more bottles of water.

"How's Vero?" Elle asked.

"Okay, I guess. Aster and Josh are with her now," Lex said.

"Aster isn't preparing as much as she should, is she?"

Lex shrugged. "I don't know. She seems to want time with Vero."

Elle felt Drake's eyes on her but didn't look up at him. Her cheeks turned red. She understood. If Drake wasn't the one teaching her, she probably wouldn't be out here. Elle thought of the list Aster brought up. Just time. She wanted more time. Was this it? Just a bit more before she was murdered on the track?

Lex suggested they spend some time at her house. A shower sounded great to Elle. Along with a bed to sleep in instead of the floor. She agreed after some convincing.

Drake led her to the car and Nate dropped them off at the house. The two of them headed back to the hospital. They'd call when they needed another ride.

Elle called the shower first and Drake let her go. He gave her the bag he brought so she could change when she finished.

She let the water take her tears with it as she thought of every possibility and outcome. Drake couldn't die. He couldn't. Not after everything. She got dressed and let Drake go next.

He cracked both doors. She figured it was a safety thing. If anything happened. But she felt safe here. She wasn't looking behind her every second. Which was probably naive of her. Elle watched him as she lay down on the side of Vero's bed. Only flashes of skin and fabric until she looked away. She watched the fan on the ceiling as she heard the turn of the knob and the water stopped.

Drake wrapped his lower half in a towel and joined her in the room. She watched him search the bag before grabbing a few items.

"I can't believe you used the silk from my old jacket," Elle mumbled with her eyes closed. She heard him approach her and opened her eyes when he brushed her cheek with his fingers.

"You didn't see the other thing," Drake said and grabbed her jacket from the chair she placed it on. He brought it to her, and she watched drops of water roll down his chest to his waist. He smirked at her.

"Sorry, what'd you say?" she said, and he chuckled.

He raised the jacket to her and she watched him raise the flap where her initials were. The small gold leaf pin.

"Robert," she whispered. Her eyes filled again with too many emotions. She sat up and put her legs on either side of him.

"Thought you might want that there."

Elle looked up at him. His hair disheveled still. But his face was clean. He didn't smell like himself though. Maybe one day she'd be able to experience that scent again. She slowly put her hand on his chest and he sucked in a breath. She watched her fingers as they trailed down to his abs to trace the scar she'd healed and up to his shoulder. She brought him down to her mouth. His hands ran down her back and a chill ran through her.

His tongue entered her mouth and she moaned into him. She let him strip her shirt over her head and he bit her bottom lip. A car backfired on the street and she jerked back from him.

He rested his forehead on hers. She rubbed his chest as he shut his eyes.

"What are you thinking?" Elle muttered. She bit her lip.

"Fuck Elle. I don't know."

"You think we're rushing into this?" Elle asked.

Drake laughed. He kissed her again. "Absolutely." She nodded and went to grab her shirt and he stopped her. He put his mouth to her ear and dug his fingers into her sides. "But we might die in a few days. And I want to know what you taste like."

twenty-nine

Drake and Elle had Nate pick them up and take them back to the hospital. They sat with Vero and Aster for about an hour. Watched her stand for the first time on her new leg. Vero was stubborn as always but Aster helped by pushing people out of the room when she started to break down. Elle felt bad but wasn't sure how to assist other than to give her space. Drake put his fingers through his hair. Held his head.

She imagined her fingers doing that to him a little while ago. She couldn't think about him like that right now.

Aster poked her head out to the hallway and waved Elle inside. She wasn't expecting Vero to ask for her. Aster shut the door but when Elle turned, she was gone. Only Elle and Vero were in the room. Somehow the room seemed smaller with just the two of them. Elle felt useless. She couldn't do anything to make Vero's situation better.

"Hey," Vero said. She wiped her eyes, and Elle went to her side. She sat on the edge of the bed. "Sorry, I know you might not want to."

"Stop. What do you need?" Elle asked.

Vero smiled shyly. She put out her hands and Elle put her palms in hers. Looking up at her dark amber eyes.

"Help me stand first."

Elle gripped onto her and stood before assisting her friend upright. Vero weighed a bit more than her and was a few inches taller too. She figured Lex was way too small. Plus, Vero would never allow Drake or Aster see her struggle. Not like this. Elle understood. Logically, she was the best choice. She was the best option for the task.

Elle loosened her hold and took a step away holding her arms out in front of her. Vero was hesitant but took a solid step with her human leg and a half step with her metal one. Elle nodded.

"Good, one more." She encouraged her enough to get three more good steps. Vero smiled up at her. Tears in her eyes. Elle wrapped her arms around her. "You got this."

"Thank you," Vero whispered.

"You're welcome." Elle grinned at her. "Now do one more."

Vero did two more before she paused and chuckled to herself. "Assholes couldn't even make the damn thing dark chocolate to match my skin. Stupid silver piece of garbage."

"You could paint it," Elle suggested.

Vero nodded with a half smile. She struggled a couple more times before she collapsed on the bed. Exhausted.

"I'm done," Vero sighed. Her skin sticky with sweat. "Now, tell me, what are you thinking?"

"I guess I'm terrified. But I'm going to race anyway."

"No." Vero chuckled. She shook her head at her. Elle stared. "Drake."

"What? What do you mean?" She blushed.

"Please." Vero bit her thumbnail. "I'm not dumb. Now spill."

"What about Aster?" Elle raised a brow at her and crossed her arms. Vero looked down at the sheets.

"Dude, I asked first!" Vero grumbled.

Elle laughed. She wanted to tell her. Spill all her deepest thoughts on the matter. How his smile weakened her at the knees. Made her anxieties and fears float away. They didn't have time. Lex knocked on the door twice before opening it.

"You bitch," Vero said.

Lex widened her eyes.

"She's kidding Lex. Come on," Elle said and waved her in.

"Shut the door!" Vero yelled and she turned to shut it on Drake.

The girls giggled at his groan. "You got ten minutes."

Lex giggled again and jumped on the end of the bed. "So, Elle, how are you feeling? You did great today on the track. You should've seen her V! She's getting faster already. You might want to start thinking of a different nickname for her."

"Nah, Vanilla fits well for her." Vero smiled. Elle didn't mind the name so much anymore.

They were quiet for a minute before Vero put her hand on top of Elle's. "You're going to survive this, dude. Remember when you told us about that crash you lived through? You're a survivor."

"About that..." Elle winced. She looked at the door thinking about Drake and what he'd say about talking about it. As far as she was concerned, it was her story too.

She told them fast about Drake being the boy who saved her. The two girls gasped and shared a look before the girl-talk became too much. Too loud. Too many giggles came from Lex and Drake knocked again. Time to go. Elle gave them both a hug and Vero winked at her.

"Don't think you're off the hook for that other story," Vero said.

"Ditto," Elle said. Lex gave her another hug before she joined Drake and Aster in the hall. Nate came with two bags of food. One he handed to Vero and the other to Drake. He nodded as a thank you.

Drake went and spoke in Vero's ear and gave her a fist bump before saying goodbye to everyone else.

"Can we see Rafael?" Elle asked.

"I saw him. He's fine. We have to go," Drake said. A Guard was heading toward them, and Drake turned and dragged her down another hallway, Nate in tow.

They eventually made it to his car and they drove fast. He dropped them off at the garage but as he was about to leave, Elle held up her finger to Drake.

"I'll meet you inside," Elle said to Drake. He gave her a head tilt and left them. Nate seemed on edge but she smiled at him and he relaxed.

"What's up?"

"Will you sign my form?" she asked, pulling it from her pocket. He was speechless for a minute. He stared at the form. Only seeing the first name. He knew he was second on her list.

"I'd be honored to." Nate grabbed a pen from the center console and signed his name under Sarah's.

"I also want to ask you something a bit more illegal."

Nate chuckled. "Oh?"

"I want to show you how to make Blue Sludge."

"What?" His jaw dropped. "Blue Sludge? How do *you* know?"

"Long story, but it's how I have so many tins all the time. Will you let me teach you? Tomorrow night?"

"Yeah, yes. Absolutely."

Nate waved from the front seat as he sped off down the brick drive. Elle gazed at the small house in front of the garage. Imagined a life where Drake had a garage in his backyard. Would she be there with him? Is that even something he would want? She wasn't sure. Could just be something she wanted.

Elle blew out an exhale straight up so it flipped her hair out of her eyes. She turned and headed inside the garage to find Drake on his back under Vero's bike again.

"What now?" she asked.

He chuckled before he sat up. "Fixing the wire for the brake. You gripped it so tight earlier. I'm shocked it's still attached."

"Oh shut up." She flipped him off and he smirked at her. "I'm going to teach Nate how to make Sludge tomorrow night."

"He agreed?"

"Yes. So, we're going to have to get back into my apartment. It should only take about two hours. Start to finish."

"Should be fine. I'm assuming they've already checked your apartment. Might be trashed though."

"That's alright." She sighed. "Not really. But, for the lesson. I hid everything under the floorboard beneath my bed. And I have two safes. One hidden."

"Who are you?" Drake chuckled and she brought her knees to her chest. Bit her lip. "What?"

"Why'd you do it?" she asked.

"Do what?" He put the tools down and wiped his hands on a nearby towel. He put it on the seat of the bike and sat up to look at her.

"Let me do the article, I guess. Why'd you let me take the photos? Then you saved me from Cyra. Why not let her kill me? I mean, wouldn't that have been easier?" she asked.

"Elle." He stared at her. A long time passed before he spoke again. She wasn't sure he would even add anything. "I agreed to the article for Lex. She had been bugging me about getting press for the last two years. Really since Vero joined. It's better for the Championship if people know who you are. My issue was that I couldn't have Cyra see my face. So, how could we get press without doing that? Once you said you could help with that, I agreed."

Elle stayed quiet. She let him speak. Not interrupting was easy when he spoke in that tone. Soft and smooth. Velvet. When it was only them. This voice was for her alone.

"I let you take my photo the first time because I keep my word. Lex would've never let me back out anyway."

Elle smiled at him. She nodded. It was true.

"When that article came out with you on the cover. I thought I was going to kill someone," he spoke softer then, letting his words trail off. "You were only getting targeted because of us. Or so I thought anyway. And that's when I realized I had feelings for you." Elle shot her eyes to his. "I searched the crowd for you before every race. My feelings for you are what pushed me to go see Sarah. I knew if I didn't do it right then, I was never going to. Even though I was a dick the night before at the party. I went to your apartment that night to apologize. Chickened out when your neighbor yelled at me for pacing the hall too long." He shook his head. "I hoped I'd see you again. I hoped that you'd forgive me. I've never done that before. Normally I don't care. Like me, don't like me. Forgive, don't. Whatever. But not with you. I wanted you to like me. Wanted you to accept my apology. Wanted you at the next race. So, I would've done anything you asked that day. No matter what it was. Reckless." He scoffed. "And then I thought you liked Gage." Drake laughed.

"Dumbass," she said.

Drake wiped his palms on his jeans and scooted a little closer to her. Would she get the chance to get used to him eliminating the space between them?

He smiled at her. "Not my finest moment. At least I didn't hit him when he kissed your cheek at the party."

"I would've never forgiven you," Elle said.

"I know, that's why I didn't." She felt his eyes trail her arms and shoulders and up to her face. Her eyes. She brushed her hair behind her ear. "I should have told you when I realized who you were. I was fucking terrified. I had just realized my feelings for you. I couldn't let you leave. At least until the Championship was over. I wasn't expecting this outcome.

But, then Cyra. It wouldn't have been easier for you to die, Elle. That's ridiculous to even suggest."

"I don't think so. Look at us. Running around and hiding. Like we're in the Cove trying not to get sent here," Elle said.

"Been there, done that. It's worse than this. Trust me," Drake said.

"I do," Elle whispered. "Trust you. I don't know how considering all the lies and secrets." She drummed her fingers on her thigh. "But yes, I do trust you."

"I know it doesn't mean much, but I am sorry I couldn't tell you the truth. So many secrets all my life. It was survival," he explained.

"I know. I just hate it. I hate not knowing all the facts," she said.

"I figured. With all the questions you ask." He smirked at her.

"Shut up," Elle said. Her hair fell in her eyes again, and she pushed it back.

"You really are beautiful," he murmured.

Her cheeks flushed as he leaned into her. Brushing his lips on hers.

"Why'd you kiss me?" he asked.

"Now or two days ago?" Elle chuckled. She knew what he meant. She bit her lip again. Tugged on it. "Because even when you're being an ass, or punching brick walls, or pushing yourself harder than you should, or saving my life..." She smiled at him. "I see you."

Elle woke up on Drake's chest. His even breaths calmed her. Even the day before the race, she felt safe with him. At ease. She'd have to tell him her plan. Prayed he would go with it.

Drake brought his hand to her hair, splayed out on his chest, and twirled a piece in his fingers. She watched him for a couple of minutes before rubbing his bare stomach with her fingers. He tensed.

"Sorry, did I wake you?" he asked.

She shook her head. He moved his hand to her lower back and rubbed her. She closed her eyes and lay there in silence with him. Elle didn't want it to end. This would be the last morning like this.

She sat up, and Drake put his hands under his head. So relaxed. He closed his eyes. She marveled at him. Memorizing every scar. Every dip. Every bump.

His phone vibrated, and he checked it with a groan. He reached over and pulled his shirt on.

"What's up?"

"They're here," Drake said. A knock on the door came, and Elle jumped. She fixed her hair quickly as Drake went to the door. He unlocked it, and Gage walked in.

Wait.

"Hey," Elle said, surprised. He walked over to her and pulled her to stand as he hugged her.

"Hey gorgeous, ready to ride?" He grinned at her.

Elle looked over his shoulder at Drake. He had his arms crossed in front of him. She chuckled at him. "You did this?" He nodded.

"He called me yesterday. He didn't tell you?" Gage chuckled.

Elle shook her head. She smiled, and they walked out to the track.

Drake joined them and started following and circling her. Getting close, backing up, making her work around him. She enjoyed the challenge. Gage was talking in her ear the whole day. Back and forth with ideas and commentary. And lots of laughs.

Lex and Nate came to watch until Gage forced her onto Rafael's bike again. Then they all were riding. Except for Nate, of course. He stood on the sidelines and pointed out certain things from his perspective.

Josh brought sandwiches for everyone, and Gage ran inside for water. Elle laid down in the yard, face-up, and tried to catch her breath. She was already exhausted, and it wasn't even noon yet.

Josh still had his arm in a sling. She wondered if using Sludge would help. Probably not. His makeup was done to the nines, and she pictured Gage getting up early to do it for him. She smiled at that. They were cute together.

Talking with Josh, she learned about Rafael. How he joined Blue Falcon out of simplicity. He needed a team, and they were willing to take a fourth. This was his second year. He was older, and they all knew he wanted an experience before his time was up.

Nate gave the update on Vero. She could walk with a cane now. At least to the end of the hallway. Elle was thrilled. Gage ran over to join them with a box of cookies. Drake broke one in half and gave the other part to Elle.

"How's Bobby?" Drake asked Gage.

"Doing good. He got your envelope. He says thanks." Gage took another bite of his sandwich. "He actually gave me something to give to you. Remind me later. I'll grab it."

"Okay," Drake said.

Elle finished her bottle of water and sat up to join the conversation. The grass on the back of her neck began to itch. Her exhaustion was getting worse as the day went on.

"Envelope?" Lex asked.

"I give Bobby part of my paycheck every month," Drake said.

Elle coughed as she choked into her hand. "What?"

"He helped me find Jane and Howard when I was a kid. I figure it's the least I could do. Plus, I get to see the kids when I stop by." Drake explained. Elle tried to comprehend that as she took another sip of water. She looked over her shoulder at the track to try and keep her calm.

"You go to Bobby's every month?" Lex hung her head. "Is everything a secret? What the heck!"

"Not anymore," Drake said.

"Bull," Lex said. "We'll be old by the time we hear about it all."

"Maybe." Drake took his last bite of sandwich.

Elle kept her eyes on the browning grass in front of her. Did he mean her? Them. If there was even a them. She thought there was. Maybe she really was alone. She cleared her throat and started to clean up.

"Where are you going?" Drake asked.

"Back to training," Elle said.

He looked at her. Too long. They were sharing a silent conversation. She didn't care anymore. She was frustrated. Sick of his secrets. Sick of his silence.

He wrinkled his brow and looked at the group before turning back to her. She rolled her eyes and was about to stand when he grabbed her arm.

"Elle, I didn't mean you." He pressed his mouth to hers, and she melted into him until she heard Lex screech across from her. She pulled away, and Drake smirked at her. Her smile was contagious. Must have been because everyone hollered and screamed.

"Knock it off. You're embarrassing me," Elle said. He kissed her cheek.

"Finally," Lex yelled.

Gage threw his fist in the air, and Josh clapped carefully with his hurt arm.

Drake flipped them off. The group laughed.

Before they got back on the bikes, Elle went over her ideas with the entire group. Their opinions and suggestions. Gage called Rafael to get his input. He was the most helpful. He was the oldest. Been around Cyra the longest.

Once Elle got going, she wasn't going to stop. The group of them tore into the dirt. Drake backed off after a while. Eventually, Gage did too. She noticed in the corner of her eye the two of them chatting. Gage even laughed a few times. Elle smiled to herself. If she did end up dying tomorrow and Drake somehow survived Cyra, she would be glad he had more people to lean on. More friends. His family was growing. He just didn't realize it.

Josh took his sling off and joined her on the track. He started to ride closer and closer. Lex got around her and slowed down. Elle hit the brake and swerved a little, but it went smoothly. She hit the jump, and Josh rammed into her back tire. They both went flying. Elle rolled to the side. The sound of metal hitting rubber wasn't a sound she wanted to hear again.

Her past came fast and hard. Blood came from a scratch on her arm. She screamed. Evelyn's body floated in front of her. Ezra's body limp in his car seat. Everest convulsed beside her. Her mother's neck slit in half and the blood pooled onto her fingers. Elle covered her face with her hands and screamed.

Screamed and screamed.

She heard the glass break behind her, and those blue eyes stared at her. Switching from a ten-year-old little boy to a twenty-five-year-old. Back and forth. Until she finally heard him.

"Come back to me," he said. Over and over.

Elle gasped and sat up straight, almost hitting her head on Drake's. Lex stood crying. Gage had his hand over his mouth. Josh nursed a bloody nose a few feet away.

"Don't look at them. Eyes on me," Drake said.

She focused on him.

He didn't touch her. Her breath came out in big spurts. Her eyes burned. Her arm stung. She looked down at Drake's hand and watched him slowly raise it to her face. Her helmet lay in the dirt. Had he taken it off? How long was she screaming?

"Breathe." He kept his voice soft. Only for her.

Lex sat down where she was. Nate joined. Then Gage and Josh. Drake kept his eyes on hers. She could hardly see him through the sheet of tears.

"I'm sorry," Elle whispered.

"Shut up, Elle," Drake said. She chuckled. Elle leaned toward him, and he wrapped his arms around her. She sobbed into him. Nobody spoke for a long time. Let the wave pass.

"What did you do to your hand?" Elle asked, finally sitting up. It was red and swollen. Drake looked at Josh. He wiped his nose again. Elle turned on Drake so fast. "You didn't!"

"It's okay," Josh said, laughing. "I get it."

"You didn't." Elle smacked Drake's arm.

He didn't react. He didn't regret it. Elle wiped her face again. Drake kissed the top of her head, and she melted into him again.

"It was an accident. He was getting me ready for the race," Elle explained. Of course, he didn't care.

Nate ran to his car for one of the tins she gave him. Drake took it and ran his finger down her scrape. The skin was back to normal, and he wiped the blood in the dirt. Elle tossed the tin to Josh. He caught it with a smile.

"I think we're done here," Gage said. "You're in good hands. See you on the track. You got this," he said and grabbed her hand in his, and gave it a squeeze. He squeezed Drake's shoulder before turning to leave.

"We good?" Josh asked.

Drake nodded. "Yeah, we're good. I'd apologize, but I'm not sorry."

Josh laughed. "Understood." He leaned down to get closer to Elle. "Gage is right. You got this. I rocked your shit. But you got us all on your team now."

She smiled at him. "Thank you. Everyone. Really." She sniffled and looked at each of them. She couldn't imagine doing this without them.

Drake let her rest in the field with another bottle of water before they headed out again. Elle held on tight as he sped out toward the safe house his family was in. Howard had a friend that had a friend that had a shed. Drake parked behind it and knocked twice fast and then ran his hand down once. The door opened, and Riley wrapped her arms around him. He picked her up and brought her inside. Howard pulled them in, and Elle sat down on the small sofa next to Drake's mother. Jane smiled at her and gave her a hug.

"I'm sorry you're going through all of this," Jane said.

"I'm glad he's not alone this time. Now he doesn't have to live in shadows and lies." Elle shrugged. "Wish our lives weren't on the line, but that's the fun of it."

"I like her," Howard said and chuckled. Drake smiled at him.

The shed they were in was quaint. Wooden boards covered the one window. A large mattress was in the corner and a tiny kitchen, if that's what you wanted to call it, was in front of them. A mini fridge and a microwave sat on a counter. A thin door was off to the right and Elle imagined it had a toilet. The little sofa Elle sat in held the mattress up to the wall and an old TV had Graves Valley News on mute.

Riley peeked up from Drake's shoulder, and he put her down. She went straight to Elle. She got in her lap, and Drake protested until Elle stopped him. Her arms wrapped around her little torso.

"You doing alright?" Elle asked. Riley nodded and gave her a big grin.

"Yeah, Mommy's teaching me codes and gave me new books that I asked for."

"Code?" Elle asked. Drake nodded. "You gonna teach me too?"

Howard shook his head no, but Drake answered before he could open his mouth. "Yeah, the second we get out alive."

"You're going to teach her?" Howard asked. Drake nodded. "Really?"

"Yeah," Drake said.

"Babe," Jane said, and Howard turned to his wife. She mouthed something to him. Drake's eyes darted to Elle.

"Oh," Howard whispered. "Ohh."

Drake put his head in his hands. "This is not happening."

"You should be glad we don't have baby photos to show her." Howard chuckled. "I could show her that video of you singing."

"No," Drake warned. "No, no."

Riley laughed and laughed. Elle smiled up at Drake. She could only imagine what his singing voice sounded like. Or what he looked like a few years after he'd saved her. When did he fill out? Was it a recent change or did he start in high school? Maybe after the first race. The lamp behind her started to flicker and Howard reached over and tapped it twice and it became steady again.

"We can't stay long. They've been following us," Drake said.

Elle jumped in before anyone else could speak. "I came for another reason, actually." Drake stared at her. "It's only fair." She glared at him. Then turned to Jane. "Will you sign my form?"

"Hey!" Drake shouted.

"Of course," Jane said. She took the paper from her and signed on the third line.

"Who's going to be the last?" Howard asked.

"It's rude to ask, babe," Jane said.

"Vero," Elle said. "I know if we win she'll get her cut anyways, but I'd rather fill my form than have a blank space. She can distribute however she wants."

"Oh, that's wonderful," Jane responded. Her voice cracked. She was holding back her sobs as Drake took Riley from Elle to give her a hug goodbye. He gave his parents an awkward one-armed hug, and they left.

The sun was going down, and Drake took a different turn. Hit the gas hard. Elle hung on tighter.

"We got company," Drake said. Elle turned to see four Guard coming up fast.

"Shit," she said. She reached for his throwing knives on the inside of his leather jacket. She tucked one into her palm. The first one shot a spear at them. Then they kept coming. One after the next. Elle blocked a few and almost had her arm taken off by another and Drake yanked her sideways.

One threw a nail bomb, and Elle screamed. Drake turned fast to dodge it. Nails shot in all directions from the explosion. Three inches long, they stuck into everything in their path. Including Drake's wrist. He hardly reacted. It was only when Elle felt the blood dripping on her leg that she saw it.

"Drake!"

"It's fine. We'll get some Sludge. You have some at your place?"

"Yes. But how are we going to lose these guys?"

"Leave it to me," he said.

Two of them came on either side.

"Left," Elle called. She sliced him in the shoulder with her knife. He yelled as he hit the curb and crashed into the brick building. Drake turned his arm to show the nail sticking through his wrist. He used the tip to jab the other Guard in the arm. But the Guard gripped Drake's arm instead. The bike squeaked on the pavement. Elle bit her tongue and held her breath. She grabbed tight to her knife and jammed it into his neck. Blood splashed her as he released Drake. He gurgled and choked as he collapsed.

"Two left," Elle said. "Right side coming up fast."

"Grip right," he mumbled, and Elle barely had time. She moved with him, and just as they were getting close, she reached down and grabbed another knife. This time Drake took it from her hand. Lined himself up and took the shot. It sliced the Guard straight in the jugular. He went down instantly. The next one jumped right over the dead body and rammed right into the side of Drake's bike. Elle shoved him as hard as she could and felt Drake wince as he held onto her leg so she wouldn't fall off the bike. He crashed into a parked car on the side of the street.

Drake sped off and made extra turns to make sure they were okay. He parked the bike in the woods behind her apartment building. He rolled off the bike and slumped in the dirt.

"Drake? Drake!" She got down. His leg was rough. Smoke came off his burning skin from his knee down to his boot. He threw his helmet a foot away. His eyes clenched. His face red. She didn't want to leave him, but she ran.

Up the steps and to the fourth floor. Her door was busted. Shit. She ran inside. Her place was trashed. She bit back the rage and slid into the side of her bed. She reached under the floor and grabbed her hidden safe. Eight tins left. She grabbed two and ran back down to Drake. He had blood rushing out of his leg.

Elle almost crashed into him, trying to go faster. She gripped his hand like before and started to coat him in the ointment. His skin began to repair.

"It's working. It's alright," she repeated as she used more. He grunted as the last part stitched itself together. She grabbed his arm, and he didn't even have time to scream before she ripped the nail out of him. She rubbed Sludge on that too.

Drake curled his arm into his chest and coughed into the grass. His jeans were ruined, but he was alive. He was okay. He was okay.

He spat into the dirt as she helped him stand. He grabbed his helmet and followed her with a limp up the back steps. Drake's shoulders slumped when he saw her door.

"It's alright," she whispered. "We knew it was a possibility."

"Yeah, but Elle."

"It's alright," she repeated harsher.

Elle called Nate to have him come help. And to bring Drake a pair of pants. Also, it was time for his lesson. While they waited, Drake lay on the floor of the kitchen. Elle imagined the tile was cool. She sat down beside him. His boots were heavy as she yanked them off his feet. Drake smirked at her when she started to unbutton his jeans. She felt the heat rush to her cheeks but kept her emotions in check. Just get them off. Focus.

Drake let out a pained cry and bit down on his fist. She rubbed more Sludge on him until he was back to normal. He slowly sat up, out of breath. Elle put the lid on the Sludge, and Drake pulled her to him. Kissed her hard.

Nate walked in and covered his eyes. "Oh no! No! My eyes!"

"Shut up," Drake said. Elle laughed.

"You're naked!"

"No, he's not," Elle started. "If he was—"

"No!" Nate covered his ears. They laughed.

Nate threw a bag at him, and he grabbed a pair of pants from it. He stood slowly, and Nate noticed the fresh blood and new skin all down his leg. His eyes became glossy.

"They really are after you," he said softly.

Drake scoffed. "You thought we were lying? This isn't a game!"

"It is a game. Remember?" Nate said.

Elle stood and turned to Nate. "Alright. Focus. You better learn fast."

Elle grabbed her safe and opened it. She explained every step to him and then demonstrated it. She brought the first concoction to the stove and heated it to 105 degrees. Once it was eighty-two, she added it to the other tube. Each ingredient was specific, and he paid close attention. Watched intently. Drake stood to the side. Gave them space to work. Once Nate finished up the tins, he grinned at Elle.

"Whoa," he said.

"Cool, huh?"

"Definitely," he mocked her. She hit his shoulder, and he turned to Drake. "You think you could make it?"

"Yeah, why not." Drake shrugged.

"Okay, wise guy. What was the first step?" Nate raised a brow.

"The pink liquid is ten milliliters. Blue liquid at five. Mix and then add the pink powder measured at two."

"Ass," Nate said. He smiled at him, and they shared a brief moment of silence. "Good to go?" Nate asked. He looked around them.

"Wait." Elle grabbed a red box from her closet and put her camera inside. She handed it to Nate. "Give this to Riley."

"Elle." Drake shook his head at her.

"I won't need it anymore. If we get out alive, I can afford to buy a new one." Elle smiled at him. Drake nodded at her. Nate took it and opened the box to her camera and all the accessories she could find that weren't broken in her mess of a home. He closed it and helped them pack up two bags of Elle's things. Nate put them in his trunk for safekeeping and hugged Elle goodbye. He fixed his glasses on his nose before forcing a half hug on Drake. He didn't reciprocate. Didn't push him away, either.

They made it to the garage to fix the fire launcher Drake had been complaining about. Elle watched as he worked to fix his bike as fast as he could. He tore apart the garage looking for a piece he needed. Elle could tell he needed to blow off some steam. She lay down and closed her eyes. The race was tomorrow. She needed to keep her focus.

Drake banged around another twenty minutes before Elle opened her eyes.

"Can I assist?" she asked.

He huffed out his breath. She expected him to yell or snap at her to leave him alone. He held out a wrench.

"Wait, really?" She smiled. She got up and grabbed it. He told her what to do and how to do it. Which bolts to tighten and which to loosen.

"We make a pretty good team, you know," Elle said.

He smiled. "I know."

Elle cleared her throat as they worked side by side on the launcher. "Why don't you want to be Superior?"

"Who says I don't?" he whispered. His eyes told her everything she needed to know. Her body went cold.

"Is that your plan?"

"It was. Things got more complicated. Don't you think?"

He was going to murder his grandmother. Take her spot. Become Superior. Drake Matthews; Superior. "You were going to kill her."

"Once I turned twenty-five, yeah." He nodded. "You can't be Superior until you're twenty-five."

"You had a plan?"

"Vero, Lex, and I made a plan to kill her after the last race. If we won. Lex wanted me to move with them to the Cove. But I'd stay here. Be Superior. Work some things out. Try and dismantle. Then maybe one day I'd be able to join them. To keep the Valley under wraps, we'd have to win. Couldn't just kill her and take her place. It would have to get done a specific way. Or else the Guard would kill me for taking her life."

"That's no longer your plan?" Elle asked. Cyra was the most ruthless woman. If they had a plan to replace her with someone who wouldn't murder people for fun, why wouldn't they?

"You want me to be Superior?" he asked. She shrugged.

"You'd be better than Cyra. You wouldn't play games with people. Or try to kill your own family to keep your position in power."

"No. I guess not," he said.

"Well, you should consider it. She's gonna die eventually. Whether it's now or twenty years from now. What then? You'll let some other dictator take the throne? What if they're worse than her? What about everyone who lives here? All the families and children," Elle continued.

"That's not my responsibility."

"It could be."

"And what the fuck would you do?" he snapped at her.

He was being an ass again. She wasn't in the mood for his bullshit. Typical. Bad timing nonsense. What was he thinking? They'd just gotten together, or whatever it was they were. He thought she was going to walk away? Go to the Cove for what? She was getting more and more heated thinking about it.

"I wouldn't leave, you idiot!" Elle kept working on the launcher and smiled when she heard it click. "Hey, I think—"

"What are you talking about, Elle?"

"The launcher." She held the wrench in her hand and bent down to look at the other side of the launcher.

"No." He grabbed her hand and pulled the wrench away from her.

"Hey!" She tried to take it back.

"If we win, you're going to the Cove." He glared at her.

"The hell I am." She scoffed.

"You'd be safe there." His forehead scrunched when he spoke.

He didn't want her to stay with him? She felt her chest collapsing in on herself.

"Is that what you want?" she asked. She had to know the answer. No matter the outcome. No matter which way. She had to know. Drake stared at her. His eyes burned a hole in hers. He wasn't going to respond now? "Is that what you want?"

"No," he mumbled. "It doesn't matter what I want."

She heard him talking, but no words registered after his admission. He wanted her. So nothing else mattered.

"I'm going wherever you go."

Drake smashed a kiss to her lips, and she breathed him in. Wherever he went, she would go too.

thirty

Gage and Aster helped Josh get geared up in the corner. Nate brought Drake his jacket and helmet. Lex handed Elle her old helmet. She pulled it on to adjust the straps.

Lex took out the Sludge and rubbed some on the back of their necks. Not taking any chances.

"Ready?" Lex asked Elle.

"Scared. Doing it anyway," Elle said.

Drake brought her to Vero's bike. He went over everything again. His breath came out hard.

"You're going to be fine," Drake whispered.

"Stop trying to convince yourself," Elle said. His eyes watered. She shook her head. "Whether I'm fine at the end of this or not, it's not your fault."

Drake clearly didn't like that answer, but he didn't respond. He slipped a small knife into her boot, and she grinned at him.

"We got this." Elle zipped her jacket up. The gold leaf pin hit her finger, and she thanked Drake silently again for putting it there.

They each got on their bikes and headed to the arena. The crowd screamed as they rolled in as a big group. Gage led the group, and Lex came in last. Groups of girls screamed as Drake passed by.

Guard members corralled them into a section of the lot before allowing them in. They entered the first gate, and the lights were dim. Drake took his helmet off. His eyes glowed in the darkness of the tunnel. Elle pulled hers off, and Lex followed.

"I'll win. I got this. You guys worry about her neck." Lex smiled.

A Guard pulled on the next gate and let them onto the track. Elle took another deep breath before the air sucked it out of her.

Sweat ran down her face. Heat hit them all with force. All she could think about was a bottle of cold water. Elle took a step into the arena, and her boot crunched on the soil. It was so dry. No green in sight. Vines wrapped around the trees that lined the path. Everything was dark and brown. Even the foliage.

Dreary.

"Elm trees," Drake murmured.

"What?" Elle asked. She looked around and noticed the larger fire pits around. No water in sight. No movement. No life.

"The trees that grow near the passages to the underworld," Drake explained. "Just another one of Cyra's games."

"Hey," Elle said. He turned to face her. "We're going to win."

"Damn right." Lex smiled at them.

Drake nodded.

Elle looked around at the screaming crowd. Lex waved to Nate. Elle felt bad he had to sit alone this time. She hoped for his sake that they survived.

The first gunshot.

Elle jumped. She dropped her helmet, and it rolled in the dust. Drake leaned down and grabbed it for her. His dark hair swayed in front of his eyes and covered his forehead. Elle reached out for the helmet, but he didn't hand it to her. He stood and went around to her bike. Did he notice something off about it? The buttons looked okay. They tested everything over and over.

Drake held out the helmet for her and once she grabbed it, he yanked. He smirked before he slammed his lips to hers. Her breath caught in her throat. The crowd yelled for them.

"Don't die," he whispered.

"Try my best." She winked at him.

Drake put the helmet on her and double-checked Lex again.

Cyra came out of her box and pressed her mouth to the microphone once more. Elle didn't want to hear her voice but knew this one she'd remember more than the others.

"This Championship is unlike any other. Any willing soul who enters may never come out. The best will cross the line." Cyra found Drake and Elle in the lineup and nodded to them. "Let the race commence."

Second gun. All the riders got in the ready position. Elle revved her engine as if she was going to hit the gas with the rest of them. Drake did the same. They had everything planned out. And it had to work. It had to. She read the rules. She listened to the speeches. Over and over. It had to work.

Third gun.

The five teams sped past her. One almost hit her in the ass. He flipped her off as he flew by. Elle waited until the last one went. The stands were silent. Elle jumped off her bike and got on Drake's back. That's when the crowd erupted.

She held on tight as he went around the first bend. The trees swayed as Drake passed them. Elle hoped Lex was in the front. Fireballs flew from the tops of the trees, and Drake swerved to miss them. Elle tapped his shoulder when a rider started to fling spikes at them. He went around the other side of them, and Elle waved as they got in front.

A soft whizz flew between them, and she jerked back.

"What?" Drake shouted. She tightened her hold on him. Not sure what it was yet, she looked around. A small black saucer skimmed her elbow.

"What is that?" Elle asked.

"Cyra's form of a ninja star but smaller. We call them Nin Spins. Sharp. Deadly." Drake said. Elle squeezed him again.

"So are we," she reassured him. He hit a button on the handle, and the back tire whirred on the charred ground. The bridge they were about to go over cracked, and pieces fell into the river of orange lava below. As it flowed under them, Elle thought hate or pain; Styx or Acheron?

Elle noticed a rider on their right and grabbed the blade from her boot. Hurt them before they can hurt Drake. Hurt them first. Just as they were about to shoot a spear, Elle flung her arm out and struck them in the forearm. They jerked into the nearest elm, and the bike exploded on impact.

Dread filled her, but they had to keep going. Too much rested on their survival. She had to survive. Because Drake had to survive. He deserved a life outside of this prison.

A group of Nin Spin's came from the trees, and she squeezed him as she tried to duck. One stabbed Drake in the leg. He grunted as blood oozed down his leg into his shoe. Elle yelled and went to grab it. He shook his head.

"Don't touch it."

"But if I pull it, I can put Sludge on it," she said.

"You have some?"

"Of course," she yelled. "On three."

"Don't do that counting thing where you pull it on—" Drake screamed as she yanked it out. "Fuck!"

"That?" she said as she shoved her fingers into his ripped jeans to his skin. He groaned as it healed.

He weaved around other riders and came up next to Gage. He saluted them and fell behind. A few riders tried to pass. Gage refused to let them. One kept growling at her every time they got close. Elle threw the Nin Spin from Drake's leg, and it struck them in the arm. It didn't stick, but would leave a bruise. They backed off, and Gage got in front of Drake.

Elle held tight as he went over a jump and looked out at the track. Lex was in second or third. It was hard to tell, but she was definitely in the front.

"Lex is alright," Elle told him, and his posture eased.

Only a few more minutes. She told herself over and over. Hold on. A little longer. Drake dodged the riders. The jumps became easier as they went over each one. It helped when four of the other riders were no longer a threat. And most of the other riders only wanted to cross the finish line first.

This race was all about speed. Elle closed her eyes for a moment and let Drake concentrate. She felt a Nin Spin whizz by and thanked the stars that it didn't strike her. The next one sliced the side of Drake's neck. He threw his helmet off so Elle could quickly seal it with the Sludge. Now he was unprotected.

"Team Blue Falcon; fatality."

Elle felt the heat around them while her body froze to the core. No. Not them. Not Gage. Josh. Aster. Who? All three of them? She shuddered. No.

"Focus." Drake pulled her back to reality. She was still in the race. They could be calling Evolution next. Calling for her. For Drake. Announcing their deaths.

Creatures came out of the lava river in droves. Fully covered in shiny black skin that wasn't affected by the heat. Three thick arms stuck out from their chests, and two legs like twigs came down to support them. But only three inches tall. They shot small fireballs from their palms, and

Drake weaved around them easier than she ever could have. She held on tighter as riders beside them started to go down with every strike.

One rider dressed in orange tried to dodge a blast against him. Ended up diving into the river. His helmet and face melted first. The rest of his body followed soon after. Bile rose in Elle's throat. Kept her focus ahead.

The lava had eaten a few more riders. She only knew because of the evidence of a bike wheel sticking out as they went across the bridge again. She didn't want to imagine drowning like her family had though drowning in lava wouldn't be like drowning at all.

A creature got too close and hit the back of his bike with a larger fireball.

Elle screamed as the bike started to go on its side. Drake hit a button, and the tire filled again. Auto-fill. Elle sighed with relief as he straightened them out. Then she noticed the metal on the bike bent in toward the wheel. It scraped the top with every rotation. They didn't have much time. They had another lap to go.

Drake slammed on the gas. They flew past riders, getting eaten and thrust against vines. Some screamed or begged for help. Elle squeezed her eyes shut at the one without limbs. His eyes glossed over as a creature pulled his torso into the lava. It stabbed him through the chest and dragged him screaming into the bright liquid.

Drake warned her as they got closer to the finish. Finally, it was in sight. The back wheel was about to give out from the pressure. Elle could feel the heat coming from the metal on the bike scraping it for too long. The bike started to tilt as Drake slid over the line sideways. Elle threw herself off while Drake tumbled over. The bike scraped his side. Elle started to run toward him when a bike crossed the line. She jumped back. A rider in all white grazed her side. Kannon. Another motorcycle was about to hit her when Drake tackled her to the dirt.

"Are you crazy?" he growled at her.

Tears ran down her cheeks as she realized they were both alive. He helped her stand, and she looked down at his side. Blood and dirt mixed on his skin. She reached for the tin. He told her no. She pulled her helmet off as Lex ran for them.

Aster ran to hug them too. She had clearly been crying. Elle looked around. Where was Josh? Gage? She shook her head. Tears in her eyes.

Gage came running at her. Relief flooded her before the sadness. Josh.

"He," Aster stopped. A sob wracked through her. Gage hit the ground on his knees. He wept into the earth. Elle bent down to hold him in her arms. Josh didn't deserve this fate.

Gage pulled himself up, and Drake sat beside him. He put his hand on his shoulder and Gage nodded to him.

"He almost made it. So close. He smiled at me when he realized his mistake on the last jump. The creature pulled him under," Gage explained, and Aster cried beside them.

Suddenly blue balloons cascaded from above them. A falcon flapped its wings on the screen, and Gage sobbed louder. Three cameramen stayed behind to get the scene captured.

Elle hugged him closer. Lex pulled Aster to her and let her grieve the loss of her cousin. Taken too young.

They stood as the arena blasted music to celebrate the winning team. The replay of Gage crossing the line first was on a loop around the stands. Lex came in second. Only a couple of feet behind him. She was smiling as she pulled her helmet off on the screen.

Blue Falcon would get out of Graves Valley. Alive. Gage and Aster. Rafael would join them, Elle was sure. But Aster... Vero. Her heart ached for her friends.

Drake spoke to Gage quietly. Couldn't hear. His mouth moved. No sound came out. She looked at Aster and realized she was standing closer than she was before. The group stared at her now.

Elle didn't understand. Tried to ask. No words would form on her tongue.

Then it went black.

thirty-one

Her eyes fluttered open, and Drake held her stomach with his hands.

"No, no, no, Elle, no. No!" Drake's screams echoed in her ear.

Lex yelled and a Guard held her back. A river flowed from Drake's eyes. Elle tried to sit up when a blinding pain in her abdomen stopped her. She looked down. Drake's hands were covered in thick, navy blood. What? But she wasn't hit. Was she?

That rider. He had grazed her.

Kannon.

She had barely felt it.

Cyra parted the group. Then Gage and Aster were being held back by Guard. Drake shoved Sludge into her wound twice already. She shrieked when he did it again. She turned to spit out a mouthful of blue blood.

"Don't," Elle warned.

"Fuckin' hell," Drake muttered over and over. He put more on her wound. It wasn't helping. The pain started to spread. Cyra looked from Lex to Drake before her eyes landed on Elle.

"Ah, you again. Elliot isn't it?" Cyra smiled.

"You fuck!" Drake screamed. The veins in his neck popped out as he yelled.

The crowd had thinned out. Music still blared from the speakers to celebrate Team Blue Falcon's victory. Only a handful of riders stood on the track with them. They were all tuned into Drake screaming above her.

"Drake, dear, is something the matter?" Cyra chuckled to herself.

Blue streamers and glitter floated around them in the arena. Elle could hear the crowd partying in the lot just out of reach. She could imagine the other teams losing their minds over another year of living in the Valley. They didn't win. They had another chance next year. All the hope they would be feeling. So many losses too. But they always had hope. Another year. Another race.

"Save her!" he wailed and nobody moved. Drake reached for his blade when Elle put her hand on it. She shook her head at him. "What are you doing?"

"I didn't die during the race. You'll live," Elle said.

"What?" He looked at her like she was insane. He was probably right.

"Don't. It's alright," Elle choked out.

"Elle, no." Drake shook his head. "No."

"See, she's ready to accept her consequences," Cyra said.

"You bitch!" Lex yelled at her. Nate ran toward them and stopped short when he came up to the scene.

Elle couldn't believe this was how she was going out. Her group of friends watching. At least Sarah wasn't here to witness. Elle got what she wanted; more time. Cyra did too. The pain started to travel up Elle's chest.

"It's alright," she told herself. Her vision began to blur. Nate's glasses were askew on his nose. His jacket was the color of moss. It reminded her of the tree she loved. She wished she was under her favorite tree now. But looking up at Drake, this was okay too. She grabbed his hand. Funny how she gave Drake such shit for accepting his deadly fate, yet here she was.

"You can't leave me. I forbid it," he whispered.

"Some things you can't control, race boy." She tried to smile at him.

"Bullshit," he said. Drake shoved more Sludge into her, and she bit down on her lip to not scream.

Cyra grabbed the tin from him and threw it to the ground.

Drake yelled and Elle pulled him back to her. "Don't."

Elle took deep breaths. Slow. Deliberate. Until the pain was going back down to her stomach. She could feel her skin repairing. He had done it. He had saved her. He just didn't know it yet. Look dammit. Look. Her silent pleas went unnoticed.

"Are the cameras still going?" she asked him quietly. He looked around and nodded.

She locked eyes with Nate and sent him their private signal. He froze before he slowly backed away from the group. At least someone got her message.

Now she needed to hold on. And stall.

"Seems we have a winner, yet nobody is happy. Why is that?" Cyra asked Gage.

"My teammate died on the track, ma'am." A sob crept from his throat. Cyra released a bored sigh.

"Aw, how tragic," Cyra said with an exaggerated frown.

He gripped his fist.

Sit up, she told herself. Sit up. Elle spat into the dirt again and slowly pulled herself up. Blue blood covered her jeans and jacket. At least this time, the blood would wipe off.

Drake had blood smeared all over his arms. His jacket was in the mud. When had he taken it off? How long was she out?

"Stupid girl thinks she can outsmart me?" Cyra snapped her fingers, and a Guard had his arm around Drake's neck. He rammed his elbow into the Guard's chest. Drake gripped his wrist and yanked so the Guard would face him. The gun from his hip suddenly aimed into the Guard's eye. He pulled the trigger. His body hit the earth hard. He turned the gun on Cyra and scowled. Elle put her hand on his shoulder. He eased up. She ran her hand down his arm and grabbed the weapon from him. He let her take it.

"Let me do it," Drake cried. His voice cracked as he spoke to her.

"You want to be Superior?" she asked.

"Not without you," he said.

"Give up already," Cyra snapped. "Twenty years ago, you got away from me. Now you want to kill me for murdering your little girlfriend?"

"You'd rather the Valley know you as a tyrant and a murderer than a grandmother? How sad," Elle finally spoke. "Maybe I should let him kill you. Would definitely be justice served. But then again, you tried to kill him when he was ten."

"Eleven," Drake corrected. His dark eyes were on Cyra's.

"When he was eleven. You tried to kill a child while killing your own son and his wife. Why? For what?"

"You think I wanted to give up my spot as Superior to my idiot son? The man who cried at every impossible task?" She cackled. "I should've had more time with him."

"You were too busy being the warden to care for your own son. He spent all his time alone. Until he met my mother. She was the toughest woman I knew. She made him stronger," Drake said through his teeth. His eyes trained on hers. He looked more like a warrior than a rider.

A loud microphone screeched. The music stopped. Everyone covered their ears. Nate got there fast. The screens all around them turned to the same recording. Nate's voice came over the speakers as hundreds of photos of Cyra being cruel cycled through. Murdering Guard as well as the other mates.

"Superior Cyra Covington, elected years ago based on her blood," Nate began slowly and uncertainly, but as it played, his voice got stronger.

The crowd started to file back into the stands. Drake's jaw dropped.

"Murderous and cruel." Nate went on, "It's time for another Superior. Seeing as she won from her blood, it would only be fair for Drake Matthews to take over." Teams from outside started to pile back into the arena to see the screens and what was going on. Lex got out of the Guard's grasp and went to Drake's side. "Or should I say, Drake Covington? Family murdered by Superior herself."

"How is this happening?" Lex asked Drake.

Elle turned to her. "Nate, he's got thousands of photos of Cyra and the Guard. He saved it. Knew he'd use it one day."

Drake smiled. It was rare to see a genuine one on him.

Photos of the Guard killing mates in the street, in their homes, at work. So much bloodshed. The photos Elle had taken with Lex at her side.

Guard started filling the arena. A large group headed right for them. Arlo, the man in the white suit, leading the army. His terrifying smile fixed on her friends. Elle gripped a knife from her boot. Aster handed Lex a blade when Gage put his hand on Drake's shoulder. He stepped in front of him and raised a small tube. Elle had never seen anything like it. Cylindrical and fit in his palm. He aimed it at Arlo. And Arlo stopped dead in his tracks before Gage pressed it.

A blinding blue light came out like a bolt of lightning. Arlo and two Guard fell to the dirt instantly. The rest stopped behind them. Shock fell across them as well as the crowd.

"No!" Cyra screeched. She turned to the frozen army. "Fools! Get them! They're spreading lies about your Superior! Kill them!"

Nobody moved.

Gage aimed the tube at the next Guard. He raised his hands and started to back up.

"Lightning Zap," Gage said. "Ashbury Valley makes these. Cute isn't it?" Gage raised his free hand in the air and made a fist. "Superior Matthews!" Gage started to rant, and some of the mates in the stands joined.

"These images are real. We've all seen it. Graves Valley might be a prison, but it doesn't need to be a death sentence." Nate's voice came through loud and clear. "Stop the murder."

"Guard!" Cyra shouted at them. Drake turned to the Guard and raised his fists.

"Anyone thinking they can beat me, feel free to try," Drake said.

A Guard stepped toward him. Elle could see his reflection staring back from the helmet. His gloves were tight on his fingers and his boots went up half of his legs.

"Jeffries." Cyra smiled.

The group backed up to give them room. It wasn't necessary. The Guard took one swing, and Drake ducked to dodge it before flinging his leg under him. He knocked him down before crashing his elbow into the man's sternum. Elle winced at the bone snap. A gasp escaped the man before he stopped moving.

The next one came at him fast. Drake ducked and backed under the Guard's raised arm before hitting him in the spine. He fell flat on his face, and Drake stomped on the back of his helmet. Blood seeped into the ground fast.

Drake motioned for another to approach him. Not a single one moved.

Nate droned on, "we're all the same inside these walls. Stop the fear! Everyone should have an equal chance to leave. But it's not equal, is it?

Once you've completed your duty, she'll murder you instead of releasing you."

Gage pointed at the photos Nate had on the screens. The photos she'd taken of the dead Guard. The ones from the office came on the screen, and Drake eyed her. It was the room he'd saved her in.

Elle held onto her stomach and teetered. Drake held her up. She put her head on his shoulder and took a breath. Exhaustion crashing over her.

"You can't be Superior." Cyra laughed.

"Yes, he can," Elle said.

"By yourself?" Cyra cackled.

"I won't be by myself," Drake said. He put his hand in Elle's.

"What about the Guard?" Aster asked.

"The Guard belong to me!" Cyra roared.

"No, they don't. They are loyal to you because that is their job. They don't belong to you!" Lex shouted.

Guard started to clang the butts of their guns on the walls of the arena. The sound echoed in the stadium. Cyra started to spin. She cried and shouted at them. Nothing stopped them.

"What about the Championship? How will you continue?"

"We'll figure it out," Elle said. "Don't worry, you won't be here to watch."

Drake approached his grandmother with the knife from Elle's hand. The tip touched the front of her neck, and she locked eyes with him. He didn't react. Held still. Waiting.

"How's that sting?" Cyra hissed at Elle.

Elle unzipped her jacket and raised her shirt. Her skin had healed, and the blood wiped off easily. Cyra gasped. Drake looked at her over his shoulder.

"Oh, did I forget to mention how I saved Drake after the second race from a sting?" Elle said to Cyra.

Aster raised her middle finger at her.

"Any last words?" Drake asked

"Could've killed me sooner. Why wait until you were twenty-five? You must have dreamt of it," Cyra asked.

"I wasn't strong enough yet," Drake said and plunged the blade into her throat.

three months later

D rake followed Vero out to the field and shook his head at her. She smiled at him over her shoulder. Elle grabbed Drake's hand and pulled him to the track. Vero swung her metal leg over her new bike.

"You don't have to do this," Drake reminded her.

"I know." Vero smiled at him. He helped her navigate the track as if it was her first day. She only fell twice before Drake forced her to be done for the day.

A Guard walked up to them, and Elle startled.

"Lincoln, what's the report?" Drake asked. He bowed and pressed his fist twice to his chest. He took his helmet off. "Quit bowing. You know I can't stand it."

"Apologies Matthews." He was an older gentleman with graying hair and a short beard. His gray eyes landed on Drake.

"Report?" he asked.

"Sir, they're willing to have a meeting. Should I gather a team?" he asked. Drake shook his head. Elle let out her sigh, and Drake rubbed her lower back.

"I'll sit with you next week to discuss who and when. Take the rest of the day. Thank you."

"Really?" His eyes floated to the group. "I mean," he cleared his throat, "thank you, sir."

Drake nodded once at him before Lincoln turned back to his bike. Elle waved as he left.

"Dinner at ours?" Elle asked, and Nate smiled.

"Sure. I'll bring the news."

They gathered around the table outside the Covington Manor. Lex brought a plate of cupcakes that Vero swore were better than Elle's. Drake wouldn't hear a word of it.

"Alright, listen up." Nate cleared his throat. "Gage reports that Riley has won an award in school. Your parents are adjusting pretty well. Apparently, they can't seem to understand the whole pet thing. Riley adopted a dog and they keep forgetting to let it inside." They all laughed at the rest of the news he had to share. Until he got to the end of the letter. "Gage also wants to let you know he made contact with Frost Valley. They're willing to meet with you. They have questions as well. Ideas to bring to the table. Maybe you should slow down?" Nate sat back on his seat and brought his cup to his lips. His camera sat on the table beside his plate.

Vero snorted. "You've met Drake, right? Slow down? Never."

"We only have one shot to do this right," Drake explained again.

"We have to figure out how many others there are before we consider slowing," Elle added. "Remember, we have so many people on our side now. Only way to defeat this is by getting more. That includes other Valleys. Hopefully."

"I'm just aching for another race," Vero groaned.

"Next year." Lex smiled at her. Vero took a swig from her can of beer and raised it to toast everyone at the table. Her eyes were red, and Elle could only guess the reason. No word from Aster. Still.

Elle looked around the table at her family and wished Sarah and Christopher could've made it. But they'd be there tomorrow for lunch.

They sat and ate together and said their goodbyes. Drake looked at the empty field as the sun began to lower.

"What are you thinking?" Elle asked her usual question as she joined him. He put his arm around her and shrugged.

"Superior Matthews, it's still strange to hear," he said. She agreed. "And your blog, how is it going?"

"Pretty good. Nobody knows my identity, of course. Luckily, I know an expert in that department." She smiled at him, and he pulled her tighter to his side.

"Ah, yes. The hot guy you met a while back, right?"

"Asshole." She sneered.

"Beautiful," he whispered in her ear.

And she kissed him.

THE END

If you loved *Acheron Ride*, please consider leaving a review on Goodreads or Amazon. Any review, no matter how long, helps get my books in the hands of new readers. As an indie author, it means the world and helps more than you can imagine.

-millie

FIND ME ON SOCIAL MEDIA
millieleighbooks

facebook
instagram
tiktok

join my newsletter for future release notifications on my website
www.millieleighbooks.com